ELTHEA'S GAMBIT

BOOK TWO IN THE STORY OF ELTHEA'S REALM

JOHN MURZYCKI

COPYRIGHT

1. Fantasy. 2. Science Fiction. 3. Techno-thriller. 4. Magical Realism. 5. Quest. 6.Epic Fantasy. 7. Artificial Intelligence. 8. Thriller 9. Metaphysical and Visionary. 10. New Adult & College. 11. Science Fantasy.

Editor: Audra Cohen Murzycki

Cover Art and Design: Paul Silva Design

To my wife, Carol, for helping me on this journey. I'm glad we're on this road together.

CONTENTS

1. A New Reality   1
2. On the Wings of an Angel   10
3. First Interlude   19
4. The Monster Inside Him   22
5. Second Interlude   36
6. Deity of the Astari   41
7. Third Interlude   56
8. A Beacon of Reason   62
9. Dinner   70
10. Fourth Interlude   78
11. A Storm Over Haven   81
12. What Once Was Good   93
13. A Stonewraith's Tale   104
14. The Dead Zone   120
15. Fifth Interlude   134
16. A Secret Entrance   138
17. Another Reality   156
18. The Lost City of the Draas   172
19. Back in the Land of the Living   192
20. Into the Sacred Forest   210
21. The Queen's Decision   228
22. The Ethwood Tree   243
23. A Single Snowflake   259
24. This is Your Time   269
25. Against All Hope   277
26. Weep for the Death of a Friend   291
27. Phil's Decision   306
28. Home   318

Author's Note 321

Next in the Series: Elthea's Paradox 323

About the Author 325

Acknowledgments 327

Also by John Murzycki 329

Preview of Elthea's Paradox 331

A NEW REALITY

I often thought about her during quiet moments like this, remembering all we had lost. A year ago our lives were full of promise, a chance for a new beginning. But that had been shattered in one terrible moment.

Was I the cause, a fatal flaw in my soul, or could there be another explanation for the darkness in my heart? Did our foe return, and unbeknownst to me, plant the seeds of destruction in my thoughts?

The global cyberattacks supported my uneasy feeling that the Bots were back, even though the rest of the world didn't yet understand the purpose of the assaults. But as bad as they were, I couldn't help spending more of my time thinking about the girl I still loved, as if driven to her by some mystical force. Cassie McKenzie was rarely far from my mind.

I took a moment now to gaze at her image, feeling the familiar ache come over me when I paid particular attention to the soft contours of her lips. It wasn't the best photo. The light was wrong; she smirked as if imploring me to get it over with, and her eyes held a hint of sadness.

Maybe those eyes saw what was to come.

Today was a date I had been dreading for weeks. One year ago, we returned from our ordeal in the place called Elthea's Realm. But there would be no grand celebration to mark this anniversary and no reunion with those who were, at that time, the closest of friends. Neither would we gather to observe a moment of silence to honor our companion Eric, who had given his life so that we could live ours.

How did I go so wrong since then?

"Philip Matherson," the receptionist called crisply, pulling me from my reverie. "Mr. Hall will see you now."

I pocketed my phone and stepped into the carpeted room, trying my best to wipe away painful memories. The view outside immediately captured my attention. His office looked out to the Custom House Tower, long ago the tallest building in Boston. Without being obvious, I took a calming breath to help me focus. This was my fifth interview in the last month, and I didn't want to give the appearance of being desperate — or worse, scatterbrained — by being too absorbed over the scene beyond his window.

I knew immediately that Mr. Hall was a no-nonsense executive. He greeted me politely but kept the small talk to a minimum. "So tell me, Philip, why did you decide to leave your last job?"

Of the many questions from interviewers, this one was the most common, so I was prepared for it. "After the Shutdown last year, I had to take extra time to deal with a personal situation. By the time I reported back to work, layoffs were already underway because of the disruptions caused by the attack. Unfortunately, being in editorial services, I was expendable, as they put it."

He looked at me for a long moment as if trying to read my body language while he processed the explanation. I always felt hiring managers didn't believe me, or maybe they wondered if there was more to the story. I decided to add, "It's no secret, Mr. Hall, that most organizations suffered because of the virus attack and they had no choice but to reduce their staff. I can tell you I'm an excellent writer, as I'm sure you can judge from my body of work."

He nodded absently as he scanned my resume. "Have you ever worked at a for-profit business before?"

This was the question I always hated. It assumed that companies were so drastically different from government. "No, but I can adapt easily, and I'm a fast learner. In my last job, I handled a wide range of writing and editing projects."

He responded with a perfunctory nod, and my enthusiasm quickly waned. His line of questioning continued, but he displayed an increasing lack of interest. I realized my fate had already been sealed.

After a brief twenty minutes that stretched agonizingly longer, he stole a glance at his watch. "You have a great background, Philip. As I'm sure you realize, we have many qualified applicants. We should decide in a few weeks and will let you know."

He stood, indicating the interview was over. I put as much gusto as I could into a handshake and thanked him graciously.

He hesitated for a moment before adding, "I'm sure you

understand that the current cyberattacks are almost as severe as the Shutdown we faced last year when most tech devices failed. Companies like us are afraid to invest right now. We don't know what's going to happen next. I wish I could hire a dozen people like you, but I only have the approval to hire one person right now, and we won't be taking on many new employees until things settle down. It's unfortunate, but this is a new reality."

It was his one sign of empathy during the interview. I wasn't sure how to respond. Was he telling me not to give up, or that there was no hope for me? Or maybe he was signaling that he would hire me. "I understand," I said, although I really didn't.

Once outside, I felt like putting my fist through something. But only steel, glass, and concrete surrounded me. The last thing I needed was to go on another interview with a broken hand, forcing me to come up with a cockamamie story about how I could type as fast with one hand as two.

I looked up to the sky and exhaled. The steel-gray clouds held the potential for snow, and the biting wind whipped around me. I pulled the coat collar tighter around my neck, feeling ever more helpless. I never loved my former job, but it provided a certain stability in my life. Now I had nothing, no anchor. And I was rapidly running out of money.

"Damn stupid Shutdown," I muttered to nobody in particular. "Goddam cyberattacks," I added for good measure. Did the world understand it had created a monster?

Probably not. But I knew.

Cybersecurity systems and governments had inexplicably

been unable to contain the attacks. I knew they would be ineffective if the Bots were responsible.

I shivered, the cold only partly the reason.

I took stock of my current situation as I walked to the transit station so that I could return to my apartment. My options were narrowing. I could ask someone to lend me money to tide me over. My parents were out of the question. They would only insist that I return home. I let out an involuntary snort as I saw myself returning to the life of an auto mechanic in my dad's shop. All these years I was running away from that possibility, and here it was, facing me once again.

I could get some non-professional job in the city. Lots of people waited tables while looking for the right job. Unfortunately, many of them found themselves in the same temporary role years later. Was that any better than moving back home?

Another option took shape in my head. Even though I had resisted it before, the thought always bubbled to the surface: ask Matt Tyler and Diane Collentenio for help.

I knew they would give it without reservation. But our relationship had become strained since my breakup with Cassie. Matt and Diane were in the middle, and I didn't want to force them to choose sides. I had taken the high road and pushed them away—at least in my mind it was the high road.

Was I being noble or a coward? Putting my life together was more difficult than I had thought. It was so much easier to rip it apart.

A small crowd clogged the entrance to the Arlington Street Station, further deepening my sour mood. I groaned, wondering why the hell it was so busy this time of day. As I came closer, I realized that a small group of people slowed the entry by handing out flyers.

I stood in line, wanting to get home and be alone. Those handing out flyers began chanting. "Technology for the people. Don't let others control our lives."

Just as I thought I could slip through without being harassed, one protester stepped directly in front of me. The young man had an unfocused, glassy-eyed expression, making me wonder if something was wrong with him. He pushed a leaflet toward me. "Return technology to the people," he demanded.

"Uh-huh," I said and grabbed the handout.

He leaned into me. "Support *The People's Response* and put an end to this madness."

I froze. Was this only a coincidence? *The Human Response* was the title of the Utopia Project paper that I had written with Matt, Diane, Cassie, and Eric. The protester saw my hesitation and used the opening. He leaned even closer, his face violating my personal space. At that moment, my surroundings fell away. His eyes became something other than human and his breath foul. "With you by our side, we will not fail this time. Your doom is preordained. You are one of us now."

I blinked, breaking whatever spell held me motionless. The person behind me shouldered his way around us to reach the entrance. I gently pushed the protester aside and stepped away.

The words of the protesters echoed in my head as I rode

down the escalator. "No more shutdowns. Free us from technology."

I suddenly felt myself begin to perspire in the cold air.

THE SCREECH OF TRAIN WHEELS AND THE DARKNESS OF the tunnel outside the windows added a surreal feeling to what just happened, as if I had once again entered another world. I ran his words over in my head. *With you by our side, we will not fail this time. Your doom is preordained. You are one of us now.*

That was bad enough. But the name of his group, *The People's Response*, was too close to the title of the college paper that had drawn us into our nightmare with the Bots.

But this protestor wasn't a Bot. At least he didn't look it.

I realized I still held the crumpled paper that he had thrust at me. I flattened it against my leg, reading the jumble of statements that took up most of the page. *Return to life as it once was. Turn back the clock on technology. Strict controls over the use of tech devices.*

A statement in large letters dominated the bottom of the page: *Prevent another Shutdown by letting us control technology.*

Were these people out of their minds? Did they think they could control technology? What did that even mean?

I pulled out my phone and searched for *The People's Response.* I tapped on an interview in a news feed. The reporter began the segment by saying, "A group calling themselves *The People's Response* is gaining momentum across the country. I'm speaking with Ben Otto Tabet, the leader of the group. Ben, what exactly do you want to accomplish?"

The man was young, maybe in his mid-twenties. What alarmed me most was a dazed look in his eyes. The protester wore a similar expression when he handed me the flyer. Tabet paused for a long moment as if considering his response before speaking. "It's clear to us we cannot continue on our current path of development. What happened during the Shutdown can, and will, happen again unless we free ourselves from the bonds of electronics."

The reporter interrupted him. "Are you advocating going back to a pre-technology society?"

His smile never reached his eyes. Once again, it seemed to take him a moment to process the question. "No, that would not be practical. Although we believe society can live without such a great dependence on tech devices, we realize that abandoning technology is not entirely possible. Our only option is to control the use and the development of all technology."

Again, the reporter interrupted, as if she were startled by his response. "And just who do you believe should control technology?"

His grin broadened as if he realized he was having his picture taken and wanted to smile, but didn't know how. "Why us of course." The reporter raised her eyebrows. But the young man continued blithely. "Our ranks already include many top technical minds. More will join us before long."

"How do you think the government will respond? Isn't this illegal?"

For a second, he didn't appear to understand the question. "Oh, no. We will work with world governments to enact laws that will grant us this power." He paused and looked at the camera. I squirmed, thinking he was looking directly at me. "It is the only way."

I fingered a tab to end the stream. "This doesn't seem right," I mumbled.

An uneasy feeling came over me. Ever since returning from the Land of Elthea, my greatest fear was facing the Bots again. I looked back at the flyer in my hand and noticed something that I had missed before. The name of the leader of *The People's Response* was Ben Otto Tabet.

His initials spelled out the word BOT.

2

ON THE WINGS OF AN ANGEL

The train ground to a stop halfway back to my apartment. The power grid had become a prime target of cyberterrorists, and it appeared they scored another hit. The remaining passengers in the car either groaned or muttered a few choice profanities. We were above ground at this point, so the conductor came through to pry open the doors and gave us the option of either walking or waiting for the electricity to return.

Like most riders, I chose to exit.

I immediately stumbled on the small rocks lining the rails once I exited the train, causing me to scuff my only interview shoes. "Friggin fantastic," I spat. This was turning out to be a day I would rather forget. The trouble was, I seemed to have too many days like this lately.

Like the rest of the passengers, I finally reached an area where I could cross the street from the rail line to a sidewalk. It was at least five miles to my apartment, but I decided to walk rather than spend the money on a cab or a ride. This area was a quiet residential section of Brighton, just outside Boston, and I knew it well. The main boulevard would soon become clogged with traffic because the signal lights were also without power and no longer operating, so rather than listen to the blare of horns, I navigated to side streets with residential homes.

I thought about what Mr. Hall had said to me at the close of the interview. *This is a new reality.*

His words caused me to think about the reality of my current life. One year ago, I was driving away from Matt Tyler's Berkshire home with Cassie McKenzie at my side, pledging my love to her. Four months later I had no friends, no job, nothing of value.

Have the first thirty years of my life become meaningless? I have nothing to show for it except one failure after another.

The threat of snow had passed, and the sun made an appearance. Although still cold, the walk and the sun soon warmed me. I spied a public park along my route. The grass was yellow and trees bare this time of year, but it was so picturesque I decided to sit for a few minutes at a bench on the edge of the grounds.

I needed time to think about what I was going to do, and this was as good a place as any. I never thought it would come to this, but for the first time, I could understand why someone would want to commit suicide. Not only was my life bereft of meaning, but I had no purpose ... nothing that mattered.

I blinked rapidly as my eyes watered. I focused my attention on the expansive grounds before me and tried to picture this place during the height of summer with children running freely, mothers out for a walk as they pushed a baby stroller, maybe a young couple playing Frisbee on the lawns. I pictured myself as a child of maybe four or five in a similar park far away. I was always running with my friends or tossing a ball. At that age, my greatest joy was hearing the jingle from an ice cream truck as it pulled up to the curb.

I smiled at the recollection. It was a time when the future was still before me. All I had to do was wait for it.

Now I had to wonder if life had already passed me by. *How will I ever be able to continue without Cassie?*

Our love for each other was so unexpected. But against all hope, we had come together. Once that happened, I loved her without reservation. And then I had done the unthinkable.

I gritted my teeth, willing myself to consider once again this People's Response group. The more I thought about it, the more I felt they had to be a front group that represented the Bots, or they were the Bots themselves who had somehow evolved and no longer appeared as monstrous, faceless figures as they had in the past.

I recalled the time a Bot nearly killed us when we arrived on the Isles of Loralee. I was so confused trying to understand how the islands could be suspended high above an ocean, waterfalls falling off the edge of the closest island, and then meeting the Astari. The Bot had charged at us from nowhere, nearly killing Matt. It was only because of the quick reaction by one of the Astari that he remained alive. We later learned the Bots evolved from Earth's virus software. They've been after us ever since, wanting us to be the face of their mission to control Earth's technology.

I considered calling Matt to warn him about this new incident.

I pulled out my phone and looked at it, trying to decide what I should say. But after moments of indecision, I realized I didn't have the fortitude to speak with him just yet. My world was falling apart, and the Bots had nothing to do with that.

I returned my cell to my pocket, closed my eyes, and put my hands on my face. Is this what it felt like to reach the end? When I was gone, would the universe even acknowledge I had existed at all?

I felt my palms turn wet with tears I could no longer contain.

"Hello, Philip."

I jerked my head up, blinking to clear my vision. I hadn't heard anyone approach. Standing ten feet away stood a child, hands at her side, a smile on her face.

"How—" I stopped speaking before forming the rest of the words. That she knew my name became less important as I realized who she was. The sharp contours of her chin and nose, green hair and short stature marked her as an Astari, not a child. Her smile broadened as if she was pleased to see me. It was the same expression worn by Damek and his companions when I first saw them on the Raised Isles. Back then, I had trouble thinking clearly at first because of the transition. Now, I was merely dumbfounded, unable to comprehend what she was doing here.

"I have a message for you," she said pleasantly as if speaking of the weather. "Damek and the others are safe. But a new danger has developed. I'm glad I have found you." She looked around at the park, a frown creasing her expression as if puzzled by what I was doing here.

Her words and appearance opened a new floodgate of emotions. I had tried to put the memories of events from Elthea's Realm out of my mind in recent months. I had too much to worry about. Suddenly that time was as vivid as if it happened yesterday: Damek, Bevon, Quintia, Riyaad, the Lady Elderphino, the Isles of Loralee all played across my vision in a flash.

"What are you doing here? How did you—"

She held up her hand to stop me. "Damek said you would have many questions. There will be time to answer all of them. But now we must go."

My mind was a jumble of thoughts and emotions. Damek and the others were safe. I had often wondered about their fate. I felt a wash of satisfaction course through me, knowing they had survived. But then I looked at her sharply. "What? Go? Go where?" I was afraid of her answer.

"Elthea's Realm, of course. Weren't you listening? I told you, there is a new danger."

"Whoa. What are you talking about?" I held my hands in front of me as if to ward her off. "I'm not going anywhere." I looked at her more closely, trying to recall if I had seen her during our last visit to the home of the Astari. "Exactly who are you anyway?"

She smiled as pleasantly as when I first saw her. "I believe you know my story." As she spoke, something extended from her back. Within seconds, angelic wings stretched out behind and above her. They were majestic and as beautiful as anything I could ever have imagined. "Come now. I will take you."

"You're the girl in the song? The one who was given wings to sail." I stammered. "So you didn't die?"

She nodded. "Yes, funny they would make a song about me. But to answer your question, my name is Arianell. I am the girl the tinkerers fitted with these wings. And I am quite alive."

My mouth hung open as I tried to grasp everything she said. And then my shoulders sagged. "I can't go with you." I thought of how I had failed at everything in my life. "I'm not the person you need or want, whatever problem facing you or the others."

She cocked an eyebrow and furled her wings back in place so you would never know they existed. She considered what I said before speaking again. "Philip Matherson, some things in life defy explanation or reason. I think maybe this is one such time." Her face softened before she continued. "I will tell you something. I did not decide to be a beacon of safety to protect the Realm of Elthea. But once the tinkerers affixed these wings to me, Elthea called upon me to protect her land from harm. So it is with you. Of all the peoples of Earth, it is you of the Utopia Project who can make a difference. I don't know why this has happened. Some people are able to choose their road while others have it unexpectedly thrust upon them. Only you can save Elthea. And in so doing, you will save your world. The two realms are inexplicably linked. If Elthea falls to the Bots, so does Earth."

Her words scared me. I was afraid. I was always too afraid. That was the true measure of my life. I never wanted to stand out, to get into a fight with a high school bully. Something inside me always held me back; the voice in my head would invariably warn me not to get involved or to step away. I almost always regretted my inaction.

Some of my reticence mitigated during my time in Elthea. But it was still inside me, threatening to rule me whenever I faced a decision such as this. "I can't," was all I could answer, my head down.

She remained silent, and for a second, I wondered if she had disappeared as silently as she had arrived. But when I looked up again, she still stood in the same spot, her mouth unsmiling now. I felt I needed to explain more. "I'm sure you can find others who are better suited for whatever it is you need. I'm not the person you think I am. I've ... changed."

Her frown deepened. "I was told this might happen."

She was about to say more, but I cut her off. "No, you don't understand. I did something horrible. I'm a broken person, and I might hurt someone again." My eyes watered and I blinked to clear my vision. "I don't want to be with the rest of the Astari, and certainly not with Cassie, Matt, and Diane. I'm not in control of my emotions. There's something evil inside me."

I had never voiced this feeling to anyone, but I needed to say it now before she made the wrong decision, before I made the wrong choice to go with her.

She nodded as if understanding, which I knew she could not. "You are the person you always were, Philip Matherson.

I understand your confusion. But you must stay true to your-self and what you believe."

"I don't know who I am or what I believe," I bit off the words and refused to look at her.

She exhaled as if disheartened. "I have a message to convey to you in the event it came to this. It is from Damek. He told me to say, 'If not you, then who? Do we simply wait and hope for others to act? Eric sacrificed himself for us all. Will you honor him now by doing what you can?' Those were his exact words."

Damek said these words back when we asked him why he felt the need to leave the Raised Isles to find a solution to fight the Bots. He now added the part about Eric.

I sat in silence, shamed by my weakness. Eric had been far from perfect. But in the end, when it most counted, he had the fortitude to save us all. What would I give to have his strength, to have him back in my life? If he were here right now, he would probably say, "Just suck it up, buddy. And stop being such a whiner. Life's too short to give up on it."

I smiled, thinking of him. I realized he was the inspiration I needed. I stood. "How exactly do you plan to bring me to Elthea?" I remembered the Lady Elderphino had explained how difficult it was to transition a person from one land to the other.

"We can sail on my wings. The tinkerers never realized the power they created with them." She stepped toward me. "Are you ready?"

I nodded, trying not to think about the voices in my head screaming for me to stop.

She covered the space between us until she stood an

arm's length in front of me. "You did not disappoint before. I pray you will not do so now."

As she moved the final step toward me, she put her arms around me as if in a hug, while her wings extended once again and also wrapped around both of us. In the next second, I lapsed into a stupor and remembered no more.

3

FIRST INTERLUDE

Cassie entered the room and time seemed to slow, as it often did when I first saw her. I watched her, unobserved, as my body and heart responded.

I instinctively knew that my life from this time forward would be altered forever. She and I had come together, and that was still remarkable in my mind. Her love for me had changed everything. From now on, my life would be right.

She gazed absently at the disarray of moving boxes in her living room, that is, our living room. Only one month back from our ordeal in Elthea's Realm, we had decided that I should vacate my smaller apartment and move into hers. She frowned. "Now that I see all your stuff here, I'm not sure I like this idea."

Since our return to Earth, she was often impulsive and prone to joking around. I was now unsure if she was serious or not. But the slightest curve of her lips gave her away. I played along. "Too late. You're stuck with me." I sidestepped an open box, grabbed her around the waist and pulled her down to the couch.

She shrieked. "Don't touch me you brute."

I slid my arms around her, feeling the shape of her waist, the smell of her smooth hair. I heard my heart beating distinctly in my chest. Thump, thump, thump.

She made a move to push me away, and I pinned her arms to the cushion. With her face inches from me, I spoke with mock seriousness. "We need to have some new rules around here." I made a move to kiss her, but she turned her head to the side, laughing and struggling to free herself. Rather than her lips, I aimed my kiss at her exposed neck. "I didn't tell you I'm a vampire." I playfully nipped her.

She laughed harder while I continued to concentrate on moving my lips lower down her neck. But she somehow managed to lift a knee and shove me off.

I landed with a bump on my backside and looked at her with chagrin. She smirked in return. "I'm the boss here and don't you forget it."

A moment later she lost her smile as a new thought entered her head. "I still can't help wonder if it was all worth it."

I knew what she meant, but I still wanted to keep it playful. Gazing around the room with a confused frown, I said, "I guess we can move everything back to my old place."

She barely smiled, even though her tone was still lighthearted. "Don't be a jackass. You know what I mean."

I sobered as I edged my butt closer to an easy chair and leaned against it for support. "We're alive. Isn't that enough?"

She frowned. "Is that your measure of success these days? Is that what we would have said in the Utopia Project?"

I thought for a moment. "Well, we did stop the Bots from becoming stronger."

"Eric stopped them. *We* might not have had the willpower."

She was right; I always believed that was why he was given the power of the invocation. I took a different approach. "We understand them now. We can be ready, just in case." I didn't want to think about them returning and having to face them again, let alone talk about the possibility.

She worked her bottom lip, and I realized too late I had gone down the wrong path. "Do you think they could return?"

I knew this was the one fear we all lived with after what we had gone through. I wanted to tell her that everything was going to be fine now. But we both knew that would be a lie. "I don't know. I wish I did. But we can't give up living."

She smiled, but I could see it was forced. She slipped off the couch to join me on the floor. "Then we'll just have to do some living." Her smile broadened. "Now, where were we?"

4

THE MONSTER INSIDE HIM

I inhaled deeply, savoring the rich scent of pine and damp earth. Streaks of yellow light shimmered through the overhanging mantle of green leaves, weaving radiant designs on the ferns and broadleaf plants closer to the ground. Beads of dew, sparkling like precious stones, hung heavy on the grass.

I knew where I was without being told. Everything was more vivid and alive here—the colors more dramatic, air purer, the music of the birds sharper. I took a moment to savor it. Unlike the feverish shock of my first arrival, I let my body absorb the richness of Elthea's Realm.

I turned my head to look for Arianell, but she was nowhere to be seen. I was sitting on the ground with my back propped against a tree. I suffered no stupor as I had on my first transition to this land, but unlike before, this time I was alone. None of my friends from the Utopia Project were by my side.

Something else was different. A feeling stirred inside me,

a potency I had never felt before. I tried to identify it, but like a breeze on my face, it was there one moment and gone the next.

I heard a voice, one I didn't recognize. "Uh-oh, he's here."

I angled my head in that direction and saw a lanky boy of no more than sixteen, an expression of confusion etched on his face. I quickly noted he wasn't an Astari. In fact, he appeared entirely human.

"Nice job, Bryson," responded a female voice. She said the words sarcastically rather than as a compliment. "Did you just wake up?" I turned my body so I could see her better. Her dark red hair blazed as the sun caught it. Freckles dotted her face. She was slightly older than the boy and looked like any girl from Earth, except for her clothes, which were more like something Robin Hood would wear. I smiled at the thought because she actually held a bow. She asked, "What about Arianell?"

"I—I didn't see her."

"It matters little," said another person. "If she wanted us to see her, she would have remained. She is in Elthea's service now."

This person sounded familiar. As I stood I saw my Astari friend, Bevon walk toward me. His eyes were bright, and he held the slightest hint of a smile. Suddenly we were hugging each other warmly, two companions who had been through much together. Of my Astari friends, I was most happy to see him again. He held me at arm's length to look at me. "You did well, Earthfriend. Not everyone could have stood up to the Bots as did you."

"I did nothing," I replied, hoping I kept the bitterness out of my voice. "Eric is the one who kept us alive."

He frowned. "You did much. You spoke out when they were about to kill Quintia. And you demanded answers from the Bots. Not everyone would have had the courage to oppose them as you did, and at a time when there was no hope left."

Just seeing Bevon again made me feel better. Something about the Astari always brought out the best in me. Riyaad had been hanging back, and he now stepped toward me. Typically, the most subdued of my Astari companions, he gazed at me with a hint of admiration before breaking out into a wide grin. "Well met, my friend. It is good to see you again." As with Bevon, we hugged each other like good buddies.

Bevon made a motion with his hand to indicate the two strangers. "This is Rae, who prefers that you not call her Rachel. She's a member of The Guard."

She made a face. "It does no good if you always say it that way. Just leave it at Rae." She extended her hand in greeting. "I'm glad to meet you. I've already heard much about you."

My face must have reflected my uncertainty. She seemed to be human. Why was she here? Had Arianell brought her as well? Was she taken from Earth?

Bevon continued speaking, not giving me the chance to ask. "And this young lad is Bryson. He is an apprentice to The Guard."

"It's my honor to meet you," he said with a bit too much enthusiasm. "I'm usually not selected for missions such as this. I was so glad the commander asked me to come along. And I'm sorry I didn't see the other Astari who brought you here, but I think there was more to it than meets the eye. As Master Bevon explained, if she didn't want to be seen, she wasn't going to. And—"

"Bryson," Rae said firmly. "It's not necessary to explain."

"Oh, okay, it's just that I wanted to—"

She held up her hand to stop him. I had to smile. He made me think of myself during another time in my life. The pause gave me a chance to speak. Looking at Bevon, I asked, "Are they human?"

He nodded. "Their parents were from Earth. They were born here. But that's a longer story—one for later."

"I can't wait to hear it," I said as I took stock of my surroundings. Small rolling hills with lush vegetation surrounded us. "We're not on the Raised Isles?" I felt a twinge of disappointment at the thought.

"No, the mainland," he answered.

"Eustoria," Rae corrected.

I shot Bevon a puzzled frown. He added, "That's the name of this area of the mainland."

"Where's Damek and Quintia?" I asked tentatively, fearing something had happened to them.

"They returned to Haven. It's their village," he said, indicating Rae and Bryson. "Arianell already transitioned the others, and they are waiting for us there."

"Others?" I asked, even though I knew the answer.

He looked at me curiously. "Yes, Earthfriends Matthew, Diane, and Cassie, of course." He paused a moment as he considered something. "When I explained we were going to meet you, they also acted strangely. Tell me, what has happened between you four?"

His question deserved an answer, but I wasn't sure how to respond. How can anyone make sense of the way I soured the relationship between myself and Cassie, and how it ended up spilling over to the rest of our friends? "I'm afraid things have changed between us." I knew it wasn't much of an explanation, but then again, I wasn't sure I could talk about it right now.

In typical Astari fashion, Bevon looked at me appraisingly for a second longer before moving on. "We all have much to discuss. For now, shall we go to Haven? I hope a warm breakfast will be waiting."

"Do you always dress like that?" Rae asked as we hiked toward the village. She looked at me sideways, and by her tone, obviously disapproved of my attire.

I still had on the suit I wore to the interview earlier today, and it was plainly not the best choice for roaming through the woods. I had immediately taken off my overcoat in this warmer climate and carried it bunched up under my arm. "Believe me, if I had any warning about what was to come, I would have picked something more appropriate."

Wanting to change the subject, I asked Bevon, "Why did Arianell drop me off in these woods rather than the village?"

He shrugged. "I can't say I completely understand. She explained that she didn't want to attract attention to herself."

"How did you find her?"

He smiled. "She is the stuff of legend among us. None of us knew she even survived her first flight. She found us. Told us she needed to bring you back here. Only then did we discover she could travel between different lands as easily as we sail from one island to another."

I thought about this as we walked. Finally, I said what was bothering me the most. "I still don't get it. Why us? Why did Arianell want to bring us back here? I don't feel I was very helpful the last time I was here."

He glanced at me thoughtfully. I had the impression he was expecting this question. "You underestimate yourself, Earthfriend. I believe you always have. You have been instrumental in our struggle against the Bots—in more ways than you realize. And now that our opponent has gained new strength, we have little resources to counter their moves." He looked at me more seriously. "We need you now more than ever."

"What do you mean they've gained strength?" I didn't like the thought of them becoming more deadly than when I last saw them. At the time they were about to carve the Astari into little pieces.

He hesitated. "We'll have plenty of time to discuss the Bots. For now, let us enjoy this pleasant walk on this fine day. The village is not far, and I'm excited for you to see it."

I suspected he wanted Damek to explain whatever problem they were facing.

My feet were beginning to hurt in these dress shoes. First a blown job interview, then I'm whisked away to another land where deadly computer viruses have come to life and wanted to kill me. Could this day get any worse?

As we walked through the woods, I took time to appreciate the richness of this place. In a brief year, I had already forgotten the vivid display of life that existed here. I recalled how my uncle once told me he had surgery to remove cataracts from both eyes and as a result, how dramatically clearer everything appeared. I could understand now what he meant as I gazed at a small pond, the blue water glinting as the sun reflected off it, insects zipping around as they skimmed the top for a second before flying away, birds chirping with the musical notes of a small symphony orchestra. It was all so beautiful.

My thoughts soon shifted to the others—those who, until a short time ago, I would call my good friends. Strangely, my anxiety about seeing them bothered me more than anything else, at least for the moment. "Did they say anything about me?"

He turned to me, puzzled.

"Diane, Matt ... Cassie," I clarified.

"Ah, your fellow Earthfriends. They are much the same as when you left us. Diane started arguing immediately." He smiled as if recalling a joke. "But as far as I know, she has not demanded to be returned to Earth."

Even I had to smile at this, recalling Diane's insistence that the Astari take us back home. The thought made me wish things were still the same between us.

"But to answer your question," Bevon continued, "yes, they did ask about you." He looked me over as if studying something. "They said they were looking forward to seeing you again." He bunched his eyebrows together as he considered saying more. Finally, he added, "Honestly, I would have thought the four of you would have remained inseparable after your experience here."

How do you explain the unexplainable? Hell, even I didn't understand it. "As you say, there's plenty of time to discuss things." But in my heart, I knew that was the last thing I wanted to talk about.

For the moment, I was content to observe everything around me: the play of the light as it reflected off the leaves, the giant butterflies that seemed to thrive in this area, the smell of flowers, more powerful and pleasant than any perfume — everything more substantial and intense than I had remembered. It felt good to clear my mind, breathe the fresh air, and feel the warmth of the sun on my face. It also felt good to walk next to Bevon, my trusted friend in this land, a better friend than I probably ever understood.

I decided there wasn't any point worrying about what was to come.

It appeared before us as we walked out of the covering of trees and bushes. Haven rose from a broad, open area. It was nothing like I expected. I thought I would find a small rustic village with maybe a handful of homes.

The place looked more like a castle than anything else. I stopped to gape, much as I had when I first stepped out to The Green on the Astari island of Tensheann to view the other raised islands for the first time.

A broad meadow occupied the space between the tree line and the village. The field gradually rose, and at its center stood a twenty-foot-high stone wall that circled the town. Round towers, connected by the wall, anchored the corners of the village. A wooden gate with massive doors was the only way in, at least without scaling the wall.

Inside the town, the homes appeared to be several floors tall and made of stone with tiled roofs. Windows with wooden shutters were scattered thinly in somewhat symmetrical patterns across most of the homes that I could see from this vantage. Smoke drifted lazily from many of the chimneys. The entire fortification looked new, but without knowing its history, I wasn't sure.

Rae caught the astonishment in my expression. "What do you think?"

I looked at her and then back to the town. "I thought I would see a simple village, not a fortress. It's massive. Did the people here build all this?"

She smiled more broadly. "Well, the truth is, we had help; maybe more than help. A race of people called the Stonewraiths constructed it for us. They saved us from the devastation that took place just after my parents and the others came here from Earth."

I looked at her blankly, not understanding.

Seeing my puzzlement, Bevon filled in the details. "The Stonewraiths are skilled at working with the rocks of the land. The devastation that Rae speaks of is what took place when the great races attacked the Bots. I hope you recall the story of the humans appearing at the time when we were fighting the Bots."

I looked at Rae and Bryson with a new understanding. "You were the major reason the great races ultimately defeated the Bots."

"Well, let's say they helped," Bevon corrected.

The single peal of a bell rang out. "That signals our arrival," said Rae. "One is for friends, two for strangers, and three for danger." The bell rang twice as we came closer. She turned to me. "That's for you."

Haven was built to be easily defended. They had cleared trees and bushes a hundred yards surrounding the walls. Nobody could sneak up on them. The wall enclosing the town was even more impressive as we came nearer. Defenders gazed down at us, watching our approach to the gate.

"I'm curious," I said. "Why such a fortification?"

"From what I've been told, the Stonewraiths insisted on it," said Rae. "They built it just after the Astari and the other races had defeated the Bots. But the Stonewraiths told the people here that there were other dangers."

"Do these Stonewraiths live here with you?"

She shook her head. "No, they visit occasionally, less so in recent years." She waved up at one of the sentries on the wall who looked down at us above the gate. "And they were right. Lately, some nasty things roam these lands, more than I've ever seen before."

An unexpected gust of chilly wind swept over us just as a cloud blocked the sun. Bevon looked up at the sky, a hint of fear creasing his face. But in a moment it passed, and the day remained as calm and sunny as a moment ago. He urged us forward. "Come on. You must see this remarkable village."

A paved courtyard that could probably fit a hundred people opened before us once we were inside the gate. I marveled at the structures rising on all sides as we passed by. Many of the stone buildings contained balconies that looked out over the plaza. I was so captivated with the surrounding structures that I hadn't noticed Matt and Diane, along with Damek and Quintia, until they approached us. I scanned the area for Cassie, but there was no sign of her.

As they came closer, I could see Matt gaze at me quizzically as if he didn't know what to expect. He regarded me for a moment before speaking as he stood before me. "I never thought we would come back to this land," he finally said.

I knew he was making small talk to break the ice, but I felt I somehow needed to explain what had come between us. But after so much pain, I was at a loss at what to say. Looking from Matt to Diane, I spoke as evenly as possible. "You understand why I stayed away from you, don't you?"

Diane launched a retort before I could say more. "Actually, we don't. I can understand things not working out between you and Cass. But you simply pushed us away." Her voice took on an accusing tone. "And after all we've been through together. I don't understand how you—" She couldn't finish as her eyes welled up.

Matt looked at me calmly and remained silent. Even after not seeing him for the past nine months, his posture and expression gave off a feeling of confidence. It was the way I always thought of him, even during our college days. But knowing him as I did, I could see the doubt in his eyes.

Meanwhile, the Astari looked at us curiously. I thought back to the time on the Raised Isles when those of us on the utopia team had argued about Matt's planned speech to the Astari. Quintia wore an expression of fascination through our heated debate. Were they measuring us, or learning from us? I never knew.

"I had to choose." I lashed out bitterly. "Cassie and I couldn't be together. You were in the middle. I understand you wanted to help. But you couldn't. It was my fault, and I didn't want to make it worse by putting you in an impossible position. I paid the price."

Matt cleared his throat, looking uncharacteristically uncomfortable. "We all paid the price, but we're together now." He hesitated a moment before putting his hand on my shoulder. "You're still our friend. Whatever happened is between you two. We need to move on from it."

So she hadn't told him. I searched Diane's eyes for some sign she understood, but saw only bitterness.

I lowered my voice and tried to speak more calmly. "I know. But it's not going to be easy."

I turned to greet Damek and Quintia, he with his blue hair and her with pink hair, defining their appearance as much as anything. I first hugged Damek. "I'm glad you survived," I said.

I turned to Quintia, and she caught me observing the long scar on the side of her face left by our attackers. "You were brave to attempt to stop them," she said kindly. "They were about to kill me." She waited before adding with a smile, "But you were very foolish. Promise me you won't try something like that again."

"Here comes the commander," Rae interrupted. My head turned in the direction she indicated, and I saw a man of maybe mid-forties march toward us. His age belied a more youthful person. He had a spring in his step as he came forward to greet us. He beamed with a broad smile. "Welcome," he said, looking directly at me. "We have few visitors of late, and now all of you here. It's a pleasure. My name is Russell Ingram, and I'm in charge of this community."

His name tickled a memory, one I couldn't place. He shook my hand; his grip was firm, and his eyes sparkled. "Damek said you would join your other friends." I winced at his description of us as friends, but he didn't seem to notice. His gaze took in Matt and Diane. "And most amazing is that all of you are from Earth. You are the first we've seen since we came here. This is remarkable. You must tell us everything."

"I'm not sure you'll like all of it," I said.

His smile never faded. "Maybe so, but it was once our home." He gazed at the business suit I still wore. "We're going to have to fit you with better clothes. I remember wearing something like that many years ago." He looked to the young lad that had accompanied us. "Would you mind, ah—" He paused, unable to remember his name.

"Bryson," Rae quickly added.

"Yes, Bryson. I'm sorry. Would you mind taking Master Philip to one of the clothing shops as soon as he's settled in?" He glanced at Matt and Diane. "And now that I think of it, all of you could use a change of clothes as well. I want to be sure your time here is comfortable."

My initial impression of Russell was that he was a typical politician, always trying to please people or say the right words, like some I had known during my time in campaign management. But I began to reconsider. Even though we had just met, I felt he was sincere and cared about us.

"We'll talk over dinner tonight," He cast a glance at Damek. "I'll see if Tess and Alan can join us."

I waited for someone to explain who Tess and Alan were, but apparently everyone except me knew. I didn't bother to question him. Russell excused himself, saying he had work to attend.

"How long have you been here?" I asked Damek.

"We arrived several months ago. After Eric's invocation, we considered returning to Loralee but decided to continue our mission to find allies. We had no idea if other Bots remained, and we didn't want to have to face them again without others to help. We learned this village was here during our travels and decided to visit. I am glad we did. We discovered something quite remarkable."

I had the impression it wasn't something he could quickly or easily explain. So I didn't ask. Besides, I had something more important on my mind. "Where's Cassie?"

Matt and Diane flicked a glance at each other. There it was again. A simple question put them in the middle. I added, "We need to resolve some things."

I still wasn't exactly sure how I was going to convince Cassie that I wasn't the monster she believed I had become. But somehow, I had to try.

The trouble was, I wasn't sure who I had become.

5

SECOND INTERLUDE

I knew it would take time to feel normal again, and I took solace knowing that I was together with the person I loved most. I don't know how I could have survived this adjustment without Cass. There were many times when we laid in bed, just holding each other, neither of us wanting to break the silence. It was as if we couldn't believe we were this fortunate.

And yet, something felt terribly wrong, as if I wasn't myself. It was as if another person was making decisions for me.

At first, I attributed the sensations to readjusting to life back on Earth after nearly a year in Elthea. I felt on edge much of the time, waiting to hear when I could report back to work, or wondering if we would receive any message from Damek and his crew, or hoping that wasn't a Bot I had seen in the distance.

I wished Cassie were next to me now as I stared at my

laptop screen, praying I would see a message from my department giving me a date to begin work. Staying home all day wasn't as enjoyable as I had thought it would be, especially with Cass back to work and me alone. Even Matt and Diane were busy most days. Diane spent much of her time interviewing at different biotech firms while he put his company back together.

Feeling drained, as if I spent the last hours running the Boston Marathon, I lay down on the couch, wondering if I was coming down with something. I decided I would try to sleep for a short time.

As I closed my eyes, I saw Cassie standing before me. She was ghostly, airy as a cloud in the sky. But even seeing her like this brought a warmth to my heart. Her lips curled upward, eyes sparkled. "We survived, Phil. You and me."

I wanted to say something, but I couldn't form the words. She continued, not realizing I wanted to respond. "We found each other on Elthea. Wasn't that grand?"

With an effort, I finally said. "We survived, and now we're together. That's all that matters."

Her eyebrows bunched downward, her expression when thinking about something important. "We've been through so much, but was any of it worth it? All that fighting and dying. What did it accomplish?"

My voice took on a pleading quality. "We stopped the Bots. Isn't that worth anything?"

She continued to frown. "But the Bots are still here. It's going to happen again, Phil. Don't you see?"

I wanted nothing more than to hold her, put my arms around her and stay that way for hours. But I needed to respond. "No matter what happens, we have to fight them together as we did before."

The slightest shake of her head told me she didn't agree. "We can't run from this. Phil, you must understand we can't win. Nothing makes sense. The world has gone crazy. It's turned upside down, and the Bots won't stop. It's how they were created. They're not like you and me. They hate us. They detest our world and everything in it."

I became desperate. "No," I cried. "We can't give up. Especially not after we've found each other. It's not fair."

She smiled again. "There's nothing fair about life. It doesn't always make sense. That's not the point of being alive, is it? We live, maybe if we're lucky we find love, other times the ones we love most are ripped away from us. What matters is what we accomplish. We can only try our best." She considered this for a moment. "Didn't Elderphino tell us that once, or was it Damek?" She shrugged as if it didn't matter.

"We fought them before, and we survived." I didn't know how else to reach her.

Her expression turned sullen, more despondent than I had ever remembered. "This is different now. We're outmatched. They hold all the cards. This time we can't win." She paused, looking as if she were about to cry. "Why does this always happen? Again the world crumbles around us."

"We won before Cass. We defeated them, even though we knew there was no hope. It was because we were together, all of us. We did it because of you, me, Diane, Matt, and especially Eric. On our own, none of us would have survived."

"Elderphino gave the gift to Eric. It's not ours to use. No, I fear we have no recourse. All is lost."

"Don't say that. We can't surrender. We have to resist them. There's always hope."

My mind suddenly gyrated, as if someone had flipped a switch. I never felt this sensation before. Adrenalin coursed through me. My muscles twitched, ready for action. I felt the strength of my body as something entirely unfamiliar took hold of me. My mind was awash in a mix of emotions. Hatred, love, envy, scorn were all jumbled together. I felt as if I would burst unless I found an outlet to release these sensations.

The sound of the apartment door opening startled me awake. I realized the room was dark, but it was early afternoon when I had rested on the couch. I realized it was only a dream as I tried to quench the fire coursing through me.

I blinked at the stab of light as Cassie turned on a lamp. "Well, well. And there we have it," she said teasingly. "I slave away all day and come home to find my lazy boyfriend sound asleep." She looked toward the dark kitchen. "I suppose you exhausted yourself preparing dinner." Her voice was melodic, full of joy even in her feigned scolding.

I had no words for her. I tried to explain, but couldn't resist the force that was taking hold of me. I was no longer Philip Matherson. That person was being replaced by a stranger I couldn't understand or control.

Cassie must have realized something was the matter with me. A note of concern, or perhaps uncertainty, entered her voice. "Phil, are you okay?" She stepped toward me. "What is it?"

Something inside me snapped. The last vestige of my self-control slipped away. The fervor of brutal injustice, intense hatred, a war that would never end, all hit me like a sledgehammer. My head was going to burst from these sensations unless I found an outlet to release them. My skin prickled and I couldn't see or hear. My entire world consisted of a burning fire of violence about to consume my soul.

And then, just as quickly as it came over me, the possession left me. I felt the intensity of emotions drain from me like an overturned bucket full of water. And with the release, so too did my vision slowly fade up from black.

I had my hands clenched around Cassie's throat as she gasped for air.

I released her, and she stumbled back. Horror and shock played across her face as I tried to make sense of what had happened. I couldn't comprehend anything in those first seconds except a single thought: I had just committed the worst act of my life. And I had no idea why.

6

DEITY OF THE ASTARI

I asked Bevon to come with me when I faced Cassie. He led me a short distance to a building in the village. Under normal circumstances, I would marvel at the sights. But right now, I had little thought for anything except facing her. My stomach churned, and I felt lightheaded. We walked to the third floor, and he offered to stay outside the closed door. "No, I need you with me," I said, hoping I didn't sound as if I were pleading with him. Bevon shot me a quizzical expression but consented, as I knew he would. "It'll be better if I'm not alone with her."

I knocked first and then opened the door to what looked like an army barracks. Rows of cots lined most of the interior room. The far end opened out to a large terrace, which is where I spotted Cassie standing with her back to us as she gazed out at the town.

Once inside, Bevon planted himself against the wall, but I motioned for him to follow. I could tell from the adjustment of her head that Cassie heard us approach, but she remained looking outward.

"I was wondering if you would come here," she said without turning, her body rigid. She didn't speak harshly, which was somewhat of a relief.

"I asked Bevon to stay with us," I responded, hoping that would provide her with a measure of comfort.

She turned to look at us. It was the first time I had seen her in the past ten months. I was relieved that no sign remained of the raw bruises on her neck that had still been visible when we last met. Her face had taken on a slightly more mature quality, particularly with her stylish hair—a vast difference from its appearance nearly two years ago when we drove to Matt's home in the Berkshires for our first fateful encounter with the Bots.

"I like your hair," I said, thinking I would start the conversation on a light note.

She scrunched her lips to the side as if frustrated by the comment, but said nothing. Now that I was standing in front of her, I wasn't sure how to move the discussion forward. I decided to be direct. "I stayed away as you asked. I never thought we would be thrown together again like this here in this land."

"You could have refused," she rasped. "Arianell wouldn't have forced you."

Now I felt frustrated. How is it that every decision I make ends up being the wrong one? "I had to do this just as you did. I owed it to Eric."

She pierced me with a look that was not friendly. "And

just what should I do now? We're back where we started. How do I know you won't try to kill me again?"

A noticeable intake of breath by Bevon was the first sound he made since entering the room. None of my past attempts to come to terms with her had accomplished anything. I had tried to plead, to reason, and to explain something that was inexplicable. Nothing had changed her opinion of me. She hated me. I knew I had to accept her feelings, but that didn't make it any easier.

"It's different here," I offered. "The Astari will protect you. I'll make sure of that."

Her gaze flickered between the two of us standing before her. She settled her attention on Bevon. "I don't want him near me. I don't want to be left alone with him." She looked around the room and added, "And I certainly don't want him sleeping in the same room with me. Can you assure me of this?"

Bevon hesitated, one of the few times I had seen him like this.

"I'll talk with Damek," I said, hoping to mitigate the pressure on him to respond.

He answered anyway. "We have always protected each of you Earthfriends since the moment you first arrived on Elthea. I see no reason we would not continue."

"That's not good enough," she said angrily. "This is different. He's not one of those other creatures out there." She swung her arm out to the space beyond the terrace. "He's one of us, and we can't trust him." Tears welled up in her eyes. I could see her pain, but I dared not make a move to comfort her. That would only make it worse.

"What do you want, Cassie?" I said.

Before I could add more, she raised her voice. "I want you to leave. Get out of my life and stay out. I never wanted to see you again."

I looked at the floor. She was right, of course. Maybe I should just go. "Okay," I said quietly. I didn't know why I thought this time things would be different for us. Our lives were too broken. "Just give me some time to figure things out. I need to decide what to do. Then I'll leave."

The bitterness in her eyes didn't moderate as I hoped it would. I waited for her to say something, anything that would give me solace. But she remained as motionless as a statue.

Without another word, I turned and marched out of the room, my heart beating in my ears, face red from shame. I heard Bevon follow.

My life had now become entirely bereft of any value. And this was after I had thought I couldn't sink any lower.

ONCE OUTSIDE I LEANED AGAINST THE SIDE OF THE building, feeling drained of all emotion. I had no more to give.

For some reason, my mind flashed back to Gary, my brother who had been dead now for over a decade. I hadn't thought of him much since my last return from Elthea. Through some magic of the Star Lights, he had appeared and talked to me while we were on the Raised Isles. He was always my crutch when I was younger; someone who would be there to help me if I was down on myself. I wondered what he would say now? Was there any hope for me?

"I do not believe you are capable of hurting Earthfriend Cassie," Bevon said as I tried to compose myself. But the truth was, Bevon's opinion didn't mean anything when it came to this. He was a good companion, but he wasn't with us at the time. Only one person mattered. And she had already pronounced judgment.

I didn't notice Rae approach until she was nearly upon us. "Let me guess, girlfriend trouble?"

I looked at her as if I misheard what she said. She took in my astonished expression. "Your friends already filled me in about you two ending your relationship. Judging by how you look, it didn't go so well, did it?"

I wanted to lash out and tell this young girl, whoever she was, that it was none of her business, that she didn't know the true story. But I controlled myself. "She's not my girlfriend."

She looked at me as if she didn't believe me. But instead of prying further, she said, "Let's go visit someone. She's always helped me when I needed it." She turned to the young lad who had come along earlier this morning. I hadn't noticed him standing back on the other side of the street. "Bry, can you go to the canteen and bring four breakfast meals to us? And grab one for yourself. We'll be in the gardens at the gaze-bo." He immediately scampered off.

The word breakfast was the best thing she had said so far. I didn't realize how hungry I had become now that my stomach stopped churning. "Thank you," I muttered.

She smiled. "Life can suck at times."

For the first time in a while, my lips curled up with a

bitter smile. I felt an affinity with her, another human who treated me like an equal and knew nothing of my failings. I knew all too well there were so few people in my life with whom I could establish a friendship. This might be the time for a new beginning; an entire village of people from Earth. It would be interesting to explore this place and hear how they ended up here. "Were your parents born on Earth?" I asked her.

She nodded. "They don't speak much of those times, but when I was a child, they often told me many bedtime stories about Earth." She led Bevon and me through the town. The people we saw took careful note of us, but nobody intruded or questioned us. Once or twice Rae would introduce us. "This is Philip, newly arrived from Earth, and Bevon, an Astari," she would say.

The town appeared large enough to fit the residents comfortably. Storefronts at street level mingled with residential homes. Everywhere people walked with heads held high, a purpose in the way they moved. I felt a vibrancy that was contagious. I realized I was at ease here, although maybe it was because the residents were from Earth. I thought back to our days on the Raised Isles and the discussion we had about potentially spending the rest of our lives there. Most of us were uneasy with that prospect. But here? From the short time since I entered the town, I could see myself fitting into a place like this, sharing it with other humans.

And then I remembered with a pang of remorse the discussion I just had with Cassie. This would not be my new home.

Bevon had been quiet until now, but he finally joined the

conversation. "These people have done well. Only several hundred people first came from Earth. Now, I'm told they number nearly three thousand."

We passed a blacksmith shop, hammers clanging on metal as forges blazed. "I've heard stories of those early days," Rae added. "Maybe you'll be able to coax Mom to tell you more."

"Tess Armstrong is an amazing lady," Bevon added. "I'm sure you are proud of her."

This was another name I recognized. I searched my memory to place the name, but Rae kept talking. "That's funny. You still call her by her maiden name even though she told you she is now Tess Marsham."

I didn't question either of them. I had too much on my mind right now. Cassie's words still reverberated in my head. I could barely control my anxiety over what to say to her the next time we would meet. It was so much easier staying away. My head hurt, and I wished I had brought some aspirin with me before I left for my interview this morning. Was it only this morning when the most important thing on my mind was getting hired as a copywriter?

I felt as if I were looking down at myself from above, somehow putting one foot in front of the other. Bevon and Rae were talking again, but I wasn't listening. I didn't feel upset. Maybe I should. Was that my problem, that I felt no remorse?

But I had felt plenty of shame, guilt, pity—you name it. Like someone who had bled too much, I had nothing left. We walked past shops of all kinds while people and children passed us, going about their everyday existence. The sun shone brightly, but I felt removed from this life as if I were watching a movie.

After some time, I realized Bevon was speaking to me. "What?" I stammered.

He looked at me curiously for a moment. "We were discussing the story of the final assault, and I asked if you recalled what Elderphino had told you about that time?"

"Oh ... yes. When the Astari, together with other races, attacked the Bots."

"Rae was explaining how her mother, Tess, and all the others were brought to this land during that time by a force we never knew existed. Damek believes it may have been Elthea herself. He wonders if we might use that power to our advantage."

My mind was too muddled to consider tactics just yet. I needed time to decompress. I was beginning to think it would have been much better if I had just walked away from Arianell rather than feeling guilty about what had happened to Eric.

It seems my life has added up to one mistake after another.

After a short walk, Rae motioned us up a flight of stairs that wound around the side of a building. Like everything else in this town, the steps consisted of stone. I tried to shake myself of the depression that threatened to overcome me by taking time to marvel at the beauty of this village. The construction of the stonework was astonishing: everything fit together perfectly, as if someone had molded into place. "You said a people called the Stonewraiths built this?"

Rae and Bevon exchanged looks, as if wondering why I had asked now. But Rae smiled as she answered. "They are a remarkable race. My Mom can tell you more about them."

The stairs spilled out to open ground with an assault of lush plants. The contrast with the rest of the village couldn't be more arresting. While the stone masonry dominated most of the town, this oasis contained an abundance of plant life. I blinked at the improbable transformation. A few dwarf trees cast some shade for the plants. Individual slate stones provided a crisscross pattern through what appeared to be patches of vegetable gardens.

"These are the common gardens," Rae explained. "People in the town can have a garden if they want. I don't, but my Mom enjoys it. So do a lot of others. Our main agricultural fields are outside the wall. This is more of a pastime with some villagers."

She led us along the stone paths toward the far side. We passed people hoeing, clipping, or reaping the benefits of their work by picking vegetables. Rae stopped at a spot with a lady bent over on her hands and knees as she loosened the dirt with a hand tool. She wore a floppy straw hat on her head and was facing away from us, so she didn't notice our approach.

"Hi, Mom. Meet one of the new arrivals from Earth."

She turned her head in our direction, shielding her eyes from the sun. She was younger than I had expected. I immediately recognized how she resembled Rae. But unlike Rae, whose hair was a stronger red, Tess's hair, which flowed from the edges of her hat, was mostly brown with only a hint of red. She stood casually to greet us and pulled off her cloth gloves. Her eyes raked over me as if evaluating my worth. I shifted uncomfortably, recalling a similar expression from Mr. Hall, who interviewed me earlier today. "I thought you might come by," she said as her eyes softened once they shifted to her daughter. "Russell was here to give me the news."

"I asked Bryson to bring us breakfast so we could join you. Have you eaten yet?" Rae asked.

She smiled. "I've been up for hours. But it's a good time for a break."

Bevon looked at Tess in admiration and then turned in my direction to say, "Tess Armstrong is one of the three most important people to the Astari."

His comment surprised me, but then I realized where I had heard her name before. With a rush, the memory came back, and I stared at her as if she were somehow not human. "You were one of the software engineers who created them," I blurted.

Bevon nodded proudly. "Her, along with Alan Sabrinsky and Russell Ingram. Thus our name A-S-T-A-R-I," he spelled out.

"But you never told me they were here in this land. I assumed they were still on Earth."

"We never knew. We learned from Earth's databanks that they had all died." He beamed. "But someone had altered those records. We were surprised to find Tess and her partner developers here a few months ago."

"Wait. The other software engineers? They're all here?"

Even as I spoke, I recalled the commander's name—Russell Ingram. An expression of recognition must have come to my face.

"You can imagine how we felt," Bevon said with a smile.

I wasn't sure how to respond to this news. The programmers who had created the Astari were like Gods to them. I now understood why they lingered here once they discovered the trio. I looked at Tess as if seeing her for the first time, like spotting a famous person. She calmly returned my gaze, seemingly unimpressed with her status among the Astari. "Let's sit in the gazebo and talk for a bit," she said. "It's a comfortable spot to enjoy our breakfast." She led us to a structure in the middle of the garden. As I followed, she turned to me. "Where are your other friends? I'd thought you'd all be together."

"Girlfriend problems," Rae quickly answered.

I grimaced. "She's not my girlfriend," I responded sourly, uncertain what else to say. Bevon remained politely quiet.

"Well, that's unfortunate," Tess answered as we reached the gazebo. I decided not to say more.

The gazebo, like all the other structures in this village, was constructed of stone with the roof consisting of slate or tiles; I wasn't sure which. Benches inside provided enough room to fit at least a dozen people comfortably. Before stepping into it, she went to a nearby hand pump and primed it with water from a bucket. Once it started flowing, she took a porcelain mug from a stack, filled it, and handed it to me before filling another for Bevon and then Rae.

"Of all the places in Haven, this is my favorite," she said as she poured a cup for herself. She took a moment to regard the lush vegetation; her forehead lifted proudly at the view. It struck me how calm she appeared, almost as if we were a group of neighbors. "This village is more than we ever could have built on our own, but I miss the open areas and working the ground."

She motioned us inside the gazebo. Once seated, she said, "Philip, I'm not sure if I can help you with your relationship trouble, but maybe I can provide you with a purpose to your time here. From what the Astari have told me, you and your friends were the reason they survived their encounter with the Bots. I would say that makes you special."

I tried to push the image of Cassie's bitter expression out of my mind. "One of our friends was responsible. He died for us."

She nodded calmly. "I've heard the story. I'm sorry. But I understand you put your life on the line to save them." She thought for a moment. "You may not yet understand, but there's more to these Bots than you realize."

I was still in a foul mood. I couldn't help feeling bitter about everything. "There's nothing good about the Bots."

She winced. "Don't judge them so easily, Philip. They were not always so."

I couldn't believe she even said it. "You must not know them as I do."

She never lost her calm countenance. "Believe me when I say, I know them better than most anyone. I lived for a time with their forefathers here in this land."

Bevon stirred in his seat as I tried to comprehend her explanation. He said, "You should understand that the creators of the Astari—Tess, Alan, and Russell—have provided us with information about how the Bots evolved to what they are now. It has helped us gain a new perspective."

A vision of Bots slashing their blades into young children during the Midsummer Celebration came to mind. I stared at Bevon. "What are you saying? You want to forgive them and forget about all the harm they've done?"

"No, I am not suggesting that. Evil lives within them. But the more we can learn about how the Bots think, the closer we are to understanding how to defeat them."

I kept my thoughts to myself. At right this moment, I didn't want to know anything else about the Bots.

Rae nodded toward the far side of the fields. "Here comes Bryson with breakfast. And it looks like he's brought Alan with him."

"Ah, the third programmer," Bevon said, a touch of reverence in his tone.

I was struck by the appearance of this new person as they approached from the other side of the gardens. Whereas I considered Tess and Russell graceful and refined, each in their own way, my first impression of Alan was the opposite. He was overweight, displayed a scraggly five-day beard, had an unhealthy pallor, and seemed to have trouble keeping his footing as he tried to swat away bugs that apparently threatened to attack him with each step.

I heard him protest as they came within earshot. "Tell me again why we need to meet in this jungle rather than my workshop?" Bryson sighed in response, offering no other explanation.

Tess called to him as they came closer. "Alan, meet our new visitor from Earth."

He didn't look convinced. He set his face in a scowl and appeared ready to protest further. But Tess didn't give him a chance. "Don't be unsociable Alan. We have a new guest."

Bryson handed each of us something wrapped in a cloth as he said, "I asked if Alan could join us since he was already at the commissary."

Rae introduced Alan. He nodded absently to me in response and took more interest in the breakfast as he reached out to take one of the wrappers.

"Master Alan is one of the developers who wrote the code that resulted in the Astari," Bevon said.

"He was also the brightest of the three of us," Tess added. I wasn't sure if she was trying to build him up or if she was telling the truth.

He smiled smugly. "Yea, but none of it would have been possible without you."

"Alan, Russell, and I came to this land when we were young," Tess responded. "We were just starting out in our professional careers. That's when we met a race of people who eventually became the Bots. But that's a longer story, one that shouldn't be told in a rush."

I felt I should ask more, but I was already having trouble following along. I took the cloth wrap off the meal that Bryson had given me, thinking this would help me feel better. Inside, I found a bread stuffed with what looked like eggs and meats.

Tess continued to talk about Haven and how the Stonewraiths constructed it for the humans. I tried to pay attention, but my thoughts were on Cassie and how I was going to exist alongside her. How could I make things right for her after what I had done? During a pause in the discussion, I finally asked, "Bevon, why did you bring us here?"

He looked confused. "We did not, Arianell did."

"Okay, then why did you ask her to bring us here?"

"You make unfounded assumptions. Damek argued against it. But Arianell was firm, saying the spirit of Elthea believed there was no other way."

In typical Astari fashion, he answered plainly but left me confused. I wanted to ask more, force him to explain exactly what they wanted me to do. None of this seemed fair to me. I was already too numb from everything that had taken place in such a short time.

My breakfast remained mostly uneaten on my lap. After only a few bites, my head began to reel, and I felt woozy. I put it back into its cloth wrapper and tried to stand. "I'm sorry, but I don't—"

Bevon was immediately at my side. As if from a distance I heard him say, "He has been through too much today. We should find him a place to rest."

What happened next was fuzzy in my head. I barely remember them leading me away from the gardens to another room where I fell into a fitful sleep.

7

———

THIRD INTERLUDE

I wasn't looking forward to this, but I had no other choice.

Matt Tyler settled into a chair across from me, and as on most days, his easygoing smile reflected his confidence and genial personality. "I'm glad you could meet me here in Cambridge. Work has been hell, and it's tough to get away from the office during the week." His eyes took in the room for a second before returning his attention to me. "This pub has great nachos. I'll order us a plate. A draft okay with you?" He waved to the waitress who promptly stepped toward our table.

I nodded, and he placed the order, turning his attention back to me. "So what have you and Cass been doing? Haven't heard from either of you in weeks. I know I've been busy getting this business up and running again, but still, no reason to be strangers."

I cleared my throat, which had suddenly become dry. "Yea, about that, it's why I wanted to talk to you."

His mouth tightened. "What's wrong?"

Now that the time had come, I wasn't sure how to begin. I had rehearsed what I was going to say in my head, but those words had somehow vanished. "We're not seeing each other any longer," I blurted.

He looked at me as if trying to figure out whether I was telling the truth or making a bad joke. "Are you serious?"

"Matt, I have some issues to work out in my head. This last year may have been too much for me to handle. What with being ripped from our normal life and taken to another world, it was a lot to deal with, but then it ended so abruptly with Eric's death. Suddenly, we were back home with Cassie and me together; it seemed so natural, but it was all so far from normal. Things happened too quickly for me to adjust." I realized I was rambling, and I forced myself to stop talking. Judging from Matt's expression, I probably wasn't making a lick of sense.

He took a long moment to process what I had said. "I still don't understand. The two of you are good together. Anyone can see it. That kind of love isn't the result of someone who's confused."

For the millionth time, I attempted to make sense of the madness that had come over me during the moment I tried to strangle Cassie. And for the millionth time, I reached the same conclusion: I was mentally unstable, or another entity had gained control over me. I would never have considered the second explanation, but I still had nightmares of the Bots saying they would hijack our minds and force us to lead their rebellion. I didn't want to voice either concern to Matt, at least not yet. "I need time on my own. I have to put my life back together, begin working again, start functioning normally before I change everything."

His expression softened. "Have they given you a date to return to work?"

I shook my head. "Nothing. I've found out that layoffs are likely. The longer they take to notify me, the more I feel I may be on the list. It's wearing on me."

The waitress returned with a bowl of nachos and two beers. After she left, I said in a lower voice, "I'm afraid I've been acting somewhat erratic lately. My behavior has caused problems between Cass and me. It's best that we go our separate ways, at least for now."

He took a sip of the beer. "Are you planning to move out of her place?"

I nodded. "Already did. I found a small place in Allston to sublet."

He lifted his eyebrows. "Already?"

I saw the concern and surprise etched on his face. Matt was a good friend; our companionship made closer by events of the past year. What I was going to say next was going to hurt. "Matt, I'm doing this for her safety."

For the first time since sitting down, shock registered on his face. "What do you mean? Who does she need to be protected from?"

I looked into his eyes for a long second before responding. "From me. I don't trust myself any longer. In some ways, I've turned into those monsters we faced in Elthea."

He stared at me unblinking for a long moment. I couldn't imagine what he was thinking. "Phil, however uncertain you are about your emotions, you're not one of them. You will never be one of those things. What happened that was so bad?"

I didn't want to tell him more. I was too mortified to even talk about it. "At times, I have no control over what I'm doing. And I'm afraid of what I might do to her."

"Maybe you should seek help, someone trained to deal with things like this."

I choked out a bitter laugh. "And tell them what? How do I explain the events that traumatized me?" I shook my head. "No, this is something I have to deal with myself. And that's the issue; I can't deal with it when I'm with Cass all the time."

We both remained silent for a time. The bowl of nachos remained untouched on the table. I knew Matt would do anything for me if I needed help, just as I would for him. But this was an illness nobody could cure except me. Just like any number of painful events I had endured during my life, I knew I had to push through this on my own. "I need you to do a couple of things for me," I asked.

His eyes brightened. "Anything. Just ask."

"First, don't say anything to Diane about what I told you. In fact, don't tell anyone. Whatever Cass tells you, never let on that I explained any of this."

That made him uncomfortable. I knew he wouldn't want to keep secrets from Diane, but this was necessary. "It'll only make things worse for all of us if Di knows I'm not in control," I added.

He didn't respond for a long time until he finally nodded his head once. "And your other request?"

"I'm not going to be part of this tight-knit circle of friends.

Cass is going to need both of you for support. I can't be part of it. I'm going to stay away from all of you. Please, don't try to contact me."

This upset him the most. "You can't just—"

I stopped him by raising the palm of my hand. "Believe me, Matt. I've thought a lot about this. It's the only way."

"Di will not let you drift away from us that easily."

My heart wrenched, thinking about how Matt, Diane, and Cassie had been my closest, dearest friends. "I realize that. But I'll take some comfort in knowing that at least you recognize what I'm going through."

"But that's the thing; I don't understand."

I exhaled a shaky breath. "Matt, I'm not as strong as you. Hell, I'm probably not as resilient as any of you." I could see he needed more of an explanation about what had happened between Cassie and me. "I tried to hurt her, Matt. I flew off the handle and didn't even realize it. I lost control. The only way I can fix this is to stay away from her. And since she needs you and Di, I have to stay away from both of you." My anger rose. "I can't spell it out any clearer."

I could see he wanted to say more, but I spoke first as I tried to say in a level voice. "You've been a good friend, but this is the only way." My chair screeched on the floor as I pushed it back. I stood to leave, taking one last look at my friend, feeling terrible seeing his confused expression. "Don't worry about me. Take care of Cass." Without another word, I turned and walked away, hoping with all my heart that he wouldn't call after me.

He didn't. And as I walked out the door, I felt as if I had

left some of me behind—the best part of the person I had been.

8

A BEACON OF REASON

My scream ended before I was fully awake. Still, the memory of the dream lingered. I had another nightmare of what I had done to Cassie.

Damek's face was before me as he held my shoulders. I realized I was sitting up on a cot in a room that wasn't familiar. I frantically searched, making sure that I hadn't strangled her. My breathing came in rapid gasps.

"You had a bad dream, Earthfriend."

I tried to calm myself, repeating in my head that it was only a dream. Damek frowned. "You scared the wits out of me with that shriek. I hope that is not a new mannerism you have acquired since your last visit."

I wanted to laugh and cry at the same time. I swung my legs over the side of the cot and rubbed my hands against my cheeks, trying desperately to erase the lingering memory of the nightmare. I shuddered. "Not everything has worked out as I planned since we left you." I realized I had only a brief conversation with Damek since Bevon brought me here to Haven earlier today.

The hard contours of his face softened. "Does anyone's life turn out the way they expected? I suspect it is a rare case when it does."

I shook my head. "This is different. It's all gone to hell."

"Bevon explained to me what had happened between you and Earthfriend Cassie. You are not a person capable of committing such an act." He searched my face as if looking for an answer. "Wickedness doesn't just suddenly come upon someone; it grows and festers for many years before striking. I know you, Philip. You are a decent, moral person."

I heard his words, but they didn't penetrate my thoughts. They were meaningless, sitting on the edge of my comprehension. I had tried to strangle her, and I might try it again. That was the only reality.

I stared at him, trying to believe what he said about me. I found it hard to accept it. "Everyone will be happier if I'm not around. I messed up, big time, and I don't deserve another chance; not with what I tried to do. There are times when I wished I were dead."

His expression moderated to one of sadness. I felt a prickle of annoyance. The last thing I wanted was pity. I could see he didn't understand the depth of my despair.

"I will make a deal with you, Earthfriend. This is a way to put thinking like this behind you. If you attempt to harm Cassie or any other person, I will personally put an end to your life."

An alarm bell went off in my head, telling me he

shouldn't make this promise. But I knew Damek wouldn't do anything rash.

"Why don't we take it one step at a time?" he said kindly. "I have drawn a warm bath for you." He stood and walked toward the door to the room, but stopped and looked back at me. "First, we need to provide something better for you to wear." He poked his head out the door and spoke to someone outside. I wasn't even interested in what he had said.

I looked down at my dirty, wrinkled business shirt and slacks. My suit coat and overcoat had been abandoned somewhere along the way. I laid back down on the bed as I considered how I would make my departure. Should I explain more to Matt and Diane? Was it best to tell them or just do it? After all, they deserved better, even though I had a valid reason to avoid them.

My head was still swirling when I heard a knock at the door. Damek opened it to the boy Bryson and a man I didn't recognize. He had dark skin and resembled someone who might have descended from India or that area of the world. "This is Sahil, our village garment maker," Bryson proudly declared, introducing the stranger as if we were at a grand ball.

I sat up, and Sahil wasted little time as he pulled out a measuring tape and motioned me to stand. "This is fine material," he said as he pulled the tape around my chest while noting my shirt. "Would you mind giving it to me once I provide your new clothes? Our weavers have made substantial progress through the years, but we still have a long way to go before we can achieve stitching this refined. It will make a good accent to a garment."

"My pleasure," I murmured. "There's also an overcoat and a suit coat I left somewhere, if you can find it."

"Oh, I have them," Bryson announced as if talking about an important discovery. "You left them at the gazebo. I told Tess that you might want them back, so I kept them for you. In fact, they're just outside. I can bring them here if you like."

I stifled a groan, thinking this youngster was just a little too chirpy for my mood. Sahil told the boy it wasn't necessary. The tailor didn't take much time as he efficiently measured my arms, waist, inseam and even the size of my foot. "I can have these ready for you within the hour." He looked at me a moment longer as he wrapped the tape into a ball. "It's a blessing to see you and your friends from Earth," he added more softly. "It's been so long since we've had others from our home. We didn't even know if it still existed." He reflected a moment, and I imagined him pulling up images of long-lost friends or relatives. I wondered once again why these people ever gave up everything on Earth to come to a strange land. I made a mental note to ask one of them before I left here.

Once Sahil had completed his task and left with Bryson, Damek led me to another room with a tub full of water. "There is soap and a washcloth on the shelf. Take advantage while you can." He shut the door behind him.

I wanted to tell him he was treating me like a child who couldn't take care of myself. But I had to admit that the steaming bath looked good. I stripped off my clothes and tested the temperature with my foot before sinking into it. The warm water soaked into my pores and began washing away my stress. Through the single window I watched the sun, now low on the horizon, cast rays across the small room.

Time passed, but I didn't care. I had nowhere to go. Someone rapped at the door and a second later Bryson stuck his head inside. He carried a bundle, which he laid on a chair. "Everything you need. Hurry now. You don't want to be late." He quickly took my old clothes and left before I could say anything. I wanted to yell at him to ask what I'd be late for. But then I remembered Russell said something about hosting us for dinner. I decided I had no intention of joining the others, primarily since Cassie would be there.

But I had soaked long enough, so I dried myself with a nearby towel and tried on the new garments. They fit surprisingly well. The dark tan pants had the ruggedness of blue jeans but were lighter weight, while the dark green shirt had the smoothness of flannel. The sturdy boots fit perfectly. I decided these refugees had done remarkably well on their own since leaving Earth.

I stepped out into the main room to find Damek waiting for me. I already knew what he was going to say, but I spoke first. "You go to this dinner without me." I didn't want to explain more.

He waited a moment before replying. "Okay, if that's what you prefer." He gave me a long look and turned to leave without me.

I had expected more of an argument from him, and for a second I felt a stab of regret at disappointing him. Damek was the last person I wanted to let down.

With one hand on the latch of the door, he stopped. "It's odd how things turn out." He turned to look at me. "I considered you the most level-headed of the utopia team. You, more than the others, were always the beacon of reason. Even when the Bots attacked us, you remained steadfast in your conviction. When it came down to it, were it not for Eric's invocation, I believe you would have been willing to sacrifice yourself to save us." He shook his head sadly. "I wonder if the Bots won after all. Did they really defeat you?"

Without looking back, he opened the door and walked away, his words echoing in my head.

I SAT BACK DOWN ON THE BED, WONDERING ONCE AGAIN how things had become so messed up in my life. Why did I ever agree to come here? Why was I even here?

Lost in my thoughts, I barely heard the soft knock on the door. I groaned again, thinking Damek wanted to change my mind. The door opened a sliver and the young boy, Bryson, stuck his head through the opening. "Will you be wanting anything to eat this evening?"

I couldn't decide if I should be angry with him for bothering me or pleased that he was so considerate of my needs. "Why do you care?" I tried to keep my voice level but didn't succeed.

He creased his forehead and entered the room uninvited. "You're not like the others, are you?"

I assumed he meant Matt, Diane, and Cassie. "No, I suppose not."

He must have expected me to say more, but I had nothing else to add. After a moment, he shrugged. "It's strange. I would die for an invitation to the commander's table. But you just ignore it."

I wanted to tell him I didn't care about the commander, or his invitation, or anything else for that matter. But all I said was, "You don't understand. It's not the commander. I have some things I have to resolve."

He took this as an invitation to enter the room further and sit on the single chair near the bed. I groaned inwardly, already regretting not telling him to find me some food so I would be rid of him.

"I can see that," he responded, more cheerfully than I felt. "Can I help?" I looked at him, not understanding what he meant. He added, "With whatever this is that you need to resolve."

There was no sense being upset with the kid. He was only trying to be considerate. "No, I don't even know if I can explain it."

He thought about this for a moment. "I guess I can understand."

Who in the world was this person, and how could he understand what I was going through? "Oh?"

"Yeah, it's the same thing I'm dealing with."

"I doubt that very much."

He frowned. "No, I bet it is. I have a decision I need to make and so do you." I looked at him askance, wondering what he was talking about. "You see, I want desperately to become a member of The Guard. I've dreamed of it all my life. But my Mom and Dad, they own a bakery shop, and they want me to take over the business someday. I mean, baking is fine, and it's a good trade. But that's not what I want. So you see, do I disappoint them and tell them I'm going to do this, or do I give in because ... well, because they've always been good to me and I owe them that much?"

I was about to say we had nothing in common, but then I thought more about what he said. It was true; I had a decision to make. I softened my reply. "Maybe you're right. Some choices are not that easy."

His face brightened. "The way I see it, you can either displease others or spend the rest of your life sad about not taking a chance." He looked down at his hands on his lap. "I don't know about you, but I'd rather not be unhappy the rest of my life."

9

DINNER

I heard the laughter before I came close to the room. I nearly lost my nerve, no longer sure I wanted to face them.

"This way, Master Philip," Bryson urged as I followed him up the steps.

We reached the third floor of the residence and Bryson led me down a passageway toward a room awash in candles. I winced as Bryson announced me with a flourish. "Master Philip apologizes for his tardiness."

I took in everyone's expression in a single glance—the hurt and uncertainty in Cassie's eyes, the grim satisfaction from Damek and Bevon, the unfeigned pleasure from Matt and Diane. Russell immediately stood and came toward me to shake my hand. His grip was firm. "Thank you for joining us."

Tess quickly added, "I hope you're feeling better. You didn't look so well earlier."

I nodded and muttered something about it being a long day.

Russell glanced at Bryson, who continued to smile broadly. "Thank you, ah—" He paused, unable to remember his name once again.

"Bryson," Tess quickly offered.

"Yes, Master Bryson, well done," Russell continued.

Bryson didn't take offense at the slight. If anything, his expression turned even more starry-eyed. "Will there be anything else you require?"

Russell thanked him again before the boy left. Once out of earshot, Tess said, "He means well. Rachel tells me he tries a little too much."

I noticed that Tess called her daughter Rachel rather than Rae. Was it a term of endearment or a mother's wish to tame the rebellious nature of a daughter?

Russell offered me a seat that was thankfully several places away from Cassie and on the same side of the table, so I didn't have to face her directly. Here again was one of the countless minor nuances I would have to consider if I stayed with them. As I sat, I noticed that Diane had a firm hold of Cassie's forearm to prevent her from leaving, at least without making a scene.

Looking at Tess, I said, "I'm sorry for leaving so abruptly earlier. I'm not sure what came over me."

"The transition by Arianell may have contributed to you not feeling well," Damek suggested. "I only wished she had stayed so we could learn more from her." Her words drifted back to me. *I'm in the service of Elthea now.* Whatever did that mean? I wondered if Damek was thinking the same.

Matt leaned forward in his chair. "I'm glad you're here. It wouldn't seem right without you." He spoke kindly, and for a moment it brought me back to the days when we were so close. How was it I had become so reticent with these once my dearest friends?

But of course, I knew the answer. I nodded at Matt, unable to offer any other response. I still didn't believe I could stay together with them, whatever their plans. But at least for now, I didn't want to let Damek down. Ever since we first met him, he had always tried to do what was best for us.

"Now that we are all here, there is much for us to discuss," said Damek. "Our time at Haven has been beneficial. But now we have important choices to make."

Quintia leaned across the table to lift a pitcher and pour a red liquid into my glass that appeared to be wine while Damek continued speaking. "Each of you Earthfriends are needed here. The lady Arianell said as much to us."

"But why?" Diane asked. "She didn't tell us anything." I recalled the conversation I had with the winged Astari and felt the same.

"The Bots have taken control of the Elementals."

If this was supposed to mean something, he lost me. He let the words hang out there with no explanation, as if we would know what he meant until finally, Matt spoke. "Ah, I don't understand. What are you talking about?"

A grin formed on my lips. Matt was usually direct.

"They are the life force of Elthea. On Earth, you would call it the environment, comprising air, water, fire, ice, and many others. We believe the Elementals remain in harmony with each other because of the force of Elthea herself."

Cassie leaned forward in her seat. "But that doesn't explain why Arianell wanted us here."

Damek took a moment before answering. "You four are needed, that's all I know. She said the spirit of Elthea told her you each have it within you the ability to impede that which the Bots hope to accomplish." He held up his hands. "I know you want something more, a deeper explanation. But there are times when you have to go in the direction of your heart. This is one of those times."

Several staff people from the kitchen forestalled discussion as they entered the room with steaming trays. Russell motioned them to place the platters on the table. "In honor of our Astari, we have mostly a vegetarian offering tonight." Eyeing Alan, he added, "But to appease some people, we've included several meat dishes."

Alan merely grunted in response.

"This is Maria," Russell said, introducing one of the waiters. "She is our chef during functions such as this."

Maria described each dish: sautéed greens, a vegetarian and another meat-filled stew, roasted potatoes, and several kinds of foods with cooked vegetables that didn't grow on Earth.

Our discussion was put on hold as we each filled our plates and passed around platters. The food smelled delicious, but my stomach was still churning. I took only a small portion from each plate.

Before we began eating, Russell said, "I hope you don't mind, but it's our custom to say a brief prayer of thanks before our evening meal."

I don't know why this surprised me, but it did. The Astari

were not particularly spiritual. And with these settlers so far removed from Earth, I didn't expect them to be either.

Russell bowed his head, and the rest of us followed. "Bless this food and bless all those around this table. We have much to be grateful for this day. We thank you for life and all that you have bestowed upon us. Guide us in the choices we make, so we always do what is best for all. Amen."

Russell eyed us once he had finished. "There are some traditions from our past that have fallen away, and some that we've kept. Even though we've left Earth far behind, we are, after all, still human. I'm not overly religious, and neither are many people in Haven, but I find that it helps to say a prayer at times like this to keep us grounded."

I couldn't help wonder if he was praying to a deity from one of Earth's religions, or to the spirit of Elthea, someone to whom they owed so much. His words caused me to consider how I could stay grounded. I risked a glance over at Cassie. Whether it was timing, or whether she had been looking unnoticed toward me all along, but our eyes met. She was hurt, I could see it. And so was I. But there was no way I could take the hurt away. I had caused enough angst in both our lives to make it right again, regardless of how much I wished I could.

My life was a dismal failure. I might as well accept it.

WE TALKED ABOUT MANY THINGS DURING THAT MEAL, but what I found most touching was the concern that our hosts had for the four of us who had once again returned to the land. "I can't help but think how you mirror our experience," Russell said. He glanced at Tess and Alan for a moment. "Each time we came here, we were so baffled by everything taking place around us. I understand how you must feel now."

Cassie spoke tentatively. "Why did you come back after returning to Earth?"

Tess cocked her eye. "It seems you have done the same. I see a lot of us in the four of you." She glanced pointedly at me for a second. "I'm sure you have your doubts and misgivings. Of all the millions of people on Earth, you can't understand why you are the ones who have been asked to make things right in this land. But, like us, I'm sure you're trying to do your best to make this a better place. I think that's one of the most endearing traits of being a human."

"But did you ever think you made a mistake coming here at all?" Diane asked.

"Sure we did," Russell said as Alan chuckled. "But now, it feels ... natural. I can't imagine any other life. This is our home." He looked around the room at the array of candles lighting the table and to the open window. A flicker of concern crossed his face. "That's not to say we're safe. The Bots are still out there. And as long as they remain, we're all at risk."

The Astari had been quiet during much of the dinner. Damek finally said, "In spite of your early misgivings, you have remained safe all this time because of help from the Stonewraiths. I would like to meet them. During our first war against the Bots, they were one of the races that had decided not to become involved. However, they lent a great deal of support to you after the war ended. Perhaps they would help us now."

Russell nodded. "Without them, we likely wouldn't have survived the devastation that followed the final attack against the Bots. They kept us safe and then constructed all this after the war ended."

Damek considered this. "That is the kind of people whose support we need."

Russell appeared hesitant to respond, but after thinking about it, he said, "I can't speak for them, but I believe their interest in the land is more fundamental." Damek looked confused, so Russell continued, "They have no love for the Bots, and they kept us safe once the war started. They said the spirit of Elthea asked it. That's why they sheltered us when the fighting began and why they built this place once it ended." His eyes became unfocused as he thought about it. "I don't know why. I can't explain it. But I'm happy someone took care of us. We were a bunch of refugees in a strange land with no idea how we would survive. It's still a wonder that we've come as far as we have."

Alan added, "We could have used them the first time we ended up here on Elthea."

Tess and Russell smiled as if agreeing.

"There's one thing I don't understand," said Matt. "How did you convince over a hundred people to leave Earth and come here?"

"Oh, that was the simple part," Tess replied. Her face

turned serious. "When you have nothing else to live for, it's an easy choice."

I sensed there was more to it, but nobody pushed her for a clearer explanation. We all saw the pain in her eyes.

10

FOURTH INTERLUDE

"I'm worried about him," Diane said as she set the table in the kitchen of their Cambridge brownstone. "It's been a month, and Phil still hasn't returned my calls. That's not like him."

Matt frowned. "Give him time. At least Cass is joining us for dinner."

Diane didn't look happy at his response as she fussed over the table settings. "I don't care if they're not a couple any longer. That's no reason for him to ignore us, especially after everything we've been through together. It makes me angry."

Matt avoided looking at her as he continued to baste the chicken that had been roasting. She picked up on his silence. "He hasn't spoken to you, has he?"

He sighed. "The last time was three weeks ago when we met at the pub near my office. I haven't heard from him since." Matt fidgeted with a pot holder before putting the chicken back into the oven. "We've got to let the two of them work this out on their own, Di. Breaking up can be difficult for anyone, but Phil had a real soft spot for her. This hit him hard."

"But did he say anything to you at the pub about not wanting to see us again?"

Matt took a long moment before replying. "He's emotional about it. We have to give him space on this. Trust me."

She was about to fire back a retort, but the chime of the doorbell forestalled her. Matt hurried off to open the front door to Cassie McKenzie. They hugged before she handed him a bottle of wine. "I think this is the brand you like," she said.

"You didn't have to, but it's perfect. It's so good to see you again, Cass. We were concerned about you."

As he helped her take off her coat, the silk scarf around her neck pulled down, revealing purple marks on her neck. His face blanched, and he tried to cover his shock by hanging her coat in the closet as she adjusted the scarf. Diane came over to greet her, and they settled into the family room while Matt stepped to the kitchen and leaned against the counter for support.

He listened to them catching up with each other as his breathing returned to normal. After another moment, he opened the bottle, poured it into three glasses and handed one to each.

Diane said, "I'm sorry you and Phil broke up. I'm sure it was difficult."

Cassie lowered her gaze and remained silent for a moment. "Some things just aren't meant to be."

Diane frowned. "Do you two still talk to each other? We

haven't heard from him." Cassie shook her head, her only response.

Diane was about to say more, but Matt interrupted by proposing a toast. "To good friends. May we always remember the remarkable events of this past year." His firm voice did little to belie his uncharacteristic nervousness. Diane shot him a puzzled frown but said nothing.

Much later, as Matt cleared the dishes from the dining table, Diane continued to question Cassie about Phil. "Do you plan to see him again, I mean after a time?"

A stillness radiated from Cassie as her eyes became unfocused. A moment later she shrugged casually. "Things don't always work out the way we planned." She thought about this, and when she spoke again, her voice cracked. "Maybe we just weren't right for each other. Despite all we went through during the Utopia Project and then in another land, I suppose I never really knew him. There's a part of him I found ... disturbing." She looked at both Matt and Diane as if awakening from a dream. "No, I don't plan to see him ever again."

11

A STORM OVER HAVEN

I stood on the parapet of the wall surrounding the town, having walked alone this morning. I thought this would be a good place to view the entire village. The few sentries didn't seem to mind; it was as if they all knew me, which I suppose they did. In a community of this size, everyone would know about visitors, particularly those from Earth.

Several days had passed since our dinner with Tess, Alan, and Russell, and I had achieved modest gains repairing my fractured relationship with Matt and Diane. I was taking it slower with Cassie, but at least we spoke to each other, her without recrimination, and me without pleading for her forgiveness. We still had miles to go before I would feel we became at least friends again.

Damek wanted to leave Haven soon to travel to the home of the Valnorians, the same race we had sought a year ago on the *Sea Spray*. But I wasn't sure I should join them. I still didn't trust myself with Cassie. What if I blacked-out and tried to do it again?

I was lost in my thoughts, so I didn't notice the thick, dark clouds that swept overhead, replacing the bright sunshine in minutes. Like a shadow passing overhead, an uncanny gloom settled over Haven and the surrounding fields. The heavens quickly transformed into a maelstrom of roiling murk spewing bolts of lightning in the distance. The storm broke before anyone could react.

A slap of wind caused me to take a few uneven steps as I struggled to keep my balance on the walkway. I decided I had better move to the street level where I would be more sheltered. This was no place to be standing right now.

With the wind increasing, I made my way to one of the stairs. That's when something awoke inside me, a malevolence that had no place within me. Yet here it was. I probed it with my thoughts, not sure if I imagined it. I recalled a feeling nearly a year ago, just before I had tried to strangle Cassie. This felt the same. But the next moment it was gone, just as when a dream flits away upon awakening.

By the time I reached the stairs, rain lashed against me. In moments, I was soaked. I had to hold on the edge of the battlement to keep my balance. People were shouting, and the bell began to ring three times, belatedly announcing danger.

I held my hands in front of me to both shield my eyes from the rain and keep my balance. As I took the first step, a burst of lightning lit the darkened sky, followed in seconds by a crash of thunder that rattled the stone under my feet.

The stone was slippery from the sheets of water that now

fell. Ribbons of lightning blinded me as flashes hit nearby rooftops and even the street below. A vision of Eric came unwittingly to mind as he had blasted the Bots with bolts of lightning. This was similar, only now the entire village was under attack. I felt as if I was in a war zone.

Once I reached the street, I looked around, disoriented and unsure of where to go. There were no shops here where I could duck into. The lightning and thunder seemed to meld into constant explosions with little or no break between each one.

I looked toward the top of the wall, my forearm shielding my face from the wind and rain. A bolt of lightning ignited one of the Guard members into a fiery explosion. Another person came to his aid and was swept over the edge of the wall by a hurricane-strength gust of wind.

I heard someone shouting my name through the clamor. I turned toward that direction, still shielding my eyes from the torrent. I spotted Bevon making his way toward me, his stock of russet-orange hair matted with water. He approached me as he fought through the gale. Hooking his arm around mine, he said, "Let us move. We have little time."

I wasn't sure what he meant, but I wasn't about to argue. He guided me along the street. Every few seconds, lightning struck the pavement in front of us, sending flashes of sparks and debris flying in the air like landmines. A step in the wrong direction could be our last.

Bevon guided me forward, searching for a doorway that would provide safety. But there was none. Some twenty yards farther down the street, a man ran from one side to the other. Before he reached the far side, a brilliant flash engulfed him, holding him in place for painstaking seconds before releasing him. His body lay limp on the ground.

I thought about my friends, hoping they were inside.

Bevon pulled me toward the closest doorway and tried the latch. It swung open just as hail began to sting my face. He pushed me inside and yanked the door shut behind us.

I found myself in a small foyer in what appeared to be someone's residence. A quick glance into one of the adjacent rooms revealed a mother and three children huddled in a corner away from the glass windows. I could see the horror on their faces as each flash of lightning lit the room. I ducked reflexively as a pane of glass shattered, sending shards flying past us. One of the little children began screaming.

"What's happening?" I asked Bevon.

His eyes blazed. "This is not natural. The Bots are attacking us." He stared outside through the broken window as if trying to understand something about the storm. "They are using the Elementals to do their work."

I wasn't sure if I should feel relieved that the creatures themselves weren't scaling the walls. This might be worse. "I'm lucky you saw me out there."

He looked at me with a strange expression. That's when I realized. "You didn't just happen to see me, did you? You were watching me."

He nodded. "We pledged to guard you," he said evenly. "That remains unchanged."

I fell silent as we both watched the deluge and the broadside of lightning explode outside. Anyone out in this wouldn't survive for long. "Do you think the others are safe?"

He understood I meant Matt, Diane, Cassie and the

other Astari. "They are watched over." He looked out the broken window with renewed interest, even though I couldn't see any change in the tempest. Lightning and thunder came in rapid bursts.

I sat on the floor, wondering how long this would last. I let the moments drag as the howling winds and eruptions of thunder continued outside. I looked up at him, surprised to see that he was in some trance, staring transfixed at the storm. His arms and hands were jerking as if he were in a bad dream. I jumped to my feet, not sure of what to do.

"Bevon. Do you hear me?" I said before deciding to shake him awake.

"Yes, Earthfriend," he answered in a whisper. "I am battling the Elementals. Can you sense them?"

I wasn't sure what he meant. But since he seemed to be unharmed, I left him alone and turned my attention to the storm. I had done meditation exercises this past year to mitigate my anxiety over what I had done to Cassie, so I practiced the technique now, clearing my mind of thoughts and focusing inward rather than on the turbulence outside the window.

Moments passed, and by slow degrees, I felt a presence outside. The feeling became stronger as I continued to concentrate. I nearly broke my trance when I felt the burning hatred of the force outside. It was lashing out at us with whatever power it had, wanting nothing more than to destroy us. I felt the loathing, the intense hatred from whatever was out there.

I realized I had felt this force before. But I had little time to think about it as this new potency washed over me. My self-control slipped away.

I fought back, pushing it away, instinctively knowing that if I stopped concentrating, it would win out and consume me. But it was so much stronger. Whatever it was, I was no match for it.

But just as I thought it was about to consume me, I felt it diminish and move away.

And then it was gone. I realized Bevon was gripping my shoulders, his face concerned. "Earthfriend, are you all right?"

I took a breath to calm myself. My legs had turned to rubber as he eased me slowly to the floor. "What was that?" I muttered.

His eyes flickered to the open window. "It is the Bots. They are much stronger now."

"You looked as if you were in a trance. I was afraid they had taken you over."

He shook his head. "We battled them—Damek, Quintia, Riyaad, and myself. But I am afraid, to little avail."

I noticed the thunder had stopped and the winds subsided. I looked up at the window to see a break in the dark clouds. "Is it over?"

His face was expressionless. "For the moment. But who knows how long."

Feeling better, I rose to my feet. A streak of sunshine reflected off the drenched pavement. "I felt them before." I looked at his calm face, wishing I didn't have to dredge up the memory. "Just before I tried to kill Cassie, I felt them. I didn't know what it was back then."

His expression turned grim, but I wondered if he even understood what I was trying to explain. He replied, "You must resist your demons, or it will be your undoing."

I knew he was trying to help, but he only made me feel more of a menace.

THE DAY AFTER THE ATTACK, I ONCE AGAIN STOOD ON the wall. For some inexplicable reason, I felt at peace with myself up here. Maybe I craved the solitude it offered with only a few other sentries who patrolled the parapet. Or perhaps I just wanted to avoid the rest of my friends. I was still uncertain about joining them when the time came for them to depart.

Today, however, was a day unlike the others. It had begun with a funeral for the nearly fifty villagers killed by the unnatural storm. Russell presided over a brief ceremony in the courtyard inside the gates for everyone to attend. For reasons of safety, he asked that only immediate family members take part in the burial, which took place in the cemetery on the edges of the field outside the wall. Everyone was still wary of another attack, and many of those killed had been caught outside the gates. A minister, or someone who assumed a similar role, led that observance.

More than ever, I believed the Bots had me in their crosshairs. Damek had it right when he said this attack was not aimed at the villagers of Haven as much as it was against me and my companions. And as long as all of us remained here, the rest of the village was in danger.

I couldn't help wonder if I was as much of a danger to my friends as the Bots if I left with them. But what about the safety of the villagers if I stayed?

From afar, I observed men lowering the simple pine coffins, one at a time, into the ground just before the tree line. A contingent of The Guard was on hand for protection, as well as Damek, Bevon, and Riyaad. I assumed Quintia remained with the rest of my companions. Bevon had explained to me that the Astari had some ability to fight the forces that controlled the Elementals. He had described the process as focusing your thoughts on the disturbance and mentally pushing it away.

I had no clue what that meant, except in the most abstract sense.

I was still watching the burial take place when I heard footsteps on the battlement behind me. It was Matt. He nodded in greeting and without a word stood next to me as we both gazed out at the service taking place.

"It seems we always end up watching funerals," he finally said. I understood he referred to the time the Bots attacked the Astari.

I shuddered, even though the day was warm. "The devil hasn't gone away," I said. "If anything, it's become stronger."

"I'm not sure if it helps us any, but at least we know the Bots are an evolution of the race that had been once alive in this land. Damek believes the Bots can tap into the essence of who they once were. That's why they've become so much more dangerous. Di suggested it's because the souls of that once living race remain somewhere here in this land, which has given them this new power."

I smiled. "She's become a lot less pragmatic, it seems."

Matt chuckled. "I wouldn't go that far." He lapsed into silence as we observed men lowering the last of the caskets. The wailing of grieving families filtered back to us, even at this distance. The permanence of death always leaves a hole in the living. Something precious had been ripped from their lives, and they would never have it back.

After a time, he said, "I'm glad I found you. Tess was hurt in the attack. She broke her leg when a gust of wind threw her down some stairs."

I raised my eyebrows and glanced at him, realizing I had never asked if the attack had injured anyone we knew. "Nobody told me. Will she be okay?"

He nodded. "I heard it's not serious. We should visit her before we leave, thank her for her hospitality."

I remained silent, still not sure if going with them was the best choice for everyone. He noticed my reticence. "Phil, I need you. We were a team once. That's the only way we're going to survive now."

For the first time in a long while, I felt a hint of the feelings I had when we were buddies in college. It was a time when we believed we could win out against all the odds. I thought about this as I watched the families out in the field slowly filter back from saying goodbye to those they loved. "Okay, I'll go with you," I responded. And a moment later added, "You've got to understand, this is going to take time. I pushed you and Di away for a reason, and I can't just turn things around again. I can't forget what I did to Cassie. And I don't think she's going to either. But more than anything, I'm afraid I could do something like that again."

He pursed his lips. "You shouldn't forget. You should be angry. But more than anything, you should get even with those dickheads who caused it."

Matt rarely used profanity. I could see he was angry. "I can't excuse it so simply." I wanted to say more, explain that if it was out of my control, then I might as well say I wasn't human anymore. But I wasn't ready to start a discussion about it, even with Matt. So instead, I added, "Let's take it one step at a time."

As we walked together away from the wall, I realized that this was the first time in nearly a year that I had made peace with Matt, a person I had once thought of as one of my closest friends.

WE CAME UPON RAE SITTING BY HERSELF ON ONE OF THE benches lining the street. Her head hung low and her body shook with sobs. She was one of the few villagers I knew, so I told Matt that I would join him later and walked over to her. "I'm sorry," I said meekly. "This must be difficult. I just found out about your Mom being hurt."

Her expression never changed, as if she hadn't heard me. But seconds later she gave me the briefest nod. "Please sit." She put her head down on her knees and wrapped her face with both hands. I thought she might start crying again, and I wasn't sure how to react. Maybe I shouldn't have interrupted her. I remained quiet.

She finally spoke quietly, almost as if to herself. "One minute they're alive, and now so many of them are dead." She looked out toward the direction of the wall. "In a town this size, everyone knows each other. Some of those killed were my childhood friends. Others made the journey from Earth for a new life here." She blinked rapidly. "It's hard to think I'll never see them again."

At this moment she looked so young and fragile. I was about the same age when I had first met Cassie and the others on the utopia team. How my life had changed since then. "It's times like this that make a person stronger," I said, wondering who spoke those words before.

She smiled weakly. "Are you trying to make me feel better? A word of caution: you're not very good at it."

I had to laugh. "I must admit that you and everyone else I've met here are remarkable. This little outpost of humanity in a land so different and so far from home. Yet you seem to thrive here. I'm sad I have to leave." I thought for a moment. "Maybe I can come back here someday when things get straightened out and spend more time in this village."

The idea seemed to surprise her and she scrunched her nose. "I had you pegged for someone cut out for more than this ... little outpost, as you call it. You might find yourself bored with life here."

"Oh, I don't know. Events have been a little too chaotic, at least for my taste."

She held her smile for only a second. "I wish I were coming along with all of you. All my life I've wanted to learn more about the rest of Elthea. Quintia told me about the Isles of Loralee. They sound amazing. I've heard about the Valnorians in their Sacred Forest. I can only imagine the wonders you'll see. It'll be such an adventure."

"Yeah, well, I'll let you in on a little secret. Adventures aren't all that they're cracked up to be. The last one we had in this land didn't pan out so well. And this one—if you want to call it an adventure—hasn't started out so great either. I'd be fine not having another one for the rest of my life."

Her face turned sad again. "Promise me one thing. Stop whoever caused this storm. It killed more people at once than anything else in my lifetime. I don't think we can survive many more."

I nodded, not knowing how to respond to such an appeal, yet wondering how I had once again found myself in the role of wanting to protect a people from a terrible evil.

12

WHAT ONCE WAS GOOD

I woke the next morning knowing that our time here was growing short. After the storm, Damek wanted to leave soon so he could seek the Valnorians for assistance.

I looked around the small, sparse room, realizing I would miss this place. A lone window looked out to the village, which was now awakening with shops opening and work crews walking out to tend the farms that lay outside the wall. The smell of freshly baked bread wafted through the open window. Groups of children, probably no more than ten or twelve years old, walked along the cobblestone street below my window, their uninhibited laughter reaching my ears. Most of them sported packs on their backs. I suspected they were on their way to school. What would a classroom be like here?

So much in Haven differed from my life on Earth. Yet in many ways, daily existence here was akin to what I had always known: adults opened their business or went to work, while children attended classes. Life here mirrored that of Earth.

Except here, there was no technology. This was a place where people didn't have to worry about a new cyberattack, or a ransomware threat, or some other form of malware targeted to prevent people from living the life they had grown accustomed to. Had humanity become so perverse that it sought to destroy itself, or was it only a few twisted individuals and leaders of rogue nation-states who wielded power, intent on bringing down the rest of civilization? Did the people of Haven represent all that was good about our race, or did they have problems I wasn't aware of yet? Maybe yesterday's storm was just another form of cyber warfare.

A rap on the door made me jump.

The smiling face of Bryson greeted me. "On orders from the commander," he said proudly as he held up a basket with a cloth covering. He looked around the room and frowned, not finding a table to place it. "I would have asked for a better room if I were you. Let's go; there's a spot right outside where you can enjoy this."

He continued as he led me along the brief passage and down the stairs to the street level. "You folks are an interesting group. I never met anyone who just came from Earth." He kept talking as he motioned me to one of the many benches that lined the street. I took a moment to marvel at the stonework that made up this town. The last days had passed in a blur, and I had been so preoccupied that I hadn't noticed the fine details. These weren't rough-edged stones that a mason had forced into place. Each stone fitted so precisely; it was as if they molded them for each particular spot.

Bryson noticed my curiosity. "It's quite amazing, isn't it? You should see a Stonewraith at work. They can melt the rocks in their hands and mold it to a particular size."

I was beginning to doubt this boy was telling the truth, but I didn't have a chance to challenge him. He continued, "You probably don't realize it yet, but each section of the town has its own unique construction. Each has a special pattern, type of stone, or color scheme."

I finally managed to say something. "The effort to construct such a place must have been enormous."

His eyes were wide. "I can only imagine. By the time I was born, they had finished most of it. But we'll often see a Stonewraith come back to change something or improve things. They always draw a crowd of onlookers when they work."

He sat next to me once we reached a bench, apparently with no intention of leaving me alone. "I have to train with the Guard later this morning," he rambled. "I'm not a member yet, but I hope someday I will." He took the cloth from the basket to uncover fruits, cheese, and dark slices of bread.

Bryson was a likable enough guy, even though he talked a lot. Oddly, he reminded me of myself during my younger high school years. It was a point in my life when I too was awkward and lacked social graces, even though I mostly wanted to please others.

As he talked, a single toll of the town bell rang out,

signaling that someone known to the village had arrived. "I wonder who that could be?" Bryson wondered out loud.

We noticed that a larger volume of people had begun streaming past us toward the direction of the main gate. Nobody appeared panicked; their faces held a look of excitement.

"I guess you must not get many visitors," I muttered.

"Come on, let's go see," he said excitedly. I smiled over his child-like enthusiasm and agreed.

A small crowd had already gathered by the time we arrived at the plaza. Russell stood at the forefront, just inside the opening of the main gate. A murmur of excitement passed through the throng as someone two feet taller than anyone else stepped through. My first reaction was that this was one of the doomed Ikhael race we had sought during our flight from the Raised Isles. But I quickly noted how this person looked different, both because of his facial features and by how vibrant and alive he seemed to be. The muscles in his arms rippled with each movement, and his skin was more like granite. Everything about him radiated strength.

"Welcome, Torermak," Russell's voice rang out. "We have missed your frequent visits. It's been too long."

It seemed to me that Russell was speaking to the crowd as much as to the newcomer. "Is that one of the stone people," I said to Bryson.

"Stonewraiths," he replied. "This one visits us more often than the others."

The giant gazed out at the villagers who had gathered to see him. "My people bring greetings to everyone. I'm here to be sure you have not chipped any of our stones." He laughed as if it were a standing joke and the crowd responded in kind.

"It's fortunate you came now," Russell continued. "We have other visitors as well, Astari from Loralee and other humans newly arrived from Earth."

The Stonewraith grunted as he considered the news. He paused another moment to take in the crowd that continued to grow. His jovial expression faded. "I'm afraid not all is well in the land." He spoke loud enough for everyone to hear. "But I am here as I always have been, to offer my assistance in times of need."

Torermak looked down to Russell. "It has been a long walk from Dal Tan. A refreshment and a sturdy bench would be most welcomed right now."

Russell led him through the crowd as we watched at the edge of the plaza. I shifted my gaze to the people still milling about, wondering if I could see myself as one of these villagers one day. Bryson began tugging on my sleeve. "Master Philip, I think he's looking at you."

I wasn't sure what he meant until I noticed that Russell and the Stonewraith had stopped walking as Torermak was staring intently in our direction. "Oh, he is one of our visitors I spoke about," Russell said, once he saw that the Stonewraith had taken an interest in me.

Torermak paid him no heed and began walking toward us. I wondered why he would be interested in me. In my new clothes, I blended in with the rest of the villagers. His expression made me uneasy, but Bryson took it as an opportunity to introduce himself. As the giant of a person approached, Bryson lifted his hand up, palm out. I remember Damek using the gesture when meeting a new race. "Greetings Torermak," he declared.

It didn't appear the Stonewraith heard him. With growing unease, I saw that he had fixed his eyes on me alone. He studied me for a long moment before speaking with a gravelly voice. "So it is true. You have been touched."

"W—What?" I croaked

He remained silent, as if trying to understand something. Russell became uncomfortable at the exchange, and he finally said, "Maybe we should all gather and discuss this."

The Stonewraith nodded absently as he finally broke his stare, looking as if he had just awoken from a trance. "That is a fine suggestion, my friend." He looked around again, his face brightening. "And where are Tess and Alan? I hope to see them."

"I'm sure they'll be glad to see you."

As they walked away, Russell looked back. "Please join us at my quarters, if you can."

Torermak's words continued to echo in my head long after they had reached the other side of the courtyard. *You have been touched.*

By the time Bryson led me to Russell's residence, Damek was already there. Russell thanked Bryson, this time remembering his name. The poor boy slumped his shoulders as he turned away.

I felt bad for him. "You were a big help this morning,

Bryson. I hope we can enjoy breakfast together again before I leave."

The boy straightened, and his face beamed. If he were a dog, his tail would be wagging at the chance to please. I smiled as I watched him leave, my smile turning to a frown as I saw the giant watching me.

Russell motioned us into one of the interior rooms on the first floor of his residence. Streaks of sunshine cast warm rays onto the quilted carpets. A white marble bench ran along one side of the room, allowing Torermak to sit comfortably, while Damek and I eased into the padded wooden chairs.

The Stonewraith rubbed his hands affectionately on the stone wall as if admiring the work. He glanced toward Russell. "Your people have done well since my last visit. I am happy for you."

He smiled. "Only because of the help from your people."

The Stonewraith's eyes shifted toward Damek. "Tell me, why is it that we meet only when trouble is at our front door?" Torermak said the words kindly, almost jokingly. "The last time those of your race visited with us, Rusgenero was trying to enlist our support in your conflict."

Damek nodded. "He perished during the final assault. Elderphino, my grandmother, became the First and served in that role until last year when she was killed during a Bot attack."

The Stonewraith lost his smile. "I am sorry. I did not know her, but he was a good person." A moment later, he added, "So why are you here? I do not recall the Astari fond of exploring unknown places."

"We are here because of the Bots. I fear they are more

deadly than we ever thought possible. They attacked Haven two days ago with a terrible storm."

Torermak didn't appear surprised by this news. "I know little of your foe. But I know what the bedrock of Elthea tells me. The old rock, especially, speaks of an approaching danger."

"The rocks talk?" I interrupted, too surprised to wait for more of an explanation.

Torermak smiled as he might to a small child. "We listen. The old stone tells us much."

"The Stonewraiths have an affinity with stones that goes beyond what we can comprehend," explained Tess.

"By approaching danger, do you mean the one we experienced?" Russell asked.

He shook his head, lost in thought. "The fabric of the world is being undone. A new power has come to the forefront. And they have taken hold of the very foundation that keeps this land alive. This storm you experienced may be the beginning of something much worse."

To my ears, he spoke in riddles. I had no more grasp on what he was talking about than when he arrived, except that he believed in an unknown threat. Besides, I was more interested in finding out what he meant when he said I was touched.

I was about to ask what he had meant, but stopped short, seeing he was now looking at me with a mixture of puzzlement and wonder, causing me to shift uneasily in my seat. "And you, my friend, have the same taint that I see in the Elementals that have turned on us."

I tried to breathe normally through a fear building inside.

"What does that mean?" Damek asked almost angrily, as if Torermak had accused me of something evil.

When he spoke again, the Stonewraith said the words soothingly. "It means that someone has changed this young man in the same way these Bots seem to have changed the Elementals." He thought for a moment before adding, "What was once good, may now be bent to their purpose. Whatever that purpose may be."

THE NEWS FROM TORERMAK THAT I HAD BEEN TAINTED hung over me like a weight that refused to go away. I couldn't dismiss it, but strangely it helped explain the cause of my attack on Cassie. The Bots had done something to me. The only question was, who was next?

I felt suffocated in the meeting room that had looked so quaint when we entered, so I explained I needed to get some fresh air.

I walked the streets in a daze, not knowing or caring where I went. I had long suspected that the Bots might have something to do with me losing control and attacking Cassie, but to have it confirmed was much different.

"You look like you've seen a ghost."

I turned my head to see Rae looking at me. A hint of sorrow clouded her eyes. She still hadn't recovered from the loss of so many friends during the storm attack. "I heard what Torermak said to you in the courtyard," she continued.

I frowned. "How did—Who told you?"

She shrugged. "Word gets around, especially the words of a Stonewraith."

"Do you understand what it means?" I wondered if she had any idea about the magnitude of my problem.

Rae nodded briefly. "It's the Bots. They're the cause of everything that's evil. They're responsible for what they did to you, the storm, other deadly things out there, more than we probably know about." She nodded in the direction of the wall.

"I'm sick. They infected me and I might not be able to control it." I felt a pleading tone enter my voice. "How can I continue knowing this is inside me?"

Her stance softened, and she looked at me with a curious expression. "You don't have an illness like my Mom did when she found out she had cancer many years ago. You've been attacked, as surely as if someone slipped a knife between your ribs. And whoever attacked you, put this ... let's call it a poison in you. It's infected you. Torermak confirmed it. He has senses we don't."

"Okay, I get that." I felt my voice rise. "I know I'm sick. But how do I get rid of it?"

"You already have your answer. You're going with your Astari friends to find the Valnorians. And from what little I know of them, they can comprehend all that is alive in the land. They have a skill with the flora, just as the Stonewraiths understand the stone."

"That's no cure," I spat. "Nobody knows if they, or anyone else, can help."

She regarded me thoughtfully. "I'd say it's a hope. At the end of the day, that's all you can ask."

"And what if I just happen to lose all sense again and kill one of my friends while we're traveling to this magical race?"

"Your Astari friends will protect the others. I've practiced fencing with Bevon and Riyaad before you arrived. They're pretty good with a lance and sword." I took in her collection of blades sheathed at her waist and leg. I had the feeling she knew how to handle them. "But I don't think they'll need to go to that extreme. I believe you're a person who will resist this, now that you know what has happened to you,"

She gazed toward the wall again. "Meanwhile, I have work to do. But I would suggest talking with your friends about this. I think you owe them at least that much, especially Cassie."

I flinched. "She hates me for what I did."

Rae shook her head. "She loves you, even I can see it. She's hurt. She feels betrayed. But she still loves you. Give it time."

I wanted to say that I gave it nearly a year and that hadn't mattered. But my throat tightened, and I wasn't sure I could say anything.

"Phil, you're going to be fine. Keep true to yourself." She gazed at me sadly for another moment and then without another word she turned and strode away from me, walking with a relaxed, carefree motion to her gait. I couldn't help wonder if all the people in this village were like her.

13

A STONEWRAITH'S TALE

The Stonewraith gazed at us without expression. If he stood unmoving for too long, I could believe he had turned into a statue. But when he spoke, he came alive, often expressing himself with sage words that revealed his wisdom. "You have taken on a worthy assignment," he said calmly, looking at each of us in turn.

Torermak was one of the few who had come out to the courtyard this early in the morning to witness our departure from Haven. The sun had barely broken the edge of the horizon, and most villagers were only now rising. I could sense that Damek was eager to begin our trek.

His short lavender hair sparkled as a ray of sun fell on it. My Astari friend gazed up at the Stonewraith with a wry smile. "We do what we must. I have never been a great believer in fate or foreordained destiny. Someone must stand up to the ones who threaten everyone." He looked over to the rest of us, and with a broader smile added, "We just happen to be available."

"Humph," said Diane, loud enough for us to hear. Damek glanced in her direction, but she remained quiet.

Cassie fidgeted with her pack, and she mostly avoided me. In many ways, her behavior was a significant improvement from the hatred she spewed in my direction whenever we came face-to-face.

"The Greylock Woods are some distance from here," said Torermak as he looked out beyond the main gate, which members of the Guard had just opened. It seemed as if he was trying to see the woods from here. "The Bots are not likely to let you pass unopposed. And there are other dangers. The lands between here and there are not so peaceful as they once were."

He wasn't doing a good job making me feel any better about this trip. Damek, however, calmly returned his gaze. "We can do little here to stop them on our own. The Bots are now beyond us in their abilities. We must gain support from the Valnorians."

"True, but perhaps you can use another ally in your journey, at least part of the way."

Damek frowned. "Who?"

The Stonewraith laughed with a rich, sonorous voice. "For all your intelligence, you Astari need things spelled out. I am talking about me. I will leave here soon anyway, and my path home to Dal Tan takes us in the same direction for some distance. I would not mind traveling with you for a portion of your journey."

Damek thought on this for a moment. "I suspect you would not need us to protect you, as would another individual."

Torermak smiled as if he thought this comment amusing. "I can assist you more than you realize. From your explanation of the storm over Haven, you were not effective at dissipating the attack. But I can help you become better. And as for safeguarding me, I suspect I would end up needing to defend you more than anything else."

Damek took a few moments to consider Torermak's offer as he regarded him. He finally said, "I accept your offer. We can all benefit by learning more from you." He turned to the rest of us. "At the very least, other predators will think twice about assaulting us once they see his size."

Torermak's face creased in a broad smile. "I will give you that. You folks are a bit on the puny side."

"How long will it take for you to make preparations to travel?"

Torermak observed the packs we all carried. He gestured with his arms to his body. "I'm ready now. I need nothing else."

Damek raised his eyes. "If you're sure, then let's be on our way."

At that moment, Bryson entered the far end of the courtyard and scampered toward us, shouting, "Wait, he's on his way."

We paused, waiting for the young man to reach us. After taking a second to catch his breath, he said, "I know you said you were leaving early, but this is really early." He looked up at the sky that was only now beginning to brighten.

"Do you mean the commander is on his way?" Damek asked.

Bryson nodded eagerly. "He told me to ask you to wait a moment."

He looked back toward the courtyard and then back to us. "Before he arrives, let me say that I am so glad to have met you all." His eyes rested for a moment on me. "And I'm especially happy to see that you, Master Philip, are feeling better. I have enjoyed our discussions together. Why I was just telling my—"

"Thank you, Bryson," I interrupted, wondering how many times others must have had to stop him from continuing. I forced as friendly a smile as I could muster, thinking once again how he was only trying to do his best. "You've been a tremendous help to me. I appreciate everything." He beamed in response.

"Thank goodness," I heard someone say behind me. I was so focused on Bryson that I hadn't noticed that Russell had approached. "I was afraid I missed seeing you off." He looked at each of us in admiration, almost as if we were part of his Guard leaving on an expedition. But most of all his eyes lingered on the Astari, the people he and his fellow computer engineers had a hand in creating. For all his imperfections, Russell struck me as a person who was trying to do his best to govern the village. Knowing a little of his background, I imagined he never aspired to a role such as commander of a community in some distant place. I had to admire him.

"I'm afraid I don't have any speech prepared or even advice to guide you on your trip," he said. "So I'll simply wish you well and hope you meet with success."

Damek accepted the words with a kind smile. "Thank

you, Commander. These last few months with you, Tess, and Alan have been remarkable. I cannot thank you enough for shedding light on the early days of our existence. And once again, all Astari are grateful for the decisions you made back then."

"In retrospect, our judgments were not always the wisest. But I'm glad that the Astari came from it."

Damek took a second to gaze at Russell as a son would to his father. I had observed it was an expression Damek wore when in the presence of each of the three programmers. "I hope to return before long. And maybe someday the three of you will come visit us on the Raised Isles." A crooked smile broke over Damek's face. "At the very least, you would serve as a pleasant detraction from the ire we're likely to face from stealing one of their sailing vessels."

Russell didn't know how to reply to this. But he smiled warmly, taking a last look at his creation. Damek then shook Russell's hand in the style of Earth. But Russell embraced him and then did the same with each of us.

"I am glad you are here," Torermak said. "I'll be traveling with them, at least for some of their journey."

Russell opened his eyes in surprise before lowering his shoulders. "I had thought you might stay with us for a time. We so enjoy your company."

The Stonewraith nodded. "Do not fear, my friend. I promise I will return soon."

Russell put on a brave smile. "Your interpretation of soon differs from ours. I hope we don't have to wait as long as your last visit."

I realized that the bond connecting the people of Haven

and the Stonewraiths was not that different from the one between the Astari and us. I wished I were here to observe the time when these people first arrived, and the Stonewraiths sheltered them during the war against the Bots, saving them from likely death.

The goodbyes finished, Damek suggested we be on our way. But as we made for the gate, we heard a voice call out from a balcony overlooking the courtyard. It was Tess, her leg heavily wrapped in a cast from her injury during the storm. Alan supported her as he stood by her side. They waved, and I heard Tess yell out, "Be safe."

As we passed through the main gate, I felt a pang of regret. I was hoping to see someone else before we left. I realized it was stupid to feel this way. I had probably not made the best impression on the people here during my short time in the village. Some thirty yards into the field surrounding Haven, I turned to scan the top of the wall. And there she was. Rae saw that I had spotted her as she stood a bit straighter. A moment later, she touched her fingers to her forehead in a casual salute. I smiled and returned the gesture.

She had been an inspiration to me. Her confidence and willingness to give heartfelt advice, especially when I needed it most, was gratifying. Without her, I might have fallen into despair.

As I quickened my pace to catch up with the others, I vowed to remember her words and not give up without a fight. I had almost let the Bots win by not even trying to reclaim the life I once had. I looked ahead and focused on the back of Cassie marching next to Diane. For the first time in a long while, I grasped that getting my life back also included winning the affection of the only girl I ever loved.

My feet were sore, and my calves were aching by the time we finally stopped for the day. I probably should have used my time in Haven to exercise more to prepare for this journey. But nothing to be done about that now except bear the discomfort. I recalled the intense workouts we went through on the Raised Isles before our departure. We did no such training before this expedition, at least I didn't.

Riyaad was already hitting a piece of flint to spark a fire with some twigs, while Quintia and Torermak gathered dry wood. We camped on a grassy knoll that would make it easier to see anyone approach. As most of the land we passed during the day, the place was primarily wooded.

I rested on the ground with my back supported by my pack. I noticed that Cassie had selected a spot far away from me. In the past, we would have congregated together without thinking about it. Diane and Matt looked at each other uncertainly before reluctantly settling down next to her. Here was yet another in a string of decisions that put them in the middle.

As I stretched the muscles in my calf, I thought back to Rae's conversation telling me that Cassie still loved me. I had doubts about it being true. But I had to hope that this journey would somehow rid me of this thing inside me. I decided to begin by taking charge of small choices such as this.

I grabbed my pack and moved over to them. "Can we talk?" I said to Cassie.

Her eyes widened, but Diane spoke first. "Cass, it can't hurt to talk."

Matt cleared his throat. "We can leave you two."

I held up my hand. "No, I want you all to hear this." But now that it came time to talk about it, I wasn't sure where to begin. I searched the surrounding space to gain a moment. "Look, Cassie, I'm only here because of what I found out at Haven, about what may have happened to me."

She frowned, as if no longer knowing how to feel about me. I rushed my words, wanting to speak before she objected. "Back on Earth, I had told you time and again that I didn't know what came over me. But now I do. The Bots infected me. Remember how we discovered they had infected the Ikhael? Only with me, it's not a disease. Believe me when I say, more than anything, I want this out of me. It's why I'm here. Otherwise, I would have stayed away from you as I did the past year. And just as Damek is hoping that these people in their Sacred Woods will help stop the Bots, my hope is that they know a way to remove this from me before something bad happens again."

I saw the uncertainty in her eyes. "You don't have to like me," I continued. "I don't expect that. But can't we just be civil to each other, at least for the time we're traveling together? You understand that Damek promised to stop me, to kill me if I lost control again. I don't know what else to do."

My emotions spent, I had nothing else to add. A vision took form in my mind of a time when life wasn't so painful. I was back at Woodbery College during the first days of our utopia team project. I was walking across campus on my way back to my dorm to read one of the books assigned as required reading for the course. Out of nowhere, Cassie called my name. My head swiveled to see her some distance behind me, walking with some other girls I didn't know but vaguely recalled seeing around campus. She said something quickly to them and jogged toward me. Her face was set in a warm smile.

"Where're you heading?" she asked.

I had felt a moment of trepidation. I was still new to the team and wanted to make a good impression on them. But Cassie was the one I felt most comfortable with right from the start. A gust of chill January wind blew a strand of hair across her face, and she angled her head and brushed it back. Her smile broadened.

During that brief walk across campus, we talked about the book I was about to begin. She had already finished it. We touched on many other topics during that short walk. She hurried through a range of subjects, and I soon realized that she wanted to know me better.

It seemed we had reached my dorm in no time. She was meeting with a professor in another building. I remember how she had captivated me with the intensity of her expression. "I'm glad you're on the team, Phil. I think we're going to have a good time with this course. Just remember what I said about Matt and Diane. They can be intense, and we're gonna have to work our tails off to keep up with them. So buckle up."

She held my eyes for long seconds before turning away. I moved toward the doors of the building, but I continued glancing over to watch her walk away. Never had I been so enamored with another person as I was at that moment.

And now, I saw mostly coldness in her eyes. "I can't forget what happened, or forgive you," she said with staccato brevity. "But I'll try to be more understanding while we're here. That's all."

I took it as a victory. "It's all I ask."

I SOON BECAME MESMERIZED BY THE CRACKLING, dancing flames of the fire as darkness settled around us. With the fragile truce declared by Cassie, I hoped that she would no longer condemn me for my violence. But I knew she might never become comfortable with me again. And that was hard for me to accept.

Matt and Diane took the opportunity as the evening passed to try to find common ground for a discussion between the four of us. After numerous failed attempts, even they lapsed into silence.

The Astari and Torermak had kept unusually quiet for some time, as if an unspoken agreement had passed amongst them to let us work this out on our own. Torermak had set a trap to catch a few small animals, which he now roasted on a spit at the fire, while Riyaad prepared a stew for the rest of us. I was still adjusting to the contrast between Torermak, a giant of a man, and the slight build of the Astari. Only a few years ago, I would have been alarmed beyond words at the sight of these other people. Now it seemed as natural as the sun rising in the sky each morning.

How far I had come in such a short time. Yet with everything I had gained, so I had lost much more.

Bevon, who sat across the fire from us, finally broke the silence by speaking in a stage whisper. "Quintia, it seems our Earthfriends do not understand this is the best part of our journey." He cast his arm out to indicate the space around us. "They sulk as if we had just lost a battle. Maybe we should tell them we are well-stocked with provisions, and this close to the village of Haven, we don't have to fear an attack by strangers."

She smiled as she placed another branch on the fire. "Maybe they miss their home. Or they may recall what happened the last time they came with us on a journey."

Bevon grunted. "I guess that did not work out so well, did it?" He thought for a moment, and his face brightened. "Maybe a ballad will cheer them." He glanced over to the Stonewraith. "Tell me, Torermak. Do your folk sing songs on nights where there is little to do but gaze at a fire and wait for dinner to cook?"

The Stonewraith had been humming softly to himself as he turned the spits. He laughed softly, a gentle rumble of a sound. "I know of many songs and tales. During our long winter nights in the fortress of Dal Tan, I have heard many stories told by our minstrels."

Everyone looked his way as he thought about it. "I cannot say I recall any about waiting for food to cook, but here is one that you might enjoy. It has long been my favorite." He took a few more moments to collect his thoughts. "This story is an old one. Our chief often recites it during the winter celebration. It tells the story of who we are today." When he began, his voice took on an even deeper resonance. I could almost feel the ground vibrate with his words.

"This tale has been told
By the Stonewraiths from long ago
Passed down from Father to Son
Mother to Daughter
Of a time when time was yet young
When the stones of the land were newly formed.

Our people were nomads during that age
We called ourselves the Nivens
We took what the Realm provided in its bounty of food
    and sustenance
Traveling to many far-flung places
Gaining knowledge from the different people and
    lands we visited.

Of the stones from the ground, we knew little
To us they were only big or small, brittle or hard, one
    color or another
Of their lore and knowledge, we were deaf
We were secure in our belief that they were dead and
    bereft of any value
Save maybe to use as a weapon to club an opponent
    over the head if the need arose
We listened only to those people who would deign to
    speak to us with their words.

So it was, our people ignorant and unaware of the
    treasure all around us
We were destined to live as wanderers with no
    purpose or rhyme to our existence
Except to follow our hearts, our feet taking us where
    they would.

What would have been the fate of our people, we will
    never know
Were it not for the Lady Elthea
Come to us as if in a dream
Explaining that she would give us a great boon.

She said, 'I have tried to protect and enrich
All the many souls who exist in my Realm
I expect each one to gain something from the whole in
    a symbiotic relationship
And I believe it is the responsibility of all to ensure
    that knowledge remains alive
Only in this way, will we benefit
So that what is precious will not die from the Realm.

'To the Nivens, I implore you to take on a unique role
Unlike that of any other
To you, I assign the most ancient entity of all
So you will watch over and learn from the very
    bedrock of my existence.

'The rock and stone of the land are the foundation
    of life

They keep alive the secrets from long ago
Ever watchful and aware of all that takes place.

'This I ask of you
Listen to this bedrock and keep their knowledge alive
Treat them as you would a priceless gift
In time, you may grow to love them and care for them
    as you would your own.
And in so doing, you enrich the life of your race
As well as that of all who live here.'

Our forefathers, however, did not understand this
    appeal
It seemed of little value or consequence
But we never forgot the summons
And as time passed, our people began to see the rocks
    of the world as something much more.

Slowly, by degrees, we attained an empathy
With what we had once thought of as only dead matter
We gained a new understanding of the rock and
    stone
And in so doing, understood the importance of our
    place in the Realm
We became the stewards of that which previously had
    meant little to us
Gaining from them not only their knowledge
But their compassion and love for the Realm.

It is then that we became the Stonewraiths

*Dedicating our lives to communing with the oldest
    entity of the land
We have assumed this charge until the end of our days
In the name of the power that is known as Elthea's
    Realm."*

WE REMAINED SILENT FOR LONG MOMENTS AFTER Torermak finished his tale. Damek finally said, "Well-spoken, my friend. It's a blessing to learn more about you and your people." He gazed at his companions. "At times like this, I wish the Astari had taken the time to delve more into the fabric of the land."

Once we had finished our meal and were about to settle in for the night, Damek sprang to his feet. "Earthfriends, I had nearly forgotten." He began rummaging through one of his sacks. "After Eric's invocation had destroyed the Bots, I collected these." He pulled out a bunch of retracted Astari swords and lances. "Your old weapons. I hope you remember how to use them," he added with a smile.

I knew he was trying to be helpful, but handling a blade was the last thing I wanted. I cast a glance at Cassie. The look of horror on her face told me exactly what she was thinking. She didn't want to have to worry about what I might do with a sword if I was afflicted once again. I caught the look of uncertainty in both Matt and Diane as they too considered the possibility. Or was I being paranoid?

He started passing them out to us, but I held up my hands before he could offer any to me. "No, Damek. You don't want me armed. If I came under the influence again..." I let the words drift off.

He caught my meaning and paused as he regarded me. "You think you are weak because you succumbed to the Bots once before. But you are stronger than you realize." He fingered the handle of a weapon. "Maybe later, when you understand yourself better. Meanwhile, I'll safeguard yours for now."

The others accepted theirs, practicing the technique of extending and collapsing the blades. I thought about Damek's words. Was I weak, or a victim of a stronger force?

14

THE DEAD ZONE

Our days were uneventful, filled with unending walking and warmhearted banter. If not for the weariness and sore feet I felt at the end of each day, it would have otherwise been a pleasant time. The terrain consisted of gentle hills with an abundance of vegetation, streams, and ponds. Torermak had no difficulty catching small game for dinner each night, which he always shared with us. We typically combined whatever he snared in his traps with the meals the Astari cooked from their supplies, usually augmented with fresh fruit or plants collected along the way.

We continued to move in a southeasterly direction, the same course we had set when the *Sea Spray* had ended its journey. We encountered no other race or people during this time. Our primary concern was another attack by the Bots similar to the storm that erupted over Haven. Remembering that attack, I often paid particular attention to the sky for any sign of trouble, and I frequently noticed that the others were doing the same.

The first sign of trouble came on the fourth day of our journey. When it came, this attack took an entirely different form.

As we walked under the canopy of tall trees, resplendent with their broad leaves, Quintia, who was in the lead, raised her hand in warning for us to stop. The other Astari immediately drew their lances. But only the natural melodies of the birds and tiny insects filtered through the air. My eyes darted up toward the billowing clouds. But they, too, looked as they always had. I saw that Quintia was looking straight ahead, not up toward the sky. I followed her gaze, and that's when I saw a distinct change in the foliage some distance ahead of us. Rather than the lush green and colorful flowers that filled the area, the land took on a rusty-brown appearance.

"What is that?" Cassie murmured.

The rest of us tried to angle our heads to see better through the covering of growth, but we were still too far away. Torermak and Damek went ahead to investigate, telling us to remain here, while Bevon, Quintia, and Riyaad spread out protectively around us.

After some time, Damek called to us and waved that we should come over. When I reached them, the sight took my breath away, but not in a good way.

My first reaction was that someone had sprayed the entire area with a pesticide that was killing all the vegetation. Giant trees had either fallen to the ground or stood naked, while everything that should have been green or flowering had withered and was nearly dead. A putrid, rancid smell permeated the area from all the freakishly decaying plant life. Even the dirt, normally a rich brown, had turned yellow. The desolation reached as far as I could see directly before us, and extended to my left and right beyond sight.

"This is not natural," said Torermak, his face drawn. I remember somebody saying the same thing when the storm struck Haven.

"It has the same feel as the storm," Damek added. "This is the work of the Bots."

"How could they do this?" Matt asked.

Torermak spoke purposefully. "Just as with the storm, they have taken control of the Elementals that make up the land. Rather than whipping the atmosphere into a frenzy, they have removed the life from plant and flora."

"How far?" I asked, looking in each direction.

They understood what I meant. Damek shrugged. "I don't know. It could go on for a few miles, or a few hundred."

I had a vision of this cancer spreading through the entire world, killing everything alive. The thought was too disturbing to consider, and I tried to put it out of my mind. "Can you restore it?" I asked, remembering how the Astari had waged a mental battle during the storm.

Damek looked at Torermak as if deferring to him. The Stonewraith thought about it for a moment before he shook his head. "This is beyond my abilities. What they have done here is something I cannot even comprehend."

Until now, we all stood on the edge of the ground that remained full of life. A sharp boundary separated the dead land from the living. I'm sure the others felt the same as me, wondering what would happen to us if we stepped into the dead area. Would we succumb to the killing force just as the plants had?

As if reading my thoughts, Damek was the first to test that premise as he scuffed the tip of his shoe through the dead soil, raising a small cloud of orange dust along with a pungent odor.

His face formed an expression of distaste "It doesn't appear to cause any harm stepping into it, but I have no desire to walk through this."

"No argument here," Cassie responded.

Damek looked in one direction and then another, trying to judge which way to take to avoid the damaged area. He looked again to Torermak for advice. "Any suggestion which way would be best?"

The giant merely shrugged. "I have no idea."

I looked again across the dead zone, trying to discern an end to the damage. As I did, a new feeling slowly came over me. My emotions did a flip and began racing for no reason. I was on the verge of screaming and lashing out without understanding why. My body quickly reached a boiling point, and I needed to do something to release it. If not, I felt as if I would explode. My breath started coming in sharp gasps, and my vision blurred.

A firm hand on my shoulder calmed me. I had no idea what had possessed me, but the grasp brought me back to a semblance of reality. "This is an unwholesome place, Master Philip. I feel your disgust," said Torermak.

His hand remained firmly on my shoulder, easing me back to whatever had come over me. I looked up at him, puzzled over why he was saying this to me. I saw the look of concern in his eyes. And then I realized that he understood what I was going through and was trying to shield it from the others.

I took a calming breath as I looked at my friends, noticing the puzzlement on Diane's face. The others seemed not to be paying attention. "I'm frightened," was all I could think of saying to mask what had come over me.

He tapped me gently before removing his hand and stepping away.

I looked inward again. The emotions of a moment ago had subsided. I thought about how close to the edge I had come, once again, to losing control.

The next time I might not be so lucky.

We soon called the damaged area the dead zone. It went on forever, or so it seemed. In two days of marching, we must have covered hundreds of acres of the devastated land. There was no way to know how far across the blight extended. We had yet to reach a point to move around it, and the frustration was showing on Damek's face as he contemplated the delay this was causing. Although, as I thought about it, I wasn't sure if he felt anguish over the delay or rather what had happened to this once beautiful land. Above everything else, the Astari had a great love of this Realm. The reason they first confronted the Bots once they arrived in this place was because the Bots had begun to defile it. I had to wonder if Damek now recalled that part of their history.

The damaged area was always within sight, but we had to

move further away as we walked parallel to it. The foul-smelling odor of the decay had made us feel ill. That alone negated any thought of trying to move through it.

As the afternoon wore on, I found myself walking next to Diane while Matt and Cassie, out of earshot from us, carried on a conversation with Damek at the front of the company. I had been walking by myself toward the rear, and I noticed Diane had purposely let herself drop back. "I couldn't help notice how you reacted to the dead zone," she said. A look of concern etched her face, and she spoke softly, with no accusation.

I shrugged, not wanting to discuss it. But I could see she was trying to be more like the friend she once was. "It's difficult to describe. I felt this horrible emotion. In some ways, it felt like it wasn't me reacting at all. It was as if I was someone else. But in another way, I had believed it was the most important emotion in my life."

I gazed at her to judge her reaction. I could see she was calculating what I had said with the precision of one trained in the sciences. As I thought about it, I added, "I'm beginning to understand something. The emotion was like the feeling I had during the seconds before I blacked out and awoke later to find that I had nearly strangled her to death. But rather than blacking out, as I did then, it was as if someone had pumped adrenaline into me. This time Torermak prevented me from going over the edge."

She nodded thoughtfully. More than anyone else on the original utopia team, Diane always looked for a logical solution to any problem, even after most of us had given up. "You don't have to answer if you don't want to, but did you take any medication or hallucinogenic drugs during the past few years?"

"No," I answered more forcefully than I had intended. "Hell, I haven't even smoked pot during the past few years." I smiled weakly. "Besides, what's happened to us since first coming to this land is more implausible than anything I could concoct under the influence of drugs."

She smiled, an expression that always warmed my heart. Ever since college, when she and Matt were first a couple, I had never considered pursuing her as someone other than a friend. As far as I was concerned, she was off-limits because of my friendship with Matt. Despite Eric's assertion, while we were drinking heavily at a bar one night that I had eyes for her, I never seriously considered that option. And it was still the case. But that didn't mean I found her unattractive or a poor choice for a companion. Even now, trudging through the wilderness for the past week, she was still the picture of athletic beauty. And it was easy to have a discussion with her, something that was missing most from my life this last year.

"I didn't understand what had happened to me after the incident with Cassie," I continued. "I thought I had gone crazy. She didn't care what had come over me, only that I had acted that way. And I don't blame her." It was always difficult to dredge up this memory of what I had done to her — doubly difficult talking with someone about it. I looked up at the sight of a huge bird floating lazily high above, noticing that it too avoided the dead zone. I brought my attention back to Diane. "But now, I know what happened. The Bots infected me. They did it to me." I felt my heart quicken from anger.

"Now that I know there's a possibility of ridding myself of this, I won't stop until it's out of me."

She smiled back at me, a brightness to her eyes.

"What?" I asked.

Her expression softened. "I was just thinking how much you just reminded me of the person I first met at Woodbery. You gave us this little speech when we met you. It was about how committed you were to a career after college." She smiled more broadly. "It was quite endearing."

I became flustered. "I thought the rest of you considered it silly. But it was important for me to be successful back then. I guess my definition of success has changed over time."

"So what does it mean to you now?"

I wasn't sure how to answer, and for a second I was sorry going down this road. I searched for the right words. I looked toward the front of the company and focused on the back of Cassie just as she turned to say something to Matt. Cassie's face was content and happy, and I felt a stab of regret over what had happened to us. I looked back to Diane as she waited expectantly. It was just like her to dig this out of me. "I want to feel good about myself again."

She looked at me quizzically. I wasn't sure if she figured out I wasn't telling all of it. The truth was, my real hope was to win back Cassie.

But even I couldn't bring myself to say those words out loud. At least not yet.

~

A RAZOR-SHARP LINE DIVIDED THE DEAD ZONE FROM THE land that flourished with life. There was no mistaking the difference. An inch in either direction and you knew you had entered one or the other.

The dead zone always followed a northeast-to-southwest course. Quintia remarked that it had been placed at precisely the angle that forced us to move away from our destination of the Valnorian forest, which was toward the southeast.

But later in the day, the line wavered, and the distinction between alive and dead became muddy. None of us were aware of the change immediately. As I trudged along, lost in my thoughts, it slowly dawned on me that the foul odor of the dead zone had become stronger. I looked toward my left, wondering if we had drifted too close to it. But, as always, it remained a few hundred feet away. I puzzled over this as I observed that there wasn't much of a breeze to carry the odor.

Damek, who was in the lead, stopped as he sniffed the air and looked around. Riyaad volunteered to scout ahead and trotted forward.

Alert to a problem, my senses came aroused. I might not have noticed it otherwise, but now I saw how the leaves on branches were drooping as if they had been without water for a long time. Everything had lost its rich, vibrant color. "They're dying," I muttered to myself.

Damek heard me. "I believe you are correct, Earthfriend. The zone is expanding."

As we waited anxiously for Riyaad to return, I realized another problem. My senses began tingling as if in response to the destruction of the plant life, or maybe it was in response to the power exerted by the Bots to extend the dead zone. I wondered if I was reacting to what was taking place, or once again falling under the influence of those who infected me. I took gulping breaths, a feeling of panic threatened to overcome me.

This time it was Matt who noticed that I was having a problem. "Stay with us, Phil. I know what you must be going through."

I didn't think he had any idea what I was going through. I wanted to shout at him or do something worse. I felt as if I were in a pressure cooker about to explode. But then he said, "Remember the Star Lights? How your brother Gary appeared? You told us what he said. Do you remember? He said you'd be challenged like never before and you would need to find your inner strength. Maybe he was talking about what's happening to you now."

I felt a conflict of emotions. But Matt's words helped me focus on the image of my dead brother as he appeared because of the Star Lights. Gary was a mainstay in my life. He was the one person I couldn't disappoint, even though he had left me many years ago.

I forced myself to breathe normally, willing my emotions to abate. I could feel the beating of my heart slow. The others remained focused on the return of Riyaad and paid no attention to my distress. That is, except for Torermak, who regarded me with a thin smile as if pleased that I had accomplished this without his help.

I looked at Matt. "Thanks."

He nodded. "We're in this together. Just like we once were."

Before he could say more, Riyaad scampered back. "The

land slowly deteriorates." He nodded in the direction he had come, which should not have been damaged if the dead zone held to its previous straight line. "By the time I stopped and turned back, it was nearly as bad as the other." He made a gesture with his hand in the direction of the dead zone we had been skirting the past two days.

Damek exchanged a look with Torermak. It was clear they had become partners in leading the expedition. "Do we try to veer around it or continue as before?"

The Stonewraith didn't answer immediately. "It's difficult to say. But it seems to me that if you intend to reach the Valnorians, the only recourse may be to fight through it. Otherwise, the Bots may continue to divert you, or worse, surround you with this destruction."

Damek nodded in agreement. He looked at the rest of us. "I agree. The Bots may want to prevent us from reaching the Greylock Woods. They may have the power to shift the damaged area indefinitely. We should move in the direction we intend. It may be the only way."

I looked around, suddenly fearful of seeing the vicious wolf-like animals that had kept us from going forward toward our intended direction during our last visit to this land. Was it happening again?

Cassie spoke hesitantly. "Do you mean to go into the dead zone?"

He nodded.

"But we don't even know how far it may extend," said Matt. "It could continue for days or weeks."

"And they can apparently keep extending it if they want," Diane added.

Damek's face softened. "All true. Which is why we should decide this as a group."

We had never faced this before. In the past, the Astari had always decided for us. Although their choices could be frustrating when we disagreed with them, in many ways it was comforting to know that they understood this land better than we did.

Damek looked at each of us. "It is easy for us to be full of bravado when first deciding to march out on a journey, whether it was to take flight with the *Sea Spray* or to leave Haven. But now, the choices become more difficult. We knew we would face adversity. The Bots have no intention of leaving us alone or of leaving Elthea's Realm or Earth in peace. We must do what we can. That's the only advice I can offer."

After a silence, Diane said, "We don't know how harmful it may be to spend time in there. It may eventually kill us as it has the vegetation."

"I've had time to analyze it," Torermak offered. "Although it is quite repugnant, I can discern no permanent damage it might have on us. But I cannot be positive."

That didn't sound like a ringing endorsement to my ears. I was already regretting standing here in the area where life had not yet been destroyed.

Damek waited patiently for other objections. One of the Astari traits that the rest of us often found frustrating was that they could be short on words, especially when it seemed they should explain their point by discussing it more fully. This was one of those times. I expected him to make a stronger argument supporting his choice, but he waited for others to comment.

For a while we remained silent. Finally, Matt spoke. "Damek, we've always trusted you to make the right choice. This is no different."

Damek scrutinized each of us for long moments as his conviction seemed to waver. "I've been loath to put you in harm's way." He raised his palm as if to forestall an expected response from Diane as he quickly added, "I know that did us no good during our last voyage. And this course may be more dangerous. But in my heart, I feel that a failure to enlist the help of the Valnorians could prove fatal to this land." He clenched his jaw as he looked in the direction of the dead zone. "We should resume our course directly toward the Greylock Woods. It's best we do it now while our supplies are ample. We don't know how long it will take to pass through it."

I noticed Diane exchanged a look with Matt that betrayed her concern. Like them, I knew it was risky.

But for all the dangers that we might face in the dead zone, I was only worried about one. What would happen to me if I became incapable of resisting that which had infected me? What if its hold over me became much stronger in that area? Maybe the Bots were intentionally trying to force me into it. Would I still be able to resist? Or would I once again commit an act of violence against one of my friends?

I tried to put the thought out of my mind as I fell in line following the others. I focused my thoughts on the memories of my brother Gary and how he would urge me to be strong and do the right thing. But the person I thought about most was Eric, my college friend who had willingly sacrificed himself so that the rest of us could survive. What kind of wretch would I be if I let his loss stand for nothing?

Above everything, I knew I had to destroy whatever these Bots had become. I owed Eric that much.

15

FIFTH INTERLUDE

WIRE SERVICE FEED — Washington, DC., USA — A recent wave of cyberattacks have decimated the United States, which has been struggling to recover from a widespread shutdown of the Internet and power grid that took place a year ago. Continuing to intensify during past weeks, cyberattacks have disrupted nearly every aspect of daily life for millions of people in this country and billions more around the globe.

The Commerce Department today stated that business output and production fell by thirty-five percent during the past month, due primarily to power outages and Internet failures. At least one-third of the country has been without power for over thirty days, a result of strategic cyberattacks on power grid substations, while the rest of the country has experienced periodic power failures for shorter timeframes. Nearly daily interruptions to online business continue to frustrate users and have resulted in dramatic losses for e-commerce businesses.

Homeland Security Director, Jeff Stewart, has continued to voice the administration's position that specific country-states and rogue terrorist groups are responsible for the problems. "The ranks of those who wish to cripple our country, and those with the ability to do so, have surged in recent years. We will employ aggressive measures to punish those countries, organizations, and individuals who inflict harm on this nation. Meanwhile, we have taken additional steps to secure our power grids," he said. However, a recent national poll reported that a majority of citizens are more concerned with how long it will take to restore Internet and power services than they are with the cause of the problem.

Disruptions in the US supply chain have resulted in severe fuel shortages throughout the country. "Even when we have electricity and the pumps are running, most stations are out of fuel," said Tim Evans, a Florida resident. Those gas stations which continue to stay in operation have no way of knowing when, or if, their dwindling supplies will be replenished. The unreliable power grid has caused similar problems for electric vehicles.

Computer science professor William Stanson at Golden Sierra University said, "The fabric of our technology, the glue that held our society together, is being torn apart. Emails, texts, phone calls, audio and video streaming, are being ripped away from every American. We have come to depend on digital transactions and communications in a way that we could not have imagined a generation ago. Ironically, what has happened now is more devastating to us and other technically advanced nations than it is to those who employ technology to a lesser extent. But we all will suffer, it is only a matter of degree. These cyberattacks are a milestone in our society. How we deal with them, how we solve these attacks will determine the fate of our society for decades, maybe centuries, to come."

Riots and looting continue to plague many major metropolitan areas. Local police are often inundated with emergency calls in those areas where phone service is available. Many 911 network centers have been out of service for extended periods of time. Other cities lack fuel for emergency vehicles, exasperating police and ambulance response.

Robert Brenderman, CEO of the consumer conglomerate Drake, and a longtime critic of current administration policies, said, "The belief that the city, or the state, or the federal government can handle this crisis is no longer a valid assumption. That belief has been seriously eroded. Most people are coming to the terrible realization that they are on their own. And that's when panic and chaos drive people to do things they would ordinarily never consider."

-END-

16

A SECRET ENTRANCE

I forced one foot in front of the other, my head bent low, no longer sure how long I could continue. The scarf covering my nose and mouth was doing little to keep out the rank odor of rotting leaves and pestilence. We paused a moment as Matt finished vomiting. Each of us had taken a turn puking until the episodes now consisted mostly of dry heaves.

The days were the worst, with the sun beating down mercilessly and nowhere to take cover. But the nights were not much better as I lay on the ground wanting to rest, but unable to sleep with the noxious ground inches from my face.

Our diminishing supply of water had become a major concern. At first, we drank freely, wanting to wash the dust and odor from our parched throats. But there was no source to replenish our water skins, so Damek needed to ration it, causing us to tire more quickly with the sun beating down on us each day. The thought of eating anything in this foul place was out of the question. The lack of both food and water were taking its toll as we moved like zombies through a land blasted by something we couldn't even imagine.

We trudged side-by-side rather than in tandem, finding that the dust kicked up by the leaders of the pack made it worse for those following. Every so often we witnessed the crash of a giant tree, no longer able to support its weight. I didn't know about the others, but I regularly searched for anything that was green, any sign that maybe we were about to exit this hellish place, or that the spell holding sway over it was weakening.

There was nothing.

Unlike the others, I had my own demons to fight. The infection that had caused me to attack Cassie was more potent than ever. It continued to increase in intensity since we entered the dead zone. Every minute of every day, I struggled to maintain control over my mind and body. I was tortured by the feeling that I might have already lost control and didn't even realize it. Only the inspiration of others, both the memories of those who had died and those by my side, kept me from surrendering to the force that threatened to overwhelm me.

Days and nights blurred into a tapestry of pain and suffering. We rarely spoke. It was too much of an effort. Besides, any conversation, except for the most necessary, would seem trivial.

I believe it was during our third day in the dead zone—although I couldn't be sure, having lost count—when Torermak's voice rang out. It was so unexpected that it startled me. Realizing that I needed to engage my brain and surface from the fog that had enveloped it, I raised my eyes.

Even then, I stood standing befuddled for long seconds, trying to make sense of the sound of his voice.

"Here," he called out. "I think I've found something."

I had trouble understanding how anything could be of importance in this place unless it was water, which I already knew was out of the question. Even if that's what he found, it would likely be tainted and undrinkable.

A rocky incline stood before us, and he was at the bottom on his hands and knees as he looked with interest at something along the base of the rise. My first thought was that he had finally cracked under the harsh environment. I had been wondering who would be the first, fully expecting it would be me.

Like the others, I shuffled over to where he kneeled, gazing at him blankly as he held his face close to a slab of rock. For the life of me, I could not understand why he cared. "This is quartz embedded in limestone," he said as he ran his hand across the face of a slab of stone that was partially covered by the side of the rise.

We all gazed at him without a response. Like myself, everyone had taken to wearing a scarf over their face to cover their mouth and nose. We looked like bandits from the wild west. With only the eyes of the others visible, it was difficult to discern anyone's facial expression. Torermak looked up at us as if wondering why we hadn't reacted. He tore the cloth from his mouth so he could speak more clearly. "This doesn't belong here. Everything else in this area is basalt or other igneous rock."

Nobody responded. He had only succeeded in fueling my belief that he had become unhinged. I vaguely wondered what Damek would do. Would he leave Torermak here or try to persuade him to continue with us? I had little doubt any of us would be successful at coercing this giant of a man with physical effort.

The rest of us remained silent, as if mirroring my thoughts that this wasn't something worth using up precious energy on. He seemed not to notice our lack of interest. "This was placed here by someone." He examined the ground around the stone. "Normally, brush and vegetation would cover this spot, rendering it hidden."

I could see the remains of what must have been plants surrounding the area. But that still didn't make it seem any more significant. Damek finally relented by asking, "Why does it matter?"

The Stonewraith grew increasingly excited and animated. I wondered how he had the strength to waste on something so trivial. "Don't you understand? It has a purpose. Someone put it here, maybe to help us. I must read it."

Even with the covering over his face, I could make out Damek's expression. Like me, he seemed annoyed that Torermak was causing a delay in us getting out of this place. His eyes regarded the stone for a moment before shifting to Torermak. "Do what you must. But please be quick. We can ill afford to stay here for long."

Torermak already had his face to the stone, both his hands rested on its surface as if looking for the right spot. After a moment, he moved his palms in a slow circle, while in a sing-song voice he began reciting an incantation using a language I couldn't understand. This continued for several minutes as I took a moment to gaze at the horizon, hoping to see some sign of a tree or a break in the devastation. But when one of the others gasped, I looked back to see that the stone under his fingers had turned into a swirling liquid. The fluid still held the shape of the original object and didn't flow to the ground.

His voice gradually became louder and his tone more expressive, even though I still couldn't understand the words. This lasted for some time. The stone regained its rigidity once he slowed his chant and stopped running his hands over it. The Stonewraith looked up at us, a glint of excitement in his eyes. "This is a door. A tunnel behind it leads underground."

I don't know if any of us expected that response. "To where?" Diane blurted.

"To the place they built," he responded as if that explained everything.

Diane squinted as she looked at Damek to gauge his response. The Astari leader hesitated for a time until he finally asked, "How will this help us?"

Torermak remained on his knees before the stone slab. "For one, we can avoid these oppressive conditions. Maybe we can find water. And possibly there's a way that will lead us to the other side of this area."

Torermak didn't wait for a response as he placed one palm firmly on the face of the slab and said some words. Soundlessly, the stone slid to the side, revealing a darkened cavern barely large enough for the Stonewraith's frame to fit.

"Who built this?" Damek asked as he tried to peer inside.

"The lost race of the Draas. They are a legend amongst my people." His voice was even more animated. "Legend has it they lived under the surface where they built an enchanted city."

"Are they still alive?" Cassie asked. It was clear everyone was now curious.

Torermak shrugged. "Nobody knows. We never knew whether the tales about them were fictional or true. This is the first sign of them I know of."

I forgot about my original skepticism. "How big is it in there?"

Ignoring my question, he asserted. "We must find out if they actually existed. Maybe they still live here." It was becoming clear that Torermak had shifted his priorities away from our mission to seek the Valnorians.

Damek, however, remained steadfast. "We have more important matters. Maybe later."

Torermak took the rebuke without expression. He gazed at the surrounding land. "Do you truly believe the Bots are going to allow us to leave this living hell? They are intent on destroying us. Keep on the current path, and they will accomplish it."

"Then how does going in there prevent them from doing so?"

For the first time since finding this entrance, Torermak appeared uncertain. "If the old enchantments of the Draas still hold sway inside their home, they may protect us from the Bots and what they are doing here above ground."

I had to admit it sounded like a weak argument. But the thought of escaping from this dead zone was appealing. For the first time, Damek appeared to consider the proposition seriously. His eyes shifted to the other Astari. I noticed a nearly imperceptible nod from Bevon.

It still took Damek several moments until he agreed. "Okay, we will enter. But at the first sign of trouble, we return."

I stifled a laugh, thinking how trouble seemed to find us, one way or another.

TORERMAK KICKED UP A CLOUD OF DUST AS HE SHIMMIED into the small opening. Damek went next, instructing the rest of the Astari to protect the rear.

Darkness engulfed me once I passed through the entrance, and I took a deep breath of the cool, moist air, such a delightful contrast to the parched, fetid heat outside. The tunnel was small, forcing us to move in single file on our forearms and knees. I felt claustrophobic from the cramped, dark space. But the Astari uncovered some glowlights they had brought with them, which helped mitigate my fear.

The walls of the cavern consisted of solid stone, and the way forward had a distinctly downward pitch. The further we went, the more I wondered how we would be able to navigate the way back up the incline if we reached a dead end. I didn't even think we could turn ourselves around if we had to.

A sharp gasp from someone ahead caused me to jerk my head up as I smacked it against the top of the tunnel. I saw a light disappear and heard the sound of boots scraping against stone. A second later the floor pivoted downward and I pitched forward. I tried to brace myself against the sides of the cave, but someone behind crashed into me. In turn, I careened into Damek who was crawling in front of me. The cries and shouts from the rest of the company echoed off the walls as we all tumbled forward. A glowlight pouch came tumbling past me. The angle of the decline increased noticeably, ending any thought of trying to stop our plunge. All I could hope for was not getting crushed by the bodies behind me or breaking bones in the slide.

At times like this, the terror of the moment can seem to last forever, even though the events take place in seconds. The cries of surprise quickly turned to shouts of pain and despair. There was nothing I could do to prevent my fall. The angle was becoming so steep that I realized we were now trapped here. There would be no way to return to the entrance.

I could do little else but try to prevent my hands, elbows, and knees from being scraped raw by rubbing against the stone walls and floor. The momentum jammed us close to each other as if gravity had brought us together for a final goodbye.

Without warning, the floor of the cave ended. I suddenly realized I was dropping through the air.

And just as quickly, I hit bottom, all of us landing on top of each other in a tangled heap. My first thought was that I was thankful Torermak had gone first.

My second thought was that I was alive.

Groans and protests accompanied the process of unraveling ourselves. This space was larger, allowing us to move and stand. As bodies shifted and rolled off one another, I found myself face-to-face with Cassie. Her eyes were opened wide in surprise. She was too stunned to react to my closeness. I heard her groan as she rolled away, and I hoped she wasn't hurt.

"Is anyone injured?" Damek shouted. I made my way clear of the rest of the jumble of bodies on the floor and tested my joints while looking at my arms for lacerations. My friends were too shocked to do much except sit with vacant expressions as they rubbed their arms or legs. Cassie had an ugly scrape on her arm, which was bleeding.

The Astari had already sprung into action as they tended to each of us. Bevon asked me if I was hurt. I shook my head dumbly. "I don't think so."

Both Damek and Torermak inspected the place, which I now saw was much larger than the tunnel from the entrance. The glowlights scattered around the floor gave enough brightness to see. But as I flexed my arms and legs to be sure I hadn't broken anything, I determined that it wasn't the glowlights that gave off the illumination. Even though we were still underground, the light came from a source I couldn't identify.

I looked up from where we had fallen. The stone ceiling was some ten feet above us. From what I could see, it was now solid with no marking to show a trap door. Torermak was already standing with his palms against the wall. My anger flared. "Great, we've gone from bad to worse. Now we're trapped here. Is this a trick by the Bots?"

Nobody answered. The others were still tending an assortment of bruises and cuts, but fortunately no broken bones. Diane had the most severe wound, a bad sprain on her ankle, preventing her from standing without help. Quintia was applying an ointment and wrapping it tightly as Matt kneeled by her side.

I glanced over to Cassie. Riyaad was helping her by applying the ointment Quintia had handed to him.

Once Bevon realized that I was uninjured, he moved over to Damek and Torermak as they examined the tunnel ahead. The Stonewraith appeared to be lost in a trance as he put his hands and now his cheek against the wall; I assumed to read them. But unlike the entrance stone, the wall remained solid.

The first thing I noticed as I looked around was that someone had taken the time to craft the stone into remarkably precise designs. Textured patterns and what might be letters were etched on the walls. I searched for the source of the light, but it seemed to come from everywhere. The cave led away from us in one direction, with us at a dead end and only one way to move.

"This makes no sense," I muttered to no one in particular.

Bevon heard me and turned with a curious expression on his face. "I agree. Why would someone want to trap us here?" Nobody responded.

Bevon and Damek waited patiently at the side of the Stonewraith as he continued his reading of the stone on the cave wall. After a short time, Torermak proclaimed, "It's as I hoped. We have found the home of the Draas."

"It's as you hoped?" Diane sputtered. "We could have been killed in that fall. Broken our necks."

He gazed at her calmly, as if not understanding the outburst. "But we were not." He looked up to the ceiling where we had fallen. "This is a very effective way to keep a large number of people from entering. It's not a method of inflicting harm." He poked his toe along the ground, and for the first time, I noticed the covering of a soft cushion of what might be moss, at least in the area below the trap door. "As you can see, it's designed to prevent injury."

Like Diane, I felt angry. I felt this was a trap. Torermak's explanation did little to change my feeling. "But now we're prisoners here."

He cocked his head. "That remains to be seen."

Cassie settled the discussion. "At least we're out of that putrid land above."

She was right. The air here was a pleasant change from our last several days. Torermak considered it settled as he went back to his examination of the cave walls. Yet, I still wasn't sure if we were better off. For all the unpleasant aspects of aboveground, at least we were not trapped in a cave. I didn't like confined places. And even though this tunnel was more spacious than the one we had entered, I still felt the weight of the ground above us.

I pushed away the thought that this cave could very well become a grave.

The salve that Quintia had applied to the injuries of both Diane and Cassie now caused them to fall into a deep sleep. From our observation of Astari medicinal properties, we knew this was part of the healing process. And after days of little rest in the repugnant dead zone, we were all weary. So this seemed like a good time to recuperate before moving forward. Damek suggested we take the time to recover.

After picking a spot and unrolling my bedroll, I quickly fell asleep, realizing for the first time in many days that I could breathe without nearly gagging on the toxic smell. My last thought before drifting off was that maybe this wasn't so bad a place after all.

~

I WOKE WITH NO IDEA HOW LONG I HAD SLEPT. IT COULD have been only seconds since I dozed off, but I felt refreshed and rested like I hadn't in days. As I sat up, I stretched sore muscles and rubbed bruises that I hadn't noticed from the slide down the cave.

Bevon caught my eye as he munched on some dried food, one of the assortment of items the Astari had prepared at Haven before leaving. For the most part, it was a sorry comparison to the food we had sampled on the Isles of Loralee. He motioned me over and handed me a pouch of food. I saw that both Diane and Cassie were still sleeping, but Matt was awake and sitting with his back against the wall not far away. He was also chewing on a piece of the rations.

"The Stonewraith and Damek are exploring the cave ahead," said Bevon. He spoke quietly so as not to wake the others. "We'll set out when they return. Diane should be recovered enough to walk."

"I don't like this," I replied. "What if the Bots are down here?" I still had nightmares of the underground Bot cavern where they intended to kill the Astari and hijack our minds.

"We have little choice now but to move forward and find a way out of here."

Matt came closer to sit next to us. "Our immediate concern is food and water. Our supplies are getting low."

Bevon nodded reluctantly but said nothing.

"And then there's the issue of the people who built this," Matt added. He looked at Bevon. "Do you know anything about these Draas that Torermak talked about? Would they be friendly if we ran into them?"

Bevon scanned the walls of the cave with its strange lettering before answering. "This is the first that I have heard of this race. But that means nothing." He brought his attention back to Matt and me. "Most of our encounters with other races were during the time we had garnered support for our attack against the Bots. At that time, we had little interest in finding a lost race." He brought his attention back to the walls. "I can see by these carvings that the Draas were intelligent, but I have no clue if they were peaceful. The trap door is a sign that they wanted to be left alone."

I had to admit he made sense, but I didn't feel any easier about this place.

Torermak and Damek returned a short time later. "This extends forward for some distance," Damek reported. "We thought it best not to stray too far."

Diane awoke and tested her ankle. She said it was a little stiff, but didn't feel any pain. Cassie woke a short time later; her wound healed with barely a sign of the laceration. Once they had time to nibble on the little remaining food, we made our way forward. The unnatural light made it easy to see our way. The tunnel was large enough for four of us to walk comfortably abreast of each other. Even Torermak's tall frame fit under the ceiling with room to spare. The path curved at times, but almost always angled downward.

After the unexpected incident with the trap door, Damek

decided he didn't want to be surprised again. He positioned Riyaad about twenty yards before the rest of us, with Quintia about the same distance behind. "Expect the unexpected," he said. "I suggest you keep a hand on your weapons."

I didn't have one, but I remained vigilant, scanning the tunnel around me for any sign of trouble. We had good reason to be wary of this place, and I was still trying to decide if we were better off here rather than remaining in the dead zone, even though the point was moot.

After an uneventful couple of hours with nothing but tunnel walls to look at, I had to keep reminding myself that this underground passage could be dangerous. The only memorable episode so far was the drop from the trap door. Bevon was walking near me, so I asked, "Do you have any idea why someone built this tunnel? It seems to go on forever and serve no purpose."

He looked to Torermak to see if the Stonewraith would answer. But the giant appeared to be in his own world, scanning the walls as if they were a treasure. Bevon responded, "It must lead to something. One does not construct a tunnel such as this without reason."

Cassie heard Bevon's answer, and she asked, "Torermak, what can you tell us about this race called the Draas?"

Her question brought back painful memories of the inquisitive nature of Cassie's personality. I missed those days, wondering if I would ever again share them with her.

Torermak blinked, realizing someone was talking to him. It took him a moment longer to recover from his preoccupation with studying the tunnel walls. "Many rumors and stories surround the race of the Draas. Which of those are true, and which were embellished through the many years, is difficult to say. It has been a millennium since they disappeared from the Realm. We know little about them. The stones of the land, however, remember. I've learned they were a race with remarkable intelligence. They ruled over much of this land above us for many centuries."

He fell silent as he tried to recollect more about them.

"What happened to them?" Cassie asked.

Torermak shrugged, a gesture that seemed remarkably human considering he wasn't remotely related to our race. "Even the oldest bedrock cannot answer that. They vanished from Elthea. But in the many centuries before then, the bedrock gives hints that they built a glorious city deep under a mountain and withdrew from the affairs of the land. They lived there until they passed from history."

"Could this lead us to their city?" asked Diane.

He glanced at her with a gleam in his eyes. "It would be remarkable for us to find it after so long. But we know little of their time underground. Even the stones have little to reveal, except that at one point all their people ceased to exist."

Diane, the biotech expert in the group, asked, "Do you think it was a plague or some disease?"

He shrugged again. "Nobody knows for sure. They have been gone for so long that most people now have never even heard of them."

Damek had been silent during the exchange, but now he asked, "Were they peaceful or warlike?"

"That's an important question for us, isn't it? It seems their history is a mix. During their reign above land, they took part in a number of wars. It was often necessary to do so during that millennium. But I don't believe they were an aggressive race."

A warning call from Riyaad at the front of the company put a stop to our discussion. He trotted back to us. "The way ahead opens to a vast cavern. It appears to be empty." This was the first variation to the monotony of the unending tunnel. Each of the Astari drew a sword before we advanced to the cusp of the hall that opened at the end of the tunnel.

Under other circumstances, I would have marveled at the breathtaking sight, made more so by the hours of passing through the uniformity of the tunnel. The walls of the room extended five or six stories and curved as it reached the top, much like the ceiling of a planetarium. Like the tunnel walls, these also displayed patterns which I still wasn't sure were lettering or a design. The far side of the room extended about half the length of a football field. A single entrance to another tunnel opened on the far end, its only exit.

"It seems these Draas want us to walk through this room to continue," said Matt, peering around the room. We all stood crammed at the entrance with our heads poking in, not wanting to be the first to step into it.

Damek frowned. "I don't like this." He glanced at the Stonewraith. "Can you determine its purpose?"

Torermak took a step into the cavern and settled on his knees to position his hands on the stone floor. As before, he paused a moment as if clearing his mind and began moving his palms in a circular motion. As I watched him, I noticed for the first time that the floor didn't have the slightest sign of dust or grime. Now that I realized it, neither did the long tunnel. The thought gave me an uneasy feeling. "Shouldn't there be some sign of decay, or at least dust, in a place that has been abandoned for centuries?" I muttered to no one in particular.

The Stonewraith began reciting an incantation, much as he did at the entrance of the tunnel. His soft voice echoed up to us as he garnered what he could from the surface of the floor. But unlike that first time, the stone never turned to a liquid, or whatever had happened. He finally stood and turned to us with a crease of puzzlement on his broad face. "Many things have taken place here, much of it I can't understand."

We waited for him to say more, as he thought about it. Diane finally asked, "What things?"

He looked at her as if not understanding the question. "I saw scenes of different places, almost as if the stone was relaying information of other locations. And it showed me a great jumble of events, much of it seemingly taking place above ground." We looked at each other, trying to figure out what he was saying. He noticed our puzzlement. "Please understand, reading a stone is an imprecise way to communicate. I can gain much history and knowledge from it, but it is filtered by both the reference of the stone itself and the method to read it. Here, it seems I lack the insight that the rock has witnessed through the ages."

I still wasn't sure what he meant. At times like this, I wondered how he could glean anything at all from solid rock. Damek inspected the room again for any other signs. "Did you sense any danger?"

Torermak frowned. "I cannot be sure." He turned away

from us. "I will pass first. If this place is a trap, it will be revealed."

Damek appeared ready to object, but the Stonewraith didn't give him a chance as he stepped forward without his approval. Nobody seemed to breathe as he cautiously put one foot in front of the other, pacing the length of the room. My eyes darted between him and the curved ceiling, looking for the slightest sign that something was about to happen.

But nothing did. The stone walls remained as dead as when we arrived. The only sign that this place held something beyond our understanding was the filtered light, which had no apparent source.

When Torermak reached the far end, he turned and waved. "It appears to be fine," he shouted.

"This still doesn't make sense," said Matt. "Why construct such a large place for no reason?"

"Maybe it once had a reason," I offered. They looked at me as if I had discovered a secret, which I hadn't. I looked at the curved ceiling and remembered my first impression. "Maybe it was a sort of planetarium where they could project views of the heavens." I knew I was reaching for straws, but nobody else offered a better one.

"Okay, let's pass through it," said Damek. I had wondered if he would have us move through the open space one at a time, but he decided to keep us together.

As I took my second step into the empty hall, the room erupted in a splash of light and colors which instantly materialized into a scene from my youth.

This was impossible.

17

ANOTHER REALITY

Waves lapped against a sandy shore. A lone seagull cried as it perched on a line of rocks that jutted from the beach. The sun reflected off the ocean, telling me it was early morning. The sky was cloudless, and the sun warmed my face. I took a deep breath, smelling the salt and brine of the sea.

My friends stood near me, as transfixed as I was.

Behind us, hugging the shore, stood a row of beach houses, mostly two-story gray-shingled bungalows with white trim. My eyes rested on the one I remembered; the house where my family had rented a room one summer when I was only five or six. A screened porch on the second floor looked out to the ocean. I would often sit in that screened porch with my parents as we looked out at the beach. A half-dozen cottages away stood a small amusement park. Its wooden roller coaster, Ferris wheel, and the ringing bells of arcades were now silent.

All was exactly as I remembered.

The only thing amiss was the absence of other people. Even this early in the morning, I would always see those who laid their blankets on the soft sand or sit under a beach umbrella.

Torermak, the giant of a man who had never graced this beach with his tall frame, came running back to us from his position further along the shore, which had been the other side of the cavern before it disappeared.

"Where the hell are we?" Matt exhaled after he recovered from the shock. Nobody responded.

The rest of the Astari had reacted instinctively by raising their weapons and crouching in a battle stance, as if expecting something or someone to rush at us. Diane and Cassie gazed around with their eyes wide.

Ever so slowly, I could see Cassie's expression change from stunned silence to glee. "We're free," she pronounced. "That room must have brought us here above ground." The rest of us remained silent, but she continued to press her point. "Damek, this must be just like your transition."

Damek and the rest of the Astari had dropped the points of their blades after seeing no immediate attack. "I would not jump to that conclusion so quickly, Earthfriend Cassie," said Damek as he sniffed the air.

"Are we back on Earth?" Cassie asked to no one in particular.

I responded after a moment. "It's an Earth from my memory, but it can't be real."

Torermak regarded me curiously. "From your memory?"

I nodded dumbly, not yet understanding what I was seeing. I thought back to the night on Tensheann when the

Star Lights floated down from the night sky and gave us the vision of a person we each loved but had since passed away. Each saw their own apparition. I couldn't help wonder if this was the same. "Is everyone seeing the same thing?" I asked. "We're on a beach with the ocean in front of us." I pointed to the seagull. "There, do you see that seagull?" I angled toward the houses. "And there, a line of houses?"

My friends looked at me as if I had gone crazy. I suspected they often wondered if I would surrender to the infection by the Bots and were probably thinking it had finally happened. Matt finally answered in a calm voice, apparently meant to soothe me, even though it only infuriated me. "Yes, that's what I see. Why?"

I looked to Damek, who was also regarding me curiously. "This is a memory from my past," I explained once again. I scraped a line of sand with the tip of my boot. "This was the exact spot my parents had taken me for a vacation one summer when I was a young child." My eyes were welling up as I recalled that my older brother Gary was still with us. He was the one who took me by my hand and led me into the water for the first time. I remember how happy I had been. What a joy it would be to relive that time in my life. "It was one of the few times we had gone anywhere on vacation. My dad had complained that it was too expensive, but mom insisted."

The Stonewraith and Damek exchanged a glance. Damek said, "I wonder why his memory was targeted?"

"What are you talking about?" Diane demanded.

The Astari shifted his gaze to take us all in. "This is an artificial reality, much like your Earth's virtual reality technology programs. Someone has created this from the memory of Earthfriend Philip." He paused a moment to let that sink in before adding. "It is not real."

Cassie was the first to object. "What? How can you say that?" She stepped over to the water's edge and scooped up a handful of wet sand. She giggled in the process. "I can feel this. It's cold, and it's wet." As if to reinforce her opinion she stepped a foot further toward the water and with both hands drew a handful of water and splashed it on her face, licking her lips around the wetness. "It's salt water, so we can't drink it. But this is real."

Damek's face softened. "Wanting it to be so, does not make it so. This has been created by the Draas."

We paused to process the information. Matt, always thinking logically, asked, "For what purpose?"

Damek thought for a moment. "I don't know." He looked at Torermak. "Any ideas?"

Torermak gazed out at the water. "Some believe the Draas were seeking evolution to another level of their existence. Maybe this has something to do with it."

"I can't imagine how," said Matt. "Although it's impressive, this artificial reality is not so far afield from our virtual reality programs already in existence."

"But they created this from Phil's memories," Diane countered.

"Which raises a question," said Torermak. "Why Philip and not anyone else? Was it random?"

Nobody offered an answer. But I did. "It's because I'm the only one infected. That's what you're thinking, isn't it?"

Torermak and Damek both remained silent. Damek

finally said, "We cannot conclude anything right now. It may be, but even if that were the case, it does not seem to matter much." He looked up and down the shoreline. "This is a pleasant view, but it serves no purpose. We should move out of here. I want to be sure we can find the exit."

The others nodded, and we turned in the direction along the beach that Torermak had been standing once the projection started.

We froze.

What had been an empty beach a moment ago was now occupied by three massive Bots about the size of the Stonewraith. They moved toward us, almost casually, as if strolling the beach like any human person. But this was a sight you would never see on any shore of Earth.

The Astari raised their lances. Damek glanced at me. "Earthfriend, were you thinking of them?"

I shook my head, unable to take my eyes off the shapes of these monsters from hell. It had been a year since I last saw them when they had captured and forced us to march to their cavern. And here they were again, looking deadlier than I remembered.

"Are you sure?" Damek insisted. The implication was that I had caused them to take form here.

I shook my head more vigorously. "No, I wasn't thinking of them at all."

Damek looked back at the direction we had come when this first started. "We can go back, probably exit from here."

"But that way through the tunnel is a dead end," Torermak insisted.

Damek nodded. "Yes, but we exit from this room and

later return. We can hope it resets into something new. Then we'll hurry toward the other side."

Torermak considered this for a moment before relenting. "It is your decision. But we do not even know if they can fight like Bots. We may push them aside without a struggle. Or they could be phantoms without substance."

"I am not willing to take that chance," Damek responded. "They look real. Besides, everything else here has substance. There is no reason to believe they are any different."

We slowly backed up, looking for the way we had entered when a wall of fire suddenly erupted in that direction. The flames were intense, and I instinctively raised my hands to protect my face as I backed away from it. The others did the same. Once a safe distance from the heat, I searched for a way around the inferno, but it stretched from the water to the houses along the shore.

"We can't get around this," I shouted.

Damek and the other Astari had already come to the same conclusion and were facing the Bots. "We must take our chances with them," Damek shouted. "Hurry, before more appear."

Torermak was the first to charge. I would have expected him to lumber forward, but he ran with surprising speed for someone so large. Just before reaching the first Bot he jumped nimbly in the air, and with his momentum still carrying him forward, kicked at the chest of a Bot, sending it crashing to the ground.

Bevon was right behind him as he charged forward with his lance extended toward another Bot. It met him with a swinging blade. Bevon jumped back and just as quickly shifted his balance forward and stuck his lance firmly into the ribs of the Bot. Meanwhile, Torermak swung his arm like a battering ram into the midsection of the final Bot, causing it to bend over. With another step forward, Torermak brought his knee up to smash it into its head, dropping the creature to the ground.

He turned to the rest of us, "Hurry, this way."

We scampered past the disabled Bots and raised our hands in front of us to find the exit. If we were actually on a beach on Earth, anyone seeing us would think we were crazy as we searched the air for something invisible. Either that, or we were practicing our pantomime. It appeared as if the beach still extended for another mile before us, but we knew the cavern wasn't that large, if we were even still inside the cavern.

I stole a glance behind us. Quintia was guarding our retreat, giving ground rapidly to the Bots who had already recovered from the blows. I was beginning to worry that there was no exit, that once activated, we wouldn't be able to find a way out of this artificial reality.

The three Bots were advancing quickly now. And behind them, another two had appeared and were also moving toward us. Damek and Riyaad turned to meet them while the rest of us frantically put our hands in front of us, searching the air for something that we couldn't see.

I heard the clash of metal on metal behind us. It sounded close. I didn't want to take the time to look. As I hunted for an opening, I realized I was unarmed, wondering now if that was the best decision.

All my self-doubts came rushing to the surface during

those frantic moments as we sought an escape. I feared I was the one preventing our way out. The simulation appeared when it keyed on a nearly forgotten memory from my youth. Maybe now I subconsciously wanted to die here, and to take all of them with me. It would be one way to end all the trouble I had caused.

I tried to push those thoughts away as I concentrated on finding an opening. Quintia cried out in pain as the fighting continued behind me.

Diane shouted, "Here it is." She was standing ankle-deep in water. One of her hands was missing; only her forearm was visible. Her hand had passed through the invisible barrier.

She stood at that spot to mark the location. Bevon pulled Matt's shoulder toward the opening, shouting, "Earthfriends, go through."

I followed the others, taking one step on an open beach, and another in a stone tunnel, made suddenly darker and smaller by comparison.

Once outside the artificial reality hall, we discovered the way back inside was blocked. Once we exited, there was no open arch or way to return, only solid stone. The tunnel looked remarkably similar to the place where we started. We were at the end of a dead end, with only one way to continue.

Damek slapped his palm against the stone where the opening should have been. "Damn. I would like to know if the reality would reset to something different if we entered again."

"It's just as well," Diane muttered. "I'm glad we're out of there. Alive."

Quintia had suffered a cut on her shoulder when fighting the Bots in the last moments before we found a way out. After treating her and wrapping the wound, she fell into a deep sleep. "It will be several hours before she wakes," Riyaad explained.

"Theories about what happened?" Damek asked, after giving up trying to return.

Everyone sat quietly for a time, causing me to wonder if they blamed me but were trying to avoid saying it. I said it for them. "My memories triggered it. The projection was a place I had visited with my family long ago."

"But your memories didn't activate the appearance of the Bots or the flames blocking our exit," Diane quickly added. "Stop putting it on your shoulders. Everything that goes wrong isn't your fault." I noticed that Cassie didn't react. Not that long ago she would have been the first to blame me.

Damek looked at us curiously, as he frequently did. I had the impression he was always analyzing human interactions. "Let's start with what we do know," he said.

"The hall is more than virtual reality," said Matt. He made a motion with his eyes toward the sleeping Quintia. "We could have been seriously hurt, maybe killed."

Damek nodded. "What I can't understand is why the reality turned deadly. Is it programmed to, or did we cause it?"

Nobody had an answer. Bevon finally suggested, "This

hall may not be the only one. The tunnel may lead to others." The thought sobered us. "We barely escaped with our lives. We need to have a plan should we encounter other rooms."

He was right, but for the moment we had no answer.

Once Quintia recovered and awoke, we trudged forward. In less than an hour, we came upon the next cavern, shaped much like the first. It also had an exit on the other side. If I didn't know better, I would swear it was the same one. I began to breathe more heavily, knowing that I was putting everyone else in danger. This bewildering underground world was wearing down my resolve, just as the dead zone above ground had before this.

"I have a plan," Damek said before anyone took a step inside the room. "For whatever reason, Philip's memory activated the first reality. Before he entered, Torermak could walk across the room to the other side. I suggest all of you except the two of us exit it on the far side before we enter."

"I volunteer to stay with Earthfriend Philip," Bevon quickly countered. "Damek, you are needed once we reach the Sacred Forest." The implication was that we might not make it through.

Damek considered this for a moment before answering with a brief nod.

Each of the others stepped carefully into the hall, looking around as if expecting another reality to take shape. Nothing happened. The stone was as cold and dead as it had been. Everyone except Bevon and myself was able to pass. Damek went first through the exit, and walked head-first into an invisible wall and bounced back, landing on his back with a surprised expression. The others approached the opening more judiciously and met the same unseen resistance.

"It appears we cannot exit," Damek called out to us after he had picked himself up off the floor. "Somehow it must know we are not together."

Everyone hesitated for a time. Riyaad skirted the perimeter of the hall, probing the walls for another way out, maybe a hidden door. But he eventually made a complete circle without finding anything. The others made their way back. "We should all enter and take our chances," said Damek. He shot me a warning look as if to admonish me about conjuring images in my head that could come to life in this place.

How was it, I wondered, that events hinged not only on what I did, but now on what I thought? I never wanted to be special. All I wanted was a rewarding life, one where I could wake each day with excitement about what was to come. I wanted someone to love, someone to love me. I wanted friends; good friends that would stick with me through thick and thin. And most of all, I wanted to believe I had done something worthwhile with my life.

I had none of those. I probably would have been better off listening to my Dad and working as a mechanic in his run-down gas station.

"Ready?" Bevon asked after positioning Riyaad on the far side of the hall just before the exit so we could find it more easily this time.

I nodded, taking a calming breath to clear my mind, or at the very least, think happy thoughts. I looked straight ahead unblinking and took several steps forward.

Once again reality folded.

An image of a honey and gold desert, sporting cactus and small patches of scraggly bushes unfolded. The vista stretched around us as far as we could see, divided by a road that cut across the landscape. We stood on the side of the road. And across the street was a one-pump gas station with a dilapidated sign bearing the logo of Amoco.

"A gas station," I muttered to myself, realizing that was one of my thoughts before entering here. But this station was nothing like the business my dad owned. I always viewed his shop as run-down, but not abandoned like this. And Rochester, NY was far from a desert.

"This looks like something out of the forties or fifties," said Matt. "Look at that logo. They haven't been around for decades."

I noticed the others casting furtive glances at me as if wondering what I was thinking.

"We can discuss this later," said Damek. "Let's first concentrate on finding our way out. Stay together."

Even as we moved forward toward Riyaad standing further along the road, I couldn't help inspect the building before us, looking for any sign that would tie it to something from my Dad's past. I could see no similarity beyond this being a gas station. Here was a place from bygone days. But not mine.

We had moved a dozen yards when the surrounding ground erupted with miniature explosions, sending sand and dust spewing into the air. What remained after the dust cleared were things that resembled snakes, only much larger and thicker.

Several had raised their heads to about the height of an Astari. They hissed, and each displayed a split tongue and a row of sharp teeth. The Astari had already extended their swords as they moved protectively around us. Meanwhile, Riyaad came charging back to us to help fend off a potential attack.

"Stay together," Damek cautioned. "Move toward the spot where Riyaad had been standing."

We inched our way forward, but one serpent lashed out in a blur. Damek somehow parried with his blade and struck the creature with a glancing blow, causing it to recoil. A second later, a snake on my other side struck at Riyaad before he could react, biting down on his forearm and causing the Astari to cry out in pain.

I cringed at an unexpected blast of noise from Torermak that I took as a battle cry. In a fluid motion, he bounded forward and grabbed a snake in both hands, wrapping his hands around its torso just below the head. The creature snapped its tail around Torermak's midsection, wrapped around him and tightened its grip. The Stonewraith squeezed harder, rasping with gritted teeth. Seconds later the snake relaxed its hold, and the Stonewraith ripped off its head; he threw it against the ground and stomped on it.

More serpents were erupting out of the ground. At least a dozen had surrounded us. And if things couldn't get worse, Riyaad, who only a moment ago had suffered a bite, now dropped to his knees unconscious as his head hit the ground.

Everyone except me and Torermak had a weapon drawn. Cassie and Diane withdrew their slingshots and were already loading them. I grabbed the prone Astari and hefted his waist over my shoulders with his head bent behind me. I tried to determine if he was breathing, but there was no time to examine him now. "Come on! Get out of here!" I shouted because it seemed like the right thing to say. But it was unnecessary since everyone was already moving toward the area where we thought the exit was located.

The first few yards went smoothly, with Torermak mostly clearing the way by scattering the snakes before us while Cassie and Diane hit a few with their slingshots and the other Astari fended off those to our sides and back with their blades.

And then things turned bad.

Out of the corner of my eye, I spotted a serpent flying through the air as it leaped at us. The snake crashed against Damek as he was striking at another attacker. Both of them landed on the ground and rolled a few times as the Astari attempted to gain his footing. But the creature had already wrapped itself around Damek's legs and before anyone could react, it sunk its fangs into his neck, biting down hard as blood spurted from the puncture.

Matt pounced with his foot on the head of the snake to dislodge it from Damek's neck. Once Matt saw an opening, he drove his blade into the creature's head.

We were all focused on what had happened to Damek, so nobody noticed that another snake had slithered around Cassie's feet until she screamed. In a split second, it wrapped itself around her thighs and reared its head poised to strike through her pant legs.

I saw it happening as if in slow motion. I reacted without thinking, lowering my shoulder as I let Riyaad slip to the ground. I lunged toward the head of the snake, putting myself between it and her leg. What happened next was more of a blur than anything else. I glimpsed the snake inches in front of my face as it was about to strike, mouth open, tongue flickering. And then a pain seared through my face as it bit my left cheek, causing me to jerk my head back against Cassie's leg.

I reached up and grab it with one hand just below the head as Torermak had done. My adrenaline was flowing as I felt a wave of anger I had never known before. I hated this thing for what it was about to do. My rage increased as I saw its head react to my grip by flailing around. I held firm and screamed out with a voice that even to my ears sounded less human and more something else.

I knew I had to kill this thing. In the deep recesses of my brain, I knew I had felt this same emotion before. In a twinkle of time, the pattern became obvious in my head. The same thing had happened when I had tried to strangle Cassie, when the storm struck Haven, and when we came upon the dead zone. It was the Bot infection causing me to awaken something they had placed in me. I wasn't sure what it was or if I could even control it.

But at this moment, I didn't care. I wanted the serpent dead. With a cold fury, I clutched what was inside me. And then I felt a cold satisfaction as I watched it burn before my eyes, knowing that I had caused it. I tilted my head to watch with pleasure as other snakes turned into ribbons of fire. The charred husks dropped to the ground with the pungent smell of burning flesh filling my nostrils.

My fury spent, I now felt an odd numbness course

through me. I protected the person I loved most, but I knew I wouldn't be able to save myself as poison from the snakebite made its way through my veins.

Her face was before me, a mixture of concern and awe in her eyes. What beautiful, penetrating eyes. "What have you done?" she whispered.

I tried to smile but couldn't feel my face. "I needed to make amends," I muttered.

The poison streamed through me. I knew I had only moments left. "You deserve better than me."

Her image blurred. I thought she might have said something in those last seconds, but I would never know. Darkness came over me, and I saw no more.

THE LOST CITY OF THE DRAAS

Who are you?

I puzzled over the words. Of course, I was Philip Matherson. But I sensed the question went further than skin deep. *I am someone without hope. My life is bereft of meaning or purpose.*

A long pause ensued, as if the other was considering my response. *Every living thing has a purpose. Why is it you alone believe you have none?*

I didn't have to think long about my reply. *Because I tried to end the life of the only person I had ever loved.*

But you failed?

It was as much a question as a statement. I thought about the difference between trying to accomplish it and not fully completing the act. *What does it matter? My meaning was clear. It ended any hope I once had.*

Ah, I see now the crux of your dilemma. You confuse action with intent.

We are all responsible for our actions. In that regard, I failed. I am paying the price for that failure.

So, you consider yourself a brave martyr? Mocking humor had crept into the sound of the words.

I thought it best not to dismiss the comment too quickly. I reflected on it for a moment and decided that I should reply honestly. *I don't know what I think of myself. But what if I did? Would that be so bad?*

It would if you do not desire to regain control. Another has already blackened your heart.

That raised another question in my mind. I knew the answer, but I had to ask it anyway. *Who or what has control of me?*

Those who have always tried to enslave others to their will. They have caught you in their snare.

The response did little to console me. *It is true then. They have infected me?*

The other seemed to pause again. *Interesting way to frame it, but I suppose you are correct. A battle between two factions is being waged within you: your essence and that of another.*

I knew all this to be true. None of it changed anything. *And how do I prevent the other from winning out?*

And here we reach the nub of the problem.

I waited for it to explain more. It took some time.

The resolution you seek cannot be answered by me or any other. It is something you must resolve. Only by comprehending what is at risk, will you achieve the ability to thwart that which seeks your soul.

I began to think the other was talking in riddles. But I sensed something there, just beyond the grasp of my understanding. *I know what's at risk. It's my life we're talking about.*

Oh no, you have it all wrong. Your life means little, considering the consequences. Much more is at stake.

An uneasy feeling came over me. Until this moment, I had thought the repercussion of my actions only mattered to myself and Cassie. *Please, you must explain. What's at stake? What should I do?*

I waited, wondering if it would again give me a vague, meaningless response. The answer, when it finally came, surprised me. *We can tell you this. The force that has taken hold of you seeks more than your life. It wants the essence of Elthea herself. And if it gains control over her, it will want the same in your world. It knows of only one existence: subjugate and tyrannize others, or allow others to do so to them. The ones you call the Bots are a mere copy, or reflection, of who they actually are. And now, these others bend your will to their ends. They intend to use your extraordinary strength for their design. When the time comes, you must decide if you use the power within you to bolster them, or for the good of all. But be forewarned, the choice given to you will not likely be easy.*

This gave me much to ponder. But I knew now was not the time. I sensed my connection with this other being was fading, and I still had one nagging question. *Tell me this, who are you?*

The response was much weaker, as if from a great distance. *This place was once our home. But it is no more.*

And then, as if spent, the voice left me alone.

My eyes fluttered open. The words I had exchanged with the unseen force still reverberated in my head. Unlike a dream which has the unsubstantial feel of something imagined, this remained as sharp as if I just had an actual conversation.

I blinked, forcing my eyes to focus on what was before me. And when the image sharpened, I saw the concerned faces of Bevon and Cassie looking down at me. I tried to push myself up into a sitting position, only to have Bevon firmly hold me down. "Stay as you are, Earthfriend. You were severely injured."

Because the conversation with an unseen force was still fresh in my mind, I had to take a second to think back to what happened before. I quickly remembered the attack by the snake-like creatures. The last thing I remembered was Cassie about to be bitten by one. As I forced my mind to relive those events, I felt the pain as the serpent sunk its teeth into my left cheek. I now instinctively brought my hand up to the wound and was surprised to feel no mark nor any discomfort from the bite.

My vision widened to take in the surroundings. Matt and Diane were standing, also looking worried. The tunnel walls and ceiling formed the backdrop. "The hall. We were able to get out?" I croaked.

Bevon considered how to respond. "We were. But it was because the artificial reality ended after the serpent had struck you down."

"It ended? Why?"

He shook his head slightly. "We don't know. But moments after the snakes and the desert scene dissolved, three small canisters appeared. Each contained a needle with a small amount of fluid in the vial. Damek, Riyaad, and you were unconscious, so we concluded whoever provided them intended to save you. Diane administered a shot to each of you."

"That makes no sense," I muttered. "First, they try to kill us and then save us." I focused on Matt and Diane. "Why?"

Their expressions told me they didn't know. Torermak, who was out of my range of vision, answered. "Maybe the Draas realize they made a mistake. Maybe we weren't meant to enter these halls and subjected to these events."

"Then why the hell did these tunnels lead through them?" Diane shot back. I sensed they had already gone through these arguments.

"How long was I out?"

Cassie answered. "It's been several hours. We were worried."

My heart skipped a beat, and not because of the snakebite. This was the first time in over a year she spoke to me with unfeigned compassion. I was so unprepared that I didn't know how to react. Afraid of saying the wrong thing, I only smiled weakly.

I still felt a little woozy, but at my insistence, Bevon helped me sit up. I was able to look around and saw both Damek and Riyaad awake and alert as they sat nearby with their backs against the wall. I could tell by their glassy expressions that they had recently recovered from the venom. Riyaad smiled. "Thank you for trying to save me," he said. "I am glad it was me you had to carry rather than Torermak."

I laughed. It was so rare this Astari tried to make a joke, even a feeble one was funny. Quintia came over with a pouch of some dried berries and nuts from our meager food supplies and offered it to me. "It's not much, but you should eat."

I gratefully took the pouch. Cassie lingered next to me as I munched on the food. She seemed unsure of herself. "I want to thank you for helping me," she said kindly. And then she quickly added, "It doesn't mean I've forgotten about what you did to me before."

I wanted to explain that I understood her reaction, but mostly I wanted her to keep talking. She looked at me with a glimmer of sadness in her eyes. "Maybe I should try to be more understanding about what happened before." A sad smile crept across her face. "That's what Matt and Diane have been telling me for a long while now."

After waiting for so long, hoping that she would just have a civil conversation with me, this didn't seem real. Maybe I was still dreaming. I didn't want to break the spell, and I was hesitant about saying the wrong thing. I couldn't take my eyes off her. Finally, I said, "So much has happened to us during these last few years, much of it difficult to explain or understand. Hell, I can't figure out half of it." I squirmed inwardly, knowing this was the chance I had been waiting for. "But I know this; I would never intentionally try to hurt you."

She nodded and lowered her eyes. "I know. That's what you've been trying to tell me all along. Only I found it difficult to believe."

I wanted to explain that it was okay, that I understood,

that I would have reacted the same way. But a memory from long ago came to me, and I followed it. "Remember when we were at Woodbery during the Utopia Project?" She nodded, uncertain where I was going with this. "You and I went out drinking one night at the Hideout Cafe, and we both had a little too much to drink. Do you remember that?" She rolled her eyes as if not wanting me to bring it up. I didn't wait for her to give me a response. "That was the night I realized that we both desperately needed to share our feelings." I tried not to sound like I was pleading. "We need that Cass, you and me. This thing, whatever is inside of me, put an end to what we had. And I don't know how to get rid of it. But I will ... or I'll die trying."

I slept for a time longer. The medication in the shot acted much like the Astari healing remedies by inducing sleep to the injured. I wasn't sure how long I was out this time, but when I woke, I felt more refreshed and energized than I had in many weeks. The poison I had felt in my body from the bite was gone.

Seeing me awake, both Damek and Torermak came to my side as if they had been waiting for me. "There is one thing we must ask, Earthfriend," said Damek. "After the serpent bit me and before I lost consciousness, I saw the snakes erupt in gouts of flame." His eyes shot to the Stonewraith. "Torermak explained that the artificial reality ended moments later." He hesitated, probably not wanting to accuse me of anything.

I nodded. "I caused it," I said calmly, as if it were something natural. I understood now that I had some power inside me I didn't have before, but it was something I didn't feel comfortable talking about just yet.

I could see my answer disturbed Damek, even though it seemed he also expected it. Torermak asked, "How did you accomplish it? From what I know of the people at Haven, your race has no such power."

I wasn't sure how to answer; I didn't fully understand it myself. "I suppose it has something to do with the Bot infection. I seem to have this new strength because of it." I licked my lips to give me a chance to frame my next thought. "I can't explain it, but I have this feeling that what's inside of me is from the forefathers of the Bots."

"Be careful," said Torermak. "It is not clear to me if this strength you command is a gift or a curse."

I smiled, but it was joyless. "Believe me, I want this out of me. It's why I'm here. It's done more to ruin my life already."

I glanced over to Cassie, who sat cross-legged as she chatted with Diane. If I could remove the backdrop of the tunnel, it might be a scene from them at Woodbery College, a time and place when we were so young and had no idea of the trouble and danger that would follow us. I brought my eyes back to Torermak and Damek. "Don't worry. I'm never going to become comfortable with whatever is inside me. And I don't think of it as a strength. To me, it's an infection."

I could tell that they both felt uncertain. But there was nothing we could do about it now except hope that the Valnorians could help. They were about to turn away when I remembered something else to tell them. "Wait. You should know what else that happened. The Draas spoke to me. Maybe it was only one of them; I don't know."

Torermak's eyebrows raised. "They're alive? What did they say? Where are they?"

"A voice came to me while I was recovering. I wasn't awake yet." His expression of surprise turned to uncertainty. But I pressed on. "They warned me about this infection. They talked about another force, I think it was the ancestors of the Bots, but they never named them. They said the Bots are a mere copy. They used the word reflection. The Draas explained that this other force infected me so I would help them."

I decided to leave out the explanation that I could use this power for something good. I had already paid a terrible price because of it. I needed it out of me. "The voice also said that this place was once their home. But it's not any longer."

Torermak's face took on a somber expression. I knew how much he was hoping to find the Draas alive. "Did they explain where they went?" he asked hopefully.

I shook my head.

Damek hesitated before saying, "You must realize, Earth-friend, it could have been a dream, perhaps the result of the medication."

"No, I considered that. It wasn't a dream. I could tell the difference."

"Did this voice tell you more," Damek pressed. "Maybe they explained how to leave here or the purpose of the artificial realities?"

"No. But I had the feeling they were puzzled about me at first. It was as if they were trying to understand who I was."

The two looked at each other as they considered this. Torermak grunted and nodded toward the direction where the hall should be, but was now solid rock blocking us from returning that way. "Then what controlled those chambers if they are no longer here?"

Damek said, "Possibly they are programmed with an autopilot. If that's the case, it may be difficult to find our way out."

I had a different opinion. "I believe the Draas are still here, at least something left of them. You said they supplied a cure for the snake venom for Riyaad and me. That tells me there's some capacity for them to understand us. And I don't believe that the one who spoke to me was some autopilot. It was too ... intelligent." I thought about it for a moment and added, "Damek, you were right about one thing. The Bots want to take the life of Elthea. And once they accomplish it, they'll do the same on Earth."

Damek took the information calmly. "All the more reason for us to continue our mission. While we wander around in this tunnel, the Bots could do more damage above ground. I have a feeling we might not have much time to stop them."

ONCE WE HAD ALL FULLY RECOVERED, WE CONTINUED TO follow the tunnel on its downward course. In a short time, we came to the opening of another chamber, much like the other two. "Damn," Matt spat. "I had hoped we were finished with these things."

I had a sinking feeling we had become trapped in a closed

loop of endless artificial reality chambers, destined to face one nightmarish episode after another, never finding a way out.

"It's interesting that this one is so close to the last," Damek added. "The others were spaced much further apart."

Torermak gazed at the Astari. "You believe that's significant?"

Damek shrugged. "I have a theory." He inspected the inside of the hall without stepping into it. "These rooms may not be the only artificial reality in this place. Maybe the tunnels are part of the game."

"We're in a game now?" Diane quipped.

"Not exactly a game, but a challenge based on gaming," Damek answered. "Possibly we will find out." Looking at me, he continued, "Earthfriend, are you ready?"

"Wait," Matt said before we could move. "That second episode was more dangerous than the first. I know enough about gaming back on Earth to understand that if that's what this is, and if these Draas follow a similar pattern, this one will be more deadly. That's the way they work. Each level becomes more challenging."

"What will you have us do?" Damek asked.

Matt blinked, glancing back along the tunnel from the way we came. It was as if he had forgotten that direction was blocked. His lips tightened. "I guess we have no choice." He took Diane's hand, and they each shared a look. It was an expression that two people convey to each other when they become one. It was an insignificant gesture, but one that reminded me again about what I had lost.

"Be ready," Damek said to the other Astari. "Earthfriend

Matthew makes a good point." Each had already drawn a blade.

I followed the others into the hall. In a blink, we were standing in a cozy room with a fire blazing in a hearth. Cloth tapestries woven with scenes or images indecipherable to me hung on the stone walls. The many shelves were lined with ornaments that made as much sense as the images on the tapestries. Several windows looked out to a sunlit field of tall grass waving in a stiff breeze.

I quickly observed all this before focusing my attention on a creature sitting behind a wooden desk. It gazed at us with interest. The skin covering its face and arms looked more like fish scales than anything else. Its large eyes appeared as if they came from an insect. It had no hair on its head, only scales like the rest of its body. The arms were much longer than a human's, and its hands had more than five fingers on each, as it interlocked them on the surface of the desk.

"That, my friends, is a Draas," Torermak whispered, afraid of breaking the silence.

The Draas angled its head as if interpreting the words. "You are correct, my dear Stonewraith." The Draas motioned with its arm, indicating chairs positioned before the desk. "Please, come sit. We shall talk."

Nobody moved, wary of another attack. The Draas must have understood this. "Do not fear. You are safe here." After a moment it added, "I apologize for putting you through the other reproductions. Unfortunately, you experienced an unintended consequence of their purpose."

"And just what is their purpose?" Diane asked before anyone else could speak.

The Draas made a gesture with its face I interpreted as a smile, although I wasn't sure. "They have many uses. My people primarily used them to challenge their physical and mental stamina. More recently, they have served as a tool to prevent those who might inadvertently enter our home from going further."

"By trying to kill them?" Diane shot back.

Ignoring the question, and as if noticing we hadn't yet moved, the Draas made another gesture with its hands to show the chairs. "Please, come sit with me. I will explain," it said in a softer voice.

We looked at each other before following Damek's lead as he moved to one of the chairs. A larger, sturdier chair fit Torermak's frame. Quintia, Bevon, and Riyaad remained standing, and they each kept one hand on the hilt of a blade. The Draas didn't seem to mind.

I knew this was a simulation, but already I was thinking of the creature as being real in the way it responded to us.

"Long has it been since any have entered these halls. Only those with the mental energies of a Draas should be capable of engaging the reality sequence." The person behind the desk turned its head to look at Diane. "To answer your question, everyone else would trip a string of events that would cause the hall to remain blank and the tunnel to lead the intruders to the surface, with no means of re-entering our home."

"None of us are Draas," Damek said caustically.

The Draas nodded calmly. It was now looking directly at

me, or maybe that was only my imagination. "One among you differs from the rest. You, Philip Matherson, have within you that which caused the reality to display your challenge."

I wasn't comforted knowing it understood my name. What else did it know?

"It could have killed us," said Diane, not giving up her line of attack. "Is that what your people find enjoyable?"

Damek shot her a stern look, but she was too incensed to notice. I could understand her anger, but I had more important things to discuss. "What's inside me? I still don't understand. And how do you know who I am?"

The Draas considered this a moment. "Certain people have a strength, call it a power, which allows them to draw from the essence of Elthea. This ability can enact changes in the land for good or ill. You have such a capacity. It was given to you by another." His face angled toward Damek. "Your people also have a limited talent for using it as well." I smiled inwardly, not sure why this made me happy, but it was the first time since meeting the Astari that anyone said a human could do something better than them. "The Draas gained this skill eons ago. We keyed our reality chambers to this power, which is the reason they activated when you entered them. As for knowing your name, that was a simple matter. Once we understood you had triggered the reality sequence, we delved more into your essence."

The figure of the Draas fell silent as we considered all this. Before anyone else could question him more about this, I asked, "Are you the one who spoke to me when I slept?"

The Draas nodded calmly. "Yes, in a way."

"You are only a representation," Torermak asserted. "Do

your people still live here? Are they alive? Can we meet them?"

The face of the Draas softened. "You may think of me as a construction of our reality sequence. But I assure you, I have memories, hopes, and a purpose in my life. My name is Enia, and my task is to keep our home safe and whole so that the others will have a place to return to if they come back. I am not alone in this task. Others assist me."

"They are all gone? Every last one of them?" said Torermak, a note of disappointment in his voice. "What happened to them?"

The simulation nodded. It held its head a little lower, as if sad. "I wish I knew, but I don't. They were about to embark on a great journey to a place far different from our physical world. You see, our people always sought to uncover the secrets of the universe and to pursue knowledge, wherever it led them. Through the eons, we learned much. But one mystery, above all others, captured our attention. We pursued the achievement of an environment where we could exist free from the physical limitations of mortality. We sought a place without pain, or suffering, or loss; an existence where contentment and happiness reigned."

I realized it was describing a utopia. I shot a glance at Matt, and it seemed he understood it as well. In moments such as this, I felt everything revolved around our participation in the college course called the Utopia Project, each of our friendships, loves, disappointments, and most of all, the threat to our survival. I wanted to explain this, but the figure continued its explanation.

"We set out to find such a place. We knew it did not exist

in our physical universe." The Draas paused as if reflecting on it. "I can only hope that the journey was successful; we had such high hopes. My people either arrived there, or they did not. But they have not returned. And I continue the charge that was given me."

Enia fell silent. I still wasn't sure if it was a male or female, but for some reason, I thought of her as a female. I reflected on this race of people in search of a perfect place. I hoped they found it. From Enia's tone and demeanor, I believed they must have been a good people.

Into the momentary silence, the wind outside the window buffeted the glass while the fire spit and hissed.

"You have been kind to explain this," Torermak finally said, keeping his voice low. "I feel the Realm of Elthea is a dimmer place because of the departure of your kin."

The figure nodded crisply. "That may be, but it's not why I speak of this. More than mere chance may have caused you to enter our home."

"Why do you say that?" Damek asked.

Enia spread her hands. "Events conspire against the Draas. A force intent on destroying the Realm of Elthea gains strength. Left unabated, I fear it may destroy our home. And even though my people are no longer here, my instructions are to protect this place in the event of their return. It appears the lot of you are in the middle of this struggle."

Enia waved her hand. At least I thought she did. Time seemed to miss a beat, and I felt strangely light-headed. I glanced over at Matt who sat next to me, curious if he had experienced anything amiss. His eyes were oddly blank, and his head nodded heavily. Alarmed, I looked at the others.

Their bearing was like that of Matt. "What have you done?" I said to the Draas.

"Do not fear. I did not harm them. Your companions will awake in a moment. I need to speak with you alone."

My stomach tightened. If she could disable us with a wave of her hand, what else was she capable of? "Anything you have to say can be said in front of them."

"I think not."

Her voice still sounded calm, but I was now fearful. I stammered an objection, but she didn't let me continue.

"You do not yet realize your capacity to destroy. And because of that, you are even more dangerous. Stop thinking of yourself as someone contaminated by the Bots."

I couldn't believe she was saying this. I thought about how I had lost control with Cassie. "You know nothing," I lashed out. "I can't go on with this inside me."

I expected her to object immediately, but she remained silent and stared at me. My heart began beating rapidly as I wondered what she was about to do. She finally pulled the words as if from deep inside her. "You do not have a simple path to follow and your choice will be difficult. As the first of your kind, you have no precedent to follow. I can only hope I make the right choice in allowing you to live." She looked weary as she drew a ragged breath. "You are not much to place my hopes upon, but you are what we have. To destroy you is not in our nature, and even if I did, it might not help."

I felt a wash of relief. "Help me. I don't know what is going on inside me. I don't know what to do."

She looked at me as if seeing me for the first time. "In the end, you must decide. Make the right decision and the land lives. Make the wrong choice, and it dies."

Again, I felt lightheaded, and just like an old projection with a jerky picture, the image of the Draas skipped a beat.

"Can you help us?" Damek asked. "We hope to unite others to our cause against the Bots."

I blinked, realizing he was reacting to the conversation before everyone blanked out.

Enia shook her head. "We cannot venture forth from here. Our charge is clear. We remain to protect our home."

She abruptly stood, extending her arms outward, palms up. "I wish you well. If there were more to tell you, I would. But I have conveyed everything you need to know." Her eyes glanced knowingly at me for the briefest second. "So now I must bid you farewell." She considered something for a moment and then added, "Tell me, where is it you were journeying to before you came here?"

Damek hesitated only a moment before answering, "We seek help from the Valnorians in Greylock Woods."

"Ah, their enchanted forest. If that is your destination, I hope they allow you entry." Again, she seemed to consider something. "Since that is your choice, you may leave the reality chamber and follow the tunnel. But before you leave, I will allow you the opportunity to glimpse a view of our home. No others have gazed upon it for many generations."

I felt agitated now that our conversation was reaching an end. I needed to know more. I still didn't understand what was in me or how to use it. As if sensing my thoughts, the simulation said, "When the time comes, you will understand what to do." I was unsure if she spoke these words to the entire company or me.

She bowed her head. Enia, and the rest of the artificial reality surrounding us winked out of existence. We stood in an empty stone hall. In front of us was an archway leading to a tunnel beyond.

After taking a moment to reflect on what had happened, Damek said, "Let us move on. We were fortunate to hear the Draas speak."

I wasn't sure I agreed with him. I decided not to mention the words Enia said to me in private. She had said so much, but it still confused me.

The tunnel curved to the left a short distance after we entered it. As we took the turn, a vista opened on one side that took my breath. We stood facing a city unlike any I had seen before. It stretched for miles in front of us, with our perch about mid-way to the top of dozens of slender spires that were as tall as any skyscraper on Earth. The golden buildings were impossibly thin as they curved and intertwined with one another. Walkways thousands of feet in the air connected some buildings. Lights flickered from inside them as if the Draas still lived here. It was all lit with a soft glow.

I recalled the moment I had first walked onto The Green on the raised island of Tensheann and marveled at the unrivaled beauty of the other islands standing before us. This was just as amazing.

"Is this another simulation?" Cassie asked in wonder.

Damek shook his head. "No, I do not believe so. I believe this is real."

"The lost city of the Draas. Who would have thought it still existed?" Torermak added with a catch to his voice. "They must have lived here for generations before moving on to their ultimate quest."

I almost expected to see other Draas walking the streets below. Fountains streamed water in the air, and the greenery of trees and parks lent a wholesome appearance to the city. I had no idea how they could grow here underground. Even though the Draas had apparently abandoned it long ago, I could see no sign of decay or disrepair.

We stood gazing at the sight before us for a long time, each of us unwilling to part. Damek finally said, "It is time for us to go. We still have the Bots to contend with."

As I left the home of the Draas, I couldn't help wonder if what I learned here would be of any help to me. I needed time to think about it. Mostly, I needed to accept that I was different now. But two things that Enia said stuck in my head. *You have the ability to stop what is happening in the land.* And then the other comment: *You are not much to place my hopes upon...*

I felt a stab of remorse, wondering if that was how everyone thought of me.

19

BACK IN THE LAND OF THE LIVING

We reluctantly turned away from the underground city of the Draas and continued to follow the tunnel. A short distance later, we reached a spiral staircase. Bevon moved around the base and looked upward to gauge the distance. "It is impossible to say how far it goes."

As he had often done during our passage, Torermak inspected the stonework. "This is well-constructed. No use worrying how far it reaches. We need to climb."

I soon lost all sense of time as we climbed the steps for what seemed like most of a day, that is if it was even day. We had lost all sensation of day or night in this perpetually lit place. Even with occasional stops to rest, I grew wearier with each step as I thought it would never end. We had depleted our water, and the little food that remained tasted too dry to eat.

My head was down as I looked at every step, careful not to trip. I hadn't noticed the others had stopped until I nearly bumped into Matt in front of me. They were standing on a small landing before a stone slab. The stairs had ended with nowhere to go. My heart sank, unable to bear the thought of walking back down the steps into the tunnel.

Torermak inspected it, and I thought he would perform another of his magical incantations as he had at the entrance of the tunnel. But as soon as he touched the surface, it slid silently to the side, revealing open sky and fertile land before us.

Cassie inhaled deeply. "It's been so long," We all understood what she meant. Finally, this was a place not tainted by the destruction of the Bots or some false projection.

"I didn't think we would ever make it out alive," Diane muttered.

The outside had the appearance of dusk, but it was difficult to tell because of the thick mantle of clouds. Rain fell steadily, occasionally whipped into sheets by a gusty breeze. Lush grass gave way to towering trees. The smell of pine and flowers never seemed so fragrant. My weariness and foreboding melted away.

As soon as we stepped away from the opening to the stairway, the stone slid back into place. From the outside, it appeared as rough stone, indistinguishable from the surrounding surface, just as the stone had appeared in the dead zone when we first entered. I was so glad to be out from underground and away from the dead zone. I didn't care about anything else.

My joy, however, was short-lived.

As soon as my clothes became soaked, I wondered if we shouldn't have waited under cover until the rain abated. We found a stream to refresh our thirst, and the Astari collected some nuts for us to munch.

As darkness descended, Bevon and Riyaad constructed a crude shelter with a blanket strung high enough for Matt, Diane, Cassie, and me to sit under. It gave us some cover, even though the ground was wet. "Welcome back to the land of the living," Torermak chided after seeing us huddle under the covering. He, along with the Astari, had no problem remaining exposed to the elements. "Be thankful that we are not still in the devastation. This is Elthea's way of welcoming us home."

"A sunny day and a lake for us to bathe in would have been better," Diane responded.

The small branches were too wet to light a fire. And without its comforting light, the surrounding area was shrouded in darkness, made more so because neither of Elthea's moons penetrated the clouds. The glowlights helped, but murky shadows surrounded us. "Does anyone know where we are?" I asked. It didn't seem like we had walked a considerable distance in the tunnels, since most of it was downhill. I assumed we had traveled just beyond the area of the dead zone.

Damek, who was sitting next to the Stonewraith, answered. "From the size of the surrounding trees, I believe we are on the outskirts of the Sacred Woods of the Valnorians. We've come many leagues from where we entered the home of the Draas."

"How did that happen?" Matt asked. "I thought you said it would take us weeks to reach their forest."

Torermak chuckled. "It seems the Draas did us a favor."

We waited for him to say more, and after a few moments, he realized we were still looking at him to explain. "Do you remember when Enia asked us where we were going?" Not waiting for a response, he added, "As Damek speculated earlier, the tunnels might also be part of their artificial reality. Either that or the last reality chamber brought us to a tunnel close to our destination."

Either way, I was thankful we didn't have to walk the long distance. I recalled what happened during our last march to the Greylock Forest. We already faced enough unpleasant encounters on this trip.

"But I have another matter to discuss now that we find ourselves here," Torermak added. His face clouded over and he fidgeted with his hands. "I am glad we are close to your destination. But it has taken me further from my home. It is past the time I make my way back to Dal Tan. In the morning I must head in a northerly direction rather than continue with you."

We had traveled together for so long that I had thought he would continue with us.

"You're gonna leave?" said Cassie.

He nodded. "I'm afraid so. I need to warn my people of this new danger from the Bots with their dead zones and control of the Elementals." His face brightened as he thought about it. "Besides, I'll be a legend among the Stonewraiths when I tell the story of how I found the Draas and gazed upon the lost city. It will be a tale that will be told again and again through the ages." He smiled broadly as if imagining the prestige it would bring him.

SOMETIME DURING THE NIGHT, THE RAIN HAD ABATED, and morning arrived with the sun shining. In spite of my weariness, I slept fitfully, unsure if it was because of the dampness or Torermak's announcement that he would leave us. Added to that, I remained bothered by Enia saying that I was dangerous. In any case, I felt miserable.

I moved my head and observed the Stonewraith standing a short distance away, his back to me as he took a measure of our surroundings. There was something different in his posture this morning. He turned to walk back to us with a lightness in his step. Seeing us awake, he said, "A good day to begin a new adventure, my friends."

None of us responded. He must have noticed our dispirited reaction as his eyes narrowed. "Let us make a pact that one day we will all meet again in Haven." He considered this a moment and then added with a smile, "Or better yet, we meet on the Raised Isles of Loralee."

"The Astari will always welcome you to our home," Damek responded. And then in a softer voice added, "Even though they may not greet the four of us quite so warmly."

Torermak laughed, having heard the story of how a year ago we snuck off with a ship from the islands. "You bring me with you and I'll pound sense into any Astari that treats you with anything but respect." A moment later he sobered and added, "I suspect I will always look back on this time with fond memories. You can rest assured that the Stonewraiths will hear about our friendship."

Damek nodded as if accepting a gift. "The Stonewraiths

and Astari may need each other in the times ahead. I am glad we spent this time with you."

Torermak bent down low to embrace Damek. After a long hug, he did the same with each of the other Astari. He then faced us. "I have known many of your fellow humans since they came here many years ago. But you have taught me much about the human spirit. For that I thank you." He paused before adding, "You will be Earthfriends to me forevermore."

He smiled and bent low to embrace each of us, turning to me last. "You, Earthfriend Philip, are a special person." And then in a lower voice for only my ears, he added, "You have it in you to do what is right. Remember that, my friend."

I nodded, unsure of how to respond. He hugged me with surprising gentleness for someone his size. He straightened up and peered at us. "Until we meet again, I wish you success."

And with that he turned and trotted away, never looking back.

WE TOOK TIME TO SPREAD OUR WET CLOTHES IN THE SUN to dry before continuing. Cassie and Diane stepped over to a cluster of bushes to remove their clothes in privacy. Diane turned to us as they walked away, admonishing us by pointing a finger. "No peeking boys." My heart leaped at the sight of Cassie smiling back at us. After being in a pitched battle with her for so long, it felt remarkably good to see Cassie react to me as a human.

Quintia and Bevon took the time to gather more greens, mushroom, fruits, nuts, and berries from the surrounding area, and Damek assented to Bevon's request that we light a fire and prepare a warm breakfast.

Once our clothes had dried, we sat around the fire and watched the Astari prepare a meal. They chopped, steamed, and used a skillet to cook an assortment of what they picked. Quintia took a portion of each mixture and placed it into a broad leaf and wrapped it tightly. She prepared one for each of us. "This may be a poor substitute for what we can cook back home, but it should suffice."

She handed me one, and I tasted it. After many days of little to eat but dry food, it was a feast. "I'm in heaven," Diane gushed between bites.

As I enjoyed the food, I reflected on similar moments during our first visit to the land, quiet times such as this when we would revel in pleasant conversation while enjoying a meal with our Astari companions. Maybe it was because we faced so many hazards that I remembered most fondly these calm reflections between one tempest or another. How I wish this could last forever as we enjoyed good food with the company of good friends.

"So how close are we to this forest of the Valnorians?" Matt asked between bites.

Damek glanced at the trees in the distance before answering. "We are close to the edge of their woods. A few hours should bring us to the outskirts."

"Now would be a good time to tell the Earthfriends more about the Valnorians," Bevon suggested.

His comment made me realize that all I knew about this

race was that the Astari trusted them and they lived in the woods, maybe that, and a few bits about them having a very contemplative disposition.

Damek hesitated. "One thing that I should tell you is that they might not welcome us with open arms."

"What!" Diane shouted. "Twice now we've risked our lives trying to get to these people, and now you tell us they may not be friendly at all?" I thought how Diane now filled the role that Eric had once held in our group of being the most outspoken.

Damek held up his hands in mock imitation of fending off an attack. "They are friends of the Astari, or at least they once were." Diane was about to erupt with another salvo, but Damek forestalled her by raising his voice and continuing rapidly. "They are a reclusive people, much like the Astari. They allow no strangers to enter their forest. But that does not make them hostile." Once he saw that he had contained her outburst, he continued in a level tone. "The Valnorians fought hand-to-hand with us during the great war against the Bots. They have no love for them. Once I explain why we are intruding on their land, I am sure they will understand."

I could see that Diane wasn't convinced, and I could understand her passion. "You realize, Damek, that we are risking everything on them," I said. "I remember the time we risked our lives when we sought help from the doomed race of the Ikhael. And now this time we were nearly killed in the Draas reality chambers. Why do you think they can help? Do you think that hating the Bots in the past is enough to move them to action?"

Damek thought about this before answering, probably to

avoid saying the wrong thing. "You saw Torermak's skill and lore with rock. Well, the Valnorians have an affinity for that which grows in the land. They've spent generations fostering a love of all that is alive. As such, they have this connection with the life force that is Elthea. Their understanding far surpasses ours, and possibly any other living race. With this knowledge, I hope that they can recognize how to counteract the control the Bots have on the Elementals."

"And you believe they will be willing to help?" asked Matt.

"I have to hope they will. If they choose not to, none of us may survive. The warning by Enia supports it."

Every time he recounted the discussion with Enia, I couldn't help think I was the real danger she was warning us about, not the Bots. During my depressed state of mind at Haven, I would have taken her words as a sign that I needed to end my life. Now, even though I believed something was wrong with me, I had more hope that the Valnorians would help.

"I want to thank all of you," I said before I could think about it.

Everyone looked at me as if not understanding, which was reasonable considering my rush to express myself. "I mean your willingness to accept me in spite of my past behavior," I clarified.

To my surprise, they remained puzzled, except for Cassie, who frowned. I realized that she might think I was blaming her for the way she had acted toward me after the incident. "I admire you, Cass. After what I had done, you could have continued to hate me, and you would have every right. But you didn't."

She wasn't sure how to respond. Into the silence, Matt said, "We're a team, remember? We've all hit rough patches in our lives. Friends get past it. Whatever caused you to hurt Cassie, we'll find the reason and cure you of it."

I lowered my head. "What if there isn't a reason? Suppose I'm just a bad person?"

"You'll be fine," said Diane. "Hopefully, these Valnorians will help get that infection out of you."

I nodded. "That, and knowing that you don't hate me any longer, Cass, keeps me going."

"I don't know if I ever hated you," she said softly. A moment later, a wry smile creased her lips. "Well, maybe I did just a little. But I didn't understand." She glanced around at the towering trees in the distance. "Anything is possible in this land, including you becoming infected. I should have realized that."

The Astari had remained silent during the exchange, preferring to observe us as they commonly did during times like this. Damek finally said, "I've noticed that many humans find and dissolve friendships like the change of seasons. Some people are not meant to be together forever. But it seems to me that yours is a different affinity. Consider it a blessing."

WE BEGAN OUR JOURNEY AGAIN BY MID-MORNING, having rested and found nourishment in both food and words.

It wasn't long before Damek announced that we had entered the Greylock Forest as the trees and the land took on a different appearance. We passed under thick vines that twisted above us as if notifying strangers that they had entered another domain. And it wasn't only the trees and vegetation that were different. The sounds of the forest increased in intensity from insects and small critters that scurried around us.

I wondered if the sights were even more dramatic because of the time we spent both underground and in the dead zone. Whatever the reason, everywhere else dimmed compared to the abundance of life and growth I now saw. And the further we traveled, the more dramatic it became.

I gazed up at the canopy of green and silver leaves as they rustled in the breeze, sounding more like the echo of voices by a group of people just out of sight as they whispered to each other. In other areas, we passed groves of trees that contained leaves of every imaginable color, a rainbow more beautiful than any I had seen in the sky after a summer storm.

In some places the trees supported impossibly large branches that hung low, bending toward the ground with their weight. We then passed trees that were lithe and sinewy, intertwining with one another in an orchestrated dance as they flexed in the breeze. In other areas the trees were stately with an appearance of being meticulously groomed, each branch extending slightly shorter from the trunk the higher they grew. These trees grew in straight rows as if planted an exact distance from one another.

I remembered the butterfly tree that we saw during the

first day on the Raised Isles as we made a mad dash from a Bot attack, and I looked for it here, but didn't see one, at least not yet. More than a dozen times I wanted to stop and stare as we came upon a place sporting another breathtaking grove of trees or flowers.

At one point we passed under trees that appeared to be a collection of branches growing from the ground to form a web of connected limbs with no central trunk. These towered high above us and I craned my neck to see the tops.

Cassie soon made her way to my side. "It's like the first time we came to Loralee, isn't it?" She said.

I tore my attention from the surrounding vista to look at her. For all the beauty and majesty before us, she was still more beautiful in my eyes. "That seemed so long ago, didn't it? We've been through so much since that day."

She smiled in the most charming way. "Those were glorious days, the first month or two on those islands. This place reminds me of that time." She looked around us as if seeing things for the first time. "Everything then was so different, like some unexplored world."

"I guess you've forgotten the attack by the Bots soon after we arrived. Most of us only wanted to go back to our normal way of life during those first weeks."

She shook her head slightly. "Not me; I never did." She looked at me as if studying something. "I knew from those first days on Loralee that I had been living under a rock. I was always afraid of being criticized, or not fitting in, or whatever. I never lived up to my potential. And I began to realize it during that time on the Raised Isles."

A fervid sentiment stirred in me. "You were always the

most creative and expressive person in our group, even when we were back at Woodbery."

She shook her head. "I lapsed into someone else in the years after college. Maybe it was a failed relationship, a dead-end job, no friends." She sighed. "I don't know; maybe I was just intimidated by everyone who was always smarter, more outgoing, more everything than I was. I became too scared to compete with them because I knew I couldn't."

I gazed ahead to Diane and Matt, who were out of earshot. I wondered if she was referring to them. I thought it best not to make this about them. "They'll always be people who are smarter, or more sociable, richer, better off—no matter who you are," I said. I felt a little uneasy talking with her about our feelings, but I knew this was my first chance in a long while to open up with her. "I've always been afraid of so much in my life. It's always held me back. I feel it still does. But I think I've come to realize that we have to be true to ourselves, but most of all, to be happy with what we have and who we are."

She chewed on her lower lip. "If I had been more under-standing, I would have realized long ago that something was wrong and you didn't intend to hurt me." I felt a stab of regret over what I had done to her and was about to interrupt to tell her again how sorry I was. She didn't give me a chance. "I was too scared that you would do it again. I didn't want an explanation." In a softer tone, she added, "I was only concerned with myself."

I wanted to reach out and hold her; tell her everything was going to be fine now. But I didn't dare. "Most people would have reacted the same way. There are forces out there trying to destroy us, and not just me, but everyone. They did something that caused me to act that way. And they're not done with me. I once thought there could be nothing worse than the Bots. But now we see that they've become more powerful than before and that they evolved from a race who lived here. It seems to get worse all the time."

I realized I wasn't helping her. Why do I always ramble? "The good news is we're not alone. We have good friends who would do anything for us. The one thing that will get us through this is our friendship."

She fell silent, her eyes downcast as she watched the ground before her. After a time, she said with a catch in her voice, "I know we can't start over, but maybe we can be friends again." She looked at me as if suddenly realizing what she had said. "Don't get me wrong; I'm still afraid that you won't be able to control this, whatever it is inside you, and that you'll try to do it again. That's going to be in my mind for a long time." She stopped walking and looked at me critically. "As long as you don't push me, I promise to try."

My heart beat a little faster. "All I ever wanted was for us to be friends." I wanted to say more, but decided now wasn't the time to tell her I still loved her.

I studied her reaction. She nodded but remained quiet. I added, "Besides, maybe these Valnorians will solve my problem." I tried to smile, even though it didn't feel like one. "And then all we have to worry about is the Bots, who now can throw a storm at us, or kill the land, or who knows what else."

She grinned, catching my attempt to be funny. "Yeah, no problem there. I mean, how difficult can that be?"

The sun still sat high above the horizon when Damek said we would stop for the night. "I think it best that we rest fully before venturing into the heart of this forest."

I took advantage of his decision and slipped off my pack and picked a soft spot on the ground to sit. I hadn't slept well in last night's rain. "Fine with me," I said, rubbing a sore calf.

"Are you worried about something?" Matt asked Damek as he unbuckled his pack, taking a moment to scan the surrounding woods.

The Astari hesitated. "No, not worried so much as that I want to make sure we don't blunder around and violate any of their customs. They are very protective of their forest home. I want to start things off on a positive note, rather than having to apologize to them."

"Tell us what to be careful about," said Diane.

Damek sat next to us. "For one thing, kill no trees or plants, no matter how small. The forest supplies the Valnorians with their food, but I am not sure which plants they consider edible and which might be sacred." He looked at his companions. "And most importantly, we must not light a fire. That is strictly forbidden."

Cassie frowned. "They don't cook their food?"

"And what about light at night?" Diane quickly added.

"They use a natural substance from the forest called fireroot. It is akin to the Astari glowlights, but it can also throw off heat. It is the root of a particular tree. The Valnorians have the skill to coax the root to function."

"The Valnorians sound a lot like the Astari," Diane said,

almost as if thinking out loud. "You have the Raised Isles; they have the Sacred Forest. You have glowlights, and they have these fireroots. Do they have different colored hair?" She smiled as she asked the last question.

Damek thought for a moment, giving Quintia a chance to answer. "The Valnorians are short in stature like the Astari, but not with multi-colored hair. They have evolved through generations to live in the forest. I recall others saying they can blend into the forest as if becoming invisible."

I suddenly realized something Damek had said a long time ago when it didn't matter much. "None of you four have ever met a Valnorian, have you?" I asked.

Damek shook his head. "No, we were all born after the war against the Bots. But the lady Elderphino and many other Astari spoke highly of them."

A nagging feeling troubled me. "How do you know they haven't changed since then? Look what happened to the Ikhael."

"We can only hope they haven't."

I exchanged a look with Matt, knowing he also felt uneasy about so much resting on this race whom none of us had ever met. We both kept our silence.

As the sun dipped toward the edge of the horizon, casting long shadows from the surrounding trees, we munched on the food picked yesterday. The temperate climate negated a need for a fire to keep us warm. But once darkness fell over us in earnest, a blaze would have been nice to keep the denizens of this strange forest away. The insubstantial glowlights of the Astari, which always seemed so bright in the past, tonight did little to dispel the darkness hovering at the edges of our camp.

Conversation dropped off quickly once we had eaten and the sun had set. We were all tired from our ordeal, first the dead zone and then the underground passages. Tonight was a night to recharge before facing our next challenge. And I was sure it would come.

A feeling of anticipation was growing stronger in me, but I wasn't sure if it was me or the infection. Or maybe it was the warning from the Draas that I had a capacity to destroy. Enia said I was dangerous. I already knew that, but she gave me the impression that it was much worse than I had imagined.

My body and mind were tired from everything that had happened to me. I soon drifted off to sleep. The sky was clear with no rain to trouble me on this evening. But sometime during the night, I awoke, and it seemed that I could hear the trees whispering to each other as eyes looked down at us.

The Astari had extinguished the glowlights and shadows cast by the eyelid of Celeus, the larger moon, rippled through the woods. I rolled over to settle into a more comfortable position, and I glanced again at the woods beyond. That's when I spotted spectral figures, too insubstantial to be real, drifting in and around the trees, moving with a grace that wasn't human. I realized these shapes differed from the shadows cast by the trees. And as my eyes adjusted to the darkness, I could see various plants and the ground itself glow with the radiance of unnatural light.

I sat bolt upright, thinking the figures might be dangerous. Riyaad was awake with his back against the trunk of a tree. He motioned me with his hand as if telling me to lie back down. He wasn't alarmed, so I took his advice.

I continued to look at the drifting apparitions for a time.

This was a different world we were about to enter, much different from the Raised Isles, or anywhere else in this land. I could feel the profound shift in my bones, like a season about to change. But did it portend an end to my troubles, or would I face something worse? Enia's words drifted back to me. *You don't yet realize your capacity to destroy.*

I soon drifted off. And somewhere between awake and sleep, I thought I heard the singing of many voices, as if from far away, chanting a mournful tune.

20

INTO THE SACRED FOREST

We set out at first light the next morning. Even though we were up early, I felt refreshed from a sound sleep in this verdant forest. Everything here grew so abundantly, the air clean with the rich smell of loam and pine. We were finally going to reach our goal of meeting the Valnorians. More than ever I believed they would remove what was inside me, as well as help us defeat the new threat from the Bots.

The morning sun dispelled any sign of the ghostly figures from last night. When I asked Riyaad about it, all he would say was that these woods held many mysteries. "Sometimes it is best not to inquire too deeply," he said.

I picked my way carefully around a cluster of bushes, remembering Damek's warning that we not kill anything until we understood what the Valnorians considered valuable. I was lost in my thoughts, recalling yesterday's conversation with Cassie, my heart warming again to think we were past the worst of our troubles.

210

A shout of harsh words I didn't understand brought my attention back to the present. The noise sounded like the squawk of a bird more than anything else, and for a second that's what I thought it was.

But when I jerked my head up, the sight of a dozen figures greeted me as they stepped out from behind a covering of bushes. They each held drawn bows aimed at us. After a second I became more confused, trying to understand why they pointed their weapons directly at me and nobody else.

Before anyone could react, two figures dashed toward me and slammed me face-first to the ground, knocking the air from my lungs. They expertly tied my hands behind my back as they searched for weapons. "Wait, you are making a mistake," Damek shouted. "Let me first explain."

The two figures pulled me to my feet and even though my wrists were bound they held my arms with a solid grip. They were strong despite their slight build and short stature. I was bewildered, not sure what to say. It all happened so quickly that I couldn't process what they wanted from me.

I assumed these people were the Valnorians. They were about the height of the Astari but looked nothing like our friends. It took me a moment to realize that it was only me they treated this way. They didn't seem concerned with anyone else. More of them stepped out from behind hiding spots and lowered their bows, relaxing the tension, even though they kept their arrows notched.

One of the newcomers took a moment to examine Damek. He said, "We will use your native speech. In answer to your claim, we have made no mistake. We will execute him."

The joy I felt just a short time ago vanished. Damek moved deftly in front of me. "Everyone here is under my protection. And as such, Philip is under the protection of all Astari. Any harm done to him will be dealt with harshly by my people." I wasn't sure that was true, but I had to give him credit for saying it.

"We have our orders," replied the one apparently in charge of this force. He spoke the words without the slightest hesitation, which didn't make me feel any better. "His execution will take place now."

Damek remained silent as he considered this. I wanted to shout at him to keep defending me.

Out of the corner of my eye, I saw Matt extend his lance. This gained him the attention of several others who returned the gesture by cocking their bows and pointing the arrows at his chest. Damek also saw it. "Hold. Do not resist. If they wanted Philip dead, they would have done so immediately."

This was his defense? Was he serious?

I caught a slight flicker in the eyes of the leader as he reacted to Damek's words. The stranger said nothing as he wet his lips while Damek waited him out. I was outraged that Damek was gambling with my life. Finally, the other said, "Out of respect for the Astari, I will allow you to explain why you bring this venom to our land."

Damek nodded curtly before taking a long moment to respond. I sensed a war of wills taking place between the two. "You have it all wrong, Valnorian," Damek finally said. "You misinterpret what you see. We bring you the only hope you have to defeat the contagion that has infected our land. You know our past. The Astari fought long and hard to rid the land of the plight posed by the Bots. The Valnorians had fought alongside the Astari and many other great races. Now the Bots threaten us again." He gestured to me with his hand. "You kill him, and you forfeit all hope of defeating that which even now threatens the Sacred Forest."

I wasn't sure about me being their only hope, but I liked what he said. His plea gave the other person a reason to pause. But as the eyes of this Valnorian raked over me, his stance hardened. "He has the taint of corruption, the same that degrades the land. We must stop it now before—"

"Yes, we must stop it," Damek interrupted. "That is the reason we are here. We travel with our Earthfriends, who can help."

The Valnorian leader frowned and flicked a gaze at my friends. "Only he is tainted." He set his jaw tight. "I order him sentenced to death before he brings the decay to our home." He motioned to several Valnorians behind him who raised their weapons at me. All I could focus on were the tips of their arrows aimed at my face. I realized that I could be dead in another heartbeat. Would I feel pain?

In quick succession, Damek held his hands high in front of me while Bevon darted in front of those aiming the arrows. Bevon said, "You will have to kill me first. I am sworn to protect the Earthfriends."

The Valnorian in charge was about to say something, but Damek cut him off. "I invoke our pact of friendship that no harm be committed between Valnorian and Astari."

Those words seemed to confuse the Valnorian. "He is not

an Astari, and as such we do not grant him protection." I could feel my heart beat wildly. This Valnorian was intent on seeing me dead.

"I demand to petition the head of your people. Does King La'Teribus still rule?"

He looked unsure about providing any information. "Queen A'Lenora is now our leader."

"The Astari have the right to petition her directly in matters of life and death."

For the first time, real uncertainty clouded the face of the Valnorian. I realized I had been holding my breath, and I forced myself to exhale before taking another gulp of air.

Damek moderated his voice and lowered his arms. "Take us to her. It is why we are here."

The Valnorian stood for long moments, still as a statue. If I didn't know better, I would swear he had gone into a trance. I wasn't sure how or what to think. Was this a prelude to them attacking me, or something else?

And then he blinked, and his face took on a natural appearance. "Very well. You have that right. The queen will pass judgment."

Damek nodded. "He is in our care and should not be bound."

He considered this for a moment. "I will consent only if the rest of you are unarmed."

That rankled Damek. "Has the trust between us sunk so low?"

The Valnorian remained resolute. "We live in troubling times. This is our home, and we are sworn to protect it."

Damek relented only after considering it for a long

moment. "Very well." He hefted the hilts of his lance and sword from a pocket on his upper leg and nodded for the others to follow. "These are the finest Astari blades. Keep them safe. A time may soon come when every blade will be needed in your defense."

The leader nodded curtly and took the weapons before handing them to another. Everyone else did likewise. "And your slingshots as well."

Damek smiled ruefully. "You know more about Astari habits than you let on."

One of the Valnorians who had knocked me to the ground cut the cord binding my wrists. He looked me in the eyes with a curious expression. I wasn't sure how to read it. Only a moment ago this person would have willingly slit my throat with his knife.

I rubbed my wrists, knowing now that we had made a horrible mistake coming here at all.

"That was close," said Matt as he edged to my side while we marched forward, surrounded by Valnorians. "It wasn't the reception I expected."

To the casual observer, Matt's comments would seem like idle talk. But I knew him better. He was trying to feel me out, to be sure I was in a positive frame of mind. Events were unfolding in a way none of us expected. And he knew as well as I did that these people wanted me dead. They might not be the saviors we had hoped for, and I might need my wits about me to fend off disaster.

"They're afraid," I replied. He looked at me curiously, not sure what I meant. "They know what's inside me. It's the same taint that was in the dead zone. It's the same carried by the storm over Haven. I didn't realize it then, but I do now."

Matt frowned. I could see it was not the response he had hoped. "You're not one of them. You're different from the Bots or their forefathers. You've got to understand that. These forest people don't realize it. That's why they want to kill you."

I nodded. I knew I shouldn't say this to him, but at this point, it didn't seem to matter. "Maybe they understand me better than I do."

He opened his mouth as if to respond and then thought better of it and closed it. I knew he was only trying to help, but this wasn't happening to him. I wasn't sure he understood what I was going through with everything that had happened to me this past year. We walked in silence for a time until he spoke again. "I don't think I ever told you, but I always thought you were the person on our team at Woodbery who always worked the hardest."

I looked at him, puzzled over why he was saying this. He smiled as if recalling our long-ago college life. "It seemed that you and Eric were complete opposites. It's funny that you would become such close friends. He would slack off and do the least amount necessary and still come out smelling like roses. You weren't like that." Matt held up his hand to forestall my retort about not being all that smart. "You worked harder than all of us because you wanted it more. You wanted to prove to your family and high school friends that they were wrong about you not being able to hack it in college. That, and probably because you had nothing to go back to."

He was right. Matt was good at understanding other people. "What's that got to do with what's going on now?"

"Everything," he responded. "You're not a quitter. But if you give in to them," he nodded to the Valnorian guards who kept pace with us some distance away, "then all you did in the past was for nothing." He looked at Cassie walking next to Diane a few steps in front of us. He lowered his voice. "And you'll give up on her." He paused to let me think about it. "Is that what you want, especially now after she's just started believing in you again?"

My eyes lingered on Cassie for a few moments. Was he right? Did the others understand me better than I did myself? "I won't give up," I told him. "I'll promise you that."

His face held a hint of sadness. He knew that forces beyond our control were working against me. What he didn't realize was that I was already beginning to feel less of the person he knew at Woodbery and more of someone I didn't recognize, someone who wasn't me at all.

We stopped for the night some hours later. Several Valnorians scavenged the surrounding area and returned with what I thought was firewood before remembering Damek's admonishment last evening that the Valnorians allowed no fires. One guard placed a small pile of what looked like dried pieces of wood on the open ground while others gathered small rocks to surround it, much like they were preparing a campfire. The guard struck several of the pieces together and took a moment to grasp the ends. Slowly the wood threw-off light. They soon became too bright to look at directly as the Valnorian dropped them to the center of the ring of rocks.

So this was the fireroot that Damek had spoken about. It soon glowed as bright as any fire. Another Valnorian positioned a pot of water on the ground next to it and sprinkled flakes of green leaves into the water. Not long after, the kettle was steaming, and the Valnorians passed out cups of the mixture along with dried bars of food. They offered to share it with us. One of the Valnorians approached me warily before handing me a bar and a warm mug that looked like a hollowed-out piece of wood. I was going to ask her what it was, but the moment I took it from her, she spun on her heels and scampered away as if I was contagious.

She was right to be concerned. I had an infection, albeit one that could not be transferred to others. I chewed on the bar, not really tasting it as I wondered if I should feel anger or fear at being taken prisoner.

I took the time to observe our captors as I took a sip of the warm drink. They were willowy and lithe, even in their simple movements. I noticed they could bend and flex their joints in ways that went far beyond the ability of humans. Like the Astari, they were slight in height and weight. Each one couldn't weigh over ninety pounds. Their faces were more elongated than ours, and their skin was the color of sand on a Caribbean beach.

At first, I had puzzled over the design of the clothes, swirls of greens and browns with a smattering of other colors mixed in. Did these represent a military rank or family heritage? But then I realized these patterns and colors served as effective camouflage. When any of them stepped a short distance away, they blended seamlessly into the foliage.

As we sat that night by the glow of the fireroot, the Valnorians talked among themselves in another language. I turned to Bevon, who sat near me. "How do they understand us? It seems they know our language."

He nodded as if understanding why I asked. "They know it is what the Astari speak. They likely didn't want us to misunderstand their commands."

Hearing this, Diane turned to us. "I thought they were your friends. That we could trust them."

She left unspoken the question about why they didn't trust us now. But I knew the answer. It was because of what I carried.

Bevon spoke without emotion. "Above all else, they seek to protect their forest. In that regard, our purpose aligns with theirs."

"Apparently, they don't believe I'm on their team," I said bitterly.

He had no answer. I took that as an indictment of the trouble I was in. This infection probably wouldn't kill me. But one of those Valnorians might. And I had walked blindly into their trap.

AS WE MOVED DEEPER WITHIN THE DOMAIN OF THE Greylock Forest, I realized more than ever that this was a land utterly alien from any woods I had known. The profusion of vegetation often became nearly impenetrable, and the trees stood massively tall, higher than I would have thought possible.

The cacophony of forest animals was frequently deafening. Creatures, both large and small, darted through bushes and trees all around us while flocks of colorful birds deftly navigated through the branches. Higher in the air, I caught glimpses of birds with astonishingly broad wingspans as they floated effortlessly near the tops of the trees.

Despite the thick canopy above us, enough light filtered through the mantle of leaves to support life, even on the forest floor. Down here on the ground, the vegetation often contained a riot of colors. It seemed to me that most of the plants could have been designed by a botanist gone crazy. We passed some vegetation that was nothing more than a single, giant leaf, while other plants floated in the air with no sign of support. Some flora darted from place-to-place as if it were more of an animal than any vegetation. I even saw one that bloomed into a giant flower as we approached, only to recede into its shell the moment we passed.

All this was only a small portion of the richness that I could observe on the forest floor. The trees above held their own mysteries that we could only glimpse at as we passed.

If I wasn't a prisoner on my way to execution, I might be more enamored with everything around us. But a dreadful weight hung over me, one that mitigated any awe I might ordinarily feel as I had during my first days on the Isles of Loralee.

After a time, the growth was so dense that it became difficult to pass. The Valnorians motioned us to a rope ladder hanging next to a tree whose trunk was so broad that four people likely could not wrap their arms around it. Each of us climbed a rung at a time, except for the Valnorians who scaled the branches and trunks of this and other nearby trees like monkeys in the jungles of Earth. Even with my despondency, I had to marvel at how expertly they moved from branch to branch, seemingly as effortlessly as I would walk on the ground.

By the time we climbed four or five stories on the rope ladder, my arms were feeling the strain. Fortunately, it wasn't much longer before we reached a platform where we could rest. I assumed this was our destination, but the Valnorian leader came alongside, balancing on a nearby limb, and said, "Keep moving, that was only the beginning." He pointed to the trunk where I now noticed rungs as if on a ladder that extended upward from the platform. The bars extended six inches from the trunk and looked so natural, as if they were part of the tree itself. I glanced down to the ground below, barely visible now with the leaves shielding it. I knew we were already high enough that a fall would likely kill us.

"You can't be serious," Cassie grumbled.

Damek spoke a few words to the other Astari. Each of them produced a length of rope from their packs and fastened an end around their waist and the other around one of us. As Bevon attached his end around me, he said, "Think of this as the first time I took you on a sail. You remember it, don't you?"

I smiled for the first time since encountering the Valnorians. "You told me some harebrained story about fastening a rope around me and having a group of other Astari from another island pull on it."

He chuckled in return, as if remembering it. "That was only to stop you from whining like a little baby." He pulled the rope tight to be sure it held. "Sailing is second nature to us Astari, just as climbing trees are to the Valnorians. You simply have to do it enough times until you become good at it."

"It may be fine for them, but I have no intention of liking it."

For good measure, Damek used another length of rope to attach to each of the Astari. I wasn't sure if that was as a safeguard in the event one of the Astari slipped, or to add extra support in case one of us lost our footing, and the single Astari wasn't able to hold on. I decided not to ask.

We continued to scale higher with each of us attached to the safety rope. I couldn't tell how far we climbed. I focused my undivided attention on reaching for the next handhold and bringing one leg up to the next rung. I kept my head straight ahead, inches from the bark of the tree, and tried not to think about how high we were.

That none of us from Earth froze or panicked during that climb was a measure of how far we had come in pushing our bodies and minds to new levels. Two years ago, I wouldn't have had the mental stamina to consider reaching for the next step. I doubt if any of my other friends would have either.

After a time, I heard grunts and boots scuffing against a surface above me. I didn't dare risk a glimpse to see if we reached our destination, thinking how disappointed I would be if we had not. I wasn't sure if I could continue this climb if it lasted much longer.

I reached for the next few rungs. Bevon soon grasped my arm to help support me as he leaned over another platform. "Well done, Earthfriend. I swear you must be getting braver each day." He wore a broad smile as he pulled me over the top.

After Damek reached the platform, with Matt behind him, we all took time to catch our breath. My fingers and arms ached from clutching the ladder. I sprawled face-down on the wooden platform. After I felt rested enough, I leaned my head over the edge to gauge our distance from the ground. The covering of leaves made it impossible to see the bottom.

"I'll take the confinement of the Draas tunnels over this any day," Cassie complained.

The Valnorian guards balanced themselves on branches around us. I was about to voice my objection to continuing any farther if they expected us to balance along tree limbs as they were doing. But then I spied a rope walkway that extended horizontally from the platform, its end lost in the covering of leaves ahead. The catwalk was wide enough for only a single person and looked far too flimsy to hold all of us at one time. But at least it provided some measure of support compared to the nearby boughs of the trees.

The Valnorian gestured to the walk. "We have these to accommodate the children and elderly."

Maybe he was only trying to be helpful, but I took the inference to mean that we were no better than a child or the aged. My opinion of these people continued to decline. Why did we ever come here?

I thought back with fondness to the time I spent at the village of Haven, which already seemed like a lifetime ago. Even though the town was so different from what I had ever experienced, the people there were civil, and they were humans from Earth like the rest of us. I felt entirely out of my element here in the trees of these woods. What I would do to be back with Tess, Russell, and Alan, people who risked so much to come to this land. But I especially longed to see Rae and even Bryson again, a new generation of humans who never set foot on Earth. All of them needed our help to stop the Bots from controlling the Elementals.

How did I end up being the one who needed to help everyone else? In my mind, I again saw the quiet confidence in the eyes of Tess as she told us how early in her life she had faced a race who had been the precursor to the Bots. Recalling her discussion, I felt a twinge of remorse knowing that she didn't ask for that responsibility, just as I didn't ask for this.

"We should be moving," said the Valnorian leader, bringing me out of my reverie. "With any luck, we'll reach the Ethwood before dusk."

I wasn't sure what the Ethwood was. I assumed it was the center of these woods. My heart sank, realizing we still had a full day on these rickety-looking rope walkways. I didn't realize how unstable they were until I stepped on it and felt the bouncing, swaying movements of the others. I held tight to the ropes near my waist on either side of me.

Diane yelped, probably believing she was going to fall. Each person's step was magnified, causing me to think we were going to pitch over at any moment. The Astari continued to keep the ropes secured to each of us, but that didn't comfort me much.

We moved one stuttering step at a time, while the Valnorians scampered effortlessly from one branch to another as if they didn't even consider their next move. No matter what I thought of them, I had to admire their agility, especially as my knuckles were already turning white from gripping the guide ropes at my side.

Once I realized that the bridge would not give way and send us falling to our death, I gained some confidence. It seemed the others did also as our pace improved. I learned the knack of adjusting my steps so that I caused less of a movement on the bridge. I thought of the expression *walking on eggshells* as an apt way to describe my stride.

The bridge spanned the length of several city blocks. It ended at a tree with a small platform, too small to fit all of us at once. Another bridge led away from us on the other side of the tree. We repeated this over again until I lost count of the number of spans we crossed.

I was able to take in the view of the surrounding forest once my fear abated. I still avoided looking down while we were on a bridge, but I did hazard a look when standing on one platform. Through the covering of leaves, I glimpsed the ground far below. I decided that looking there was not the best idea as a new panic came over me. Although we were a considerable distance from the ground, these walkways were only about half-way to the tops of the massive trees. The crown of the forest was still far above us. I could only glimpse small slivers of blue sky through the mantel overhead.

I began to take more time to observe the surrounding

woods as we moved forward. It seemed a good way to dispel my sour mood at being taken captive. The more I saw of this place, the more I couldn't help become fascinated with the beauty and majesty of this forest with its incredible profusion of life. Although thick vegetation always surrounded us, I never thought of it as a jungle. That would imply a wild, untamed growth with horrific bugs and mosquitoes, at least in my mind. The amount of foliage was staggering, but the place still had a cultivated, natural appearance. Branches never blocked our way on the bridge, even with many of them growing all around us.

One thing, however, that reminded me of a jungle was the increase in humidity. I had shed my long-sleeved shirt long ago in favor of my lighter undershirt. I now wished we had brought shorts with us. An occasional spray of raindrops would often strike us, the patter of the drops hitting the leaves blended with the melody of birds and small critters. I was never quite sure if the sprinkles were caused by water falling off the leaves above or the result of a brief shower.

"We seem to have drawn a crowd," said Bevon, who now walked behind me. I wasn't sure what he meant until I noticed that many more Valnorians than the original party shadowed us. They blended in so well with the forest that it was difficult to see them until I focused on the surrounding branches. But once I trained my eyes to peer past the nearest leaves and branches, I was surprised at the number. All of them flitted from one limb to another as if they had no fear of crashing to the ground.

Damek, who was several paces in front, replied, "They

likely don't see many strangers. We must be a wonder to them."

"It's not a surprise they don't get visitors," I grumbled. "They're not the friendliest people I've ever met."

Damek turned with a frown, even as he continued to keep his pace. "I fear you've misjudged our hosts. They are a kind, caring race. They hate the Bots as much as the Astari. Don't judge them by their reaction to your infection. Once Queen A'Lenora fully understands what has happened to you, she will rectify any ill will the others may have."

Although I had serious doubts about what Damek said, I kept my feelings to myself.

21

THE QUEEN'S DECISION

Valnorians lived in homes that were as much a part of the natural landscape as the trees in their forest. "Look there," Quintia pointed as we continued to march single-file on the rope walkways. I squinted, trying to find what she meant. My first thought was that she spotted what looked like odd irregularities in the shape of a tree. Only after I looked more closely did I realize it was a dwelling nestled along the sides of an enormous trunk and supported by sturdy branches. If Quintia hadn't called my attention to it, I might have continued walking without ever realizing the house existed.

Once I spotted one home, I was able to find many others. It was as if pieces of a puzzle had suddenly become clear. Just like the Valnorians, who darted along the limbs of trees, their homes blended almost unseen into the woods all around us.

I soon noticed residents standing on what can only be described as a front porch or back deck of their homes, looking at us with unconcealed curiosity, often pointing us out to their children. The flock of other Valnorians traveling along with us also increased until it seemed a small army shadowed us.

We soon reached another platform at the end of one bridge, but this time three walkways extended on the other side of the trunk. Riyaad, who was now in the lead, hesitated until a Valnorian shimmied along a branch and landed on the platform. He smiled and bowed his head, the first sign of civility by a Valnorian that I had witnessed. His eyes were wide as he took us in. "I will show you the rest of the way. Please follow me." He took a step onto the middle of the three bridges and waited until he was sure we followed.

The forest began to modify as we continued. My previous fascination with these woods paled in comparison. Not only was the surrounding vista teeming with flora, but here was a city as grand as that of the lost race of the Draas, although much different. Unlike the Draas, with only simulations remaining, the Greylock Forest was full of life. And although there were no grand towers or plazas with fountains, life teemed all around us from birds fluttering on nearby branches, small creatures similar to chipmunks scurrying on the walkways ahead, larger animals the size of monkeys roaming from tree-to-tree, and unseen insects filling the air with their gentle melodies. For all the beauty of the Draas city, I was beginning to realize how sterile a place it was compared to this.

What amazed me most were the numerous homes that hugged the sides of towering trees or sat on massive branches. Rope walkways crisscrossed the area as they stretched from one colossal trunk to another; limbs, the size of immense trees on Earth, branched off main trunks, each of them holding homes of the Valnorians; and everywhere the Valnorian people went about their daily lives.

"Look at this place," Cassie marveled as we came to a spot with an unobstructed view of the area. "I never could have imagined a place like this."

Damek smiled at her comment. "It's likely you never suspected that places such as the Raised Isles, or the lost city of the Draas existed before you came to this land. It's sad to realize they may all be at risk."

We continued to follow our Valnorian guide, who turned around regularly, probably to be sure we hadn't fallen off the edge of the walkway. Our bridge soon split and widened so it could accommodate several people at a time, which was a good thing as it became more populated. We began passing groups of others moving in the opposite direction from us. We still drew their attention, but it seemed most of the Valnorians were now concerned with their task of getting from one place to another rather than us.

We finally came to the center of the woods. Nobody needed to tell us; we knew it as soon as we arrived at a broad area free of the massive trees and limbs. A meadow dotted with flowers covered the floor far below us. A tree stood in the center of the field, one unlike any I had ever seen. It was taller than the surrounding ones, and it reminded me of the thin towers in the Draas city. Unlike all the surrounding trees, which contained sprawling branches, this one was rela-tively compact, which only highlighted how massive it was. Rather than extending outward from its central trunk, the branches wrapped around it in spirals. Even from this distance, I could see a maze of stairs surrounding its central trunk. A series of rope walkways connected the tree to the rest of the woods, like spokes on a wheel with it at the center.

The Valnorian leading us paused, looking pleased as we took a moment to gaze in awe at the view. "This is the Ethwood Tree, the most magnificent in our forest, don't you think?"

I stood still and gaped at the sight. It impressed even the Astari. "Come along," he said after another moment. "The queen is waiting for you."

"What's your name?" Matt asked as we continued.

He appeared surprised that one of us would want to know. "I am Ja'Krill." He seemed as if he wanted to say more, but then thought better of it. He motioned us forward. "This way."

We passed over the grassy clearing below. The absence of branches and leaves below us accentuated our height from the ground, which renewed the fear I had when first stepping onto the walkway. I noticed that my friends gripped the guide rope and walked more gingerly as we passed the line of trees onto the open land below us.

I focused my attention on that tree and saw that within its spiral branches, Valnorians sat or stood in what I can only describe as airy rooms that were part of the tree itself. Other people moved up or down stairs or across rope walks from one side of the trunk to the other. Once we reached the tree, our guide led us up a stairway that wound around the center. I couldn't help compare this spiral staircase with the one we walked when leaving the confinement of the Draas tunnels. This, however, was made of wood, not stone, and life existed all around us. As I looked down, careful not to trip, I noticed that these steps weren't constructed of wood, as I first thought. I realized they were part of the natural growth of the tree.

All of us, even our Astari friends, were too amazed to say anything as we continued up the broad steps, frequently rubbernecking as if our heads were on a swivel. I felt my legs begin to tire from the walk up the stairs, but each new level brought another fascinating sight as I observed some rooms as large as banquet halls.

Ja'Krill finally led us off the staircase onto a flat surface that was the tree itself. A short distance later, he motioned us to enter a room that contained silver leaves draped on its walls and ceiling.

A group of Valnorians clustered on the far side of the room. My eye was immediately drawn to a female among the group; she was the only one sitting. The ornate chair could only be described as a throne. It was positioned on a raised dais so even sitting she was several heads higher than the others. Her face was impassive and cold. She appeared remarkably young to be their leader. A contingent of other Valnorians stood respectfully around her or along the edges of the large room. I recognized the Valnorian soldier who had intercepted us on the outskirts of the forest as he stood next to her.

She waited for us to approach, making no move to welcome us, as she sat unmoving, except for her eyes, which scrutinized each of us with an intensity that made me wonder if she could read our thoughts. Damek bowed with a flourish, his hand sweeping out before him and reaching the floor, as he stopped several paces before the throne. His movement caused me to recall the first moment I had seen him on the Raised Isles. He had greeted us with a similar gesture.

"We bid you well, Queen A'Lenora," he said once he straightened. "The Astari and the Valnorians have long been allies against those that threaten our existence. We are here now because we face—"

"How dare you bring that one here," she interrupted, raising a slender arm as she pointed her finger at me.

A fresh wave of despair came over me as I realized this queen was my last hope at both remaining alive and removing this infection from me.

Damek continued calmly, as if he had expected this reaction. "He is our friend. He has been attacked by the Bots and has suffered, much as the land is now suffering."

She didn't give him the chance to explain more. "We are well aware of the tactics of our enemy. Don't presume to lecture me."

"Do you know they have removed all life from plant and flora? We passed great patches of land destroyed by them."

For the first time, I saw uncertainty in her eyes. A second later, her face hardened once again. "We are aware of the danger. While the Astari remain safe on your islands, we have been waging a battle to protect our forest. My soldiers should have killed him as I had ordered, pact or no pact." She flashed a gaze toward the nearby Valnorian who had agreed not to kill me, causing him to blanch noticeably.

Damek raised his voice. "Would you also destroy your forest because some of it has come under the curse of the Bots? I believe you would instead attempt to make it right again. That is what we now face with Earthfriend Philip. He and his companions come from another land. The Bots believe they are a threat, which should make them your partner as well as ours."

She glared at him. It seemed she was not accustomed to someone disagreeing with her. Once again, I wondered why Damek sought these people for assistance. I could see this leader had no intention of wanting to work with us. Damek licked his lips. This conversation was rapidly spiraling out of control.

"I understand the past friendship of our people, but in this matter, I don't care," she continued. "We must eliminate any taint that enters our forest before it causes more harm. We must kill him."

I had a sinking feeling. This queen spoke with authority, and it seemed she brokered no room for disagreement. It was clear she was intent on having her orders obeyed. I was a danger, and that was all she cared about right now.

Damek's face was stern, an expression I had rarely seen from him. I'm sure he would draw a weapon right now if he hadn't been forced to hand it over to the Valnorians. I noticed that Bevon inched closer to my side, although I wasn't sure what any of them could hope to accomplish.

"If I may," I said without thinking. She raised her eyebrows, shocked that I even dared to speak. I decided I needed to continue before she could object. Still not sure what I was going to say, I blurted, "I don't blame you for wanting to kill me. I thought about doing it myself once after this poison inside me changed my life." My eyes fixed on

Cassie for a second. "It took away everything important to me."

"That's all very well and good, but it doesn't change my decision," she said, her voice rising a notch louder than before. "I have a responsibility to our forest, which is paramount. Everything else is secondary, including your life. Once we allow this pathogen to enter our home, it may destroy us all."

"But you're wrong," said Cassie meekly. I turned my head, wondering if I heard her speak or if it was my imagination. I frowned, realizing that if this ruler decided Cassie was also a threat, she might suffer from the queen's wrath. I wanted to tell her to remain quiet, that it didn't matter if they killed me. That was better than putting everyone else at risk.

Cassie paused a moment as she collected her thoughts. But the queen was impatient. "I'm wrong about what?" she snapped, causing Cassie to cringe.

"It's just that, it seems to me that as a ruler, your responsibility is to Elthea's Realm, not only your forest." Her eyes glanced around the room. "This place is beautiful, and I can understand why you love it, but the reason we came here was because we thought you would be willing to oppose the Bots, who are trying to destroy everything. That's what you did in your war against them, wasn't it? You worked together." She nodded at me. "He's an example of why we should fight them. We may all become infected soon if we don't stop them."

Her words were so disarming that Queen A'Lenora became silent. I noticed that Damek wore a grim smile while Matt and Diane looked at Cassie with admiration. Whatever happened to me now, I knew that some feelings she once had for me remained.

The queen stared at Cassie. But then, surprisingly, A'Lenora's face softened, and her eyes touched on me before returning to Cassie. "Even if I agree with what you say, he is still a danger to us."

And that was the crux of the problem. Even I knew I was a threat. I had already proved it.

Cassie was momentarily unsure of herself, which allowed Matt to speak. "It might help if you first consider something about the Astari. They were created on our world to stop the Bots. At that time, the Bots were a deadly virus, occupying whatever they came in contact with. But the Astari didn't stop the Bots by killing the host when they became infected by the Bots. They concentrated on destroying what made the host malfunction. They killed the virus." He paused for a moment, probably wondering if this explanation was too vague. The queen looked at him without expression. He pressed on. "That's what has happened to our friend. He's a host. The Bots occupied him. They infected him with a deadly virus. It's the same thing they did on my world, and it's now happening to the rest of this land. They're destroying it with their virus."

He gave this time to sink in. The queen's face remained stoic, but she no longer interrupted us at each step.

"The Bots continue to gain a foothold while we bicker," Damek said into the silence. "The Astari are responsible for the Earthfriends. Because of his infection, I have already pledged that Earthfriend Philip would not be permitted to harm another Earthfriend. I extend that oath to include the

Valnorians. I vow to end his life should he inflict harm on any of your people or to your Greylock Forest."

I saw no uncertainty in Damek's expression as he spoke, but there was plenty of doubt in my heart. I could feel this venom in me growing ever stronger since arriving in this land. If I somehow lost control, I wondered if Damek could keep his promise.

It seemed an eternity before the queen reacted. She sat stone-faced for the longest time, just as she had when we first entered the chamber. I knew this was Damek's last appeal. If it failed, my life was done.

She finally pursed her lips before saying, "I will grant your request with one warning. And on this, I will stand firm." She looked at me again, this time with an expression of distaste. "If that one does any harm to us or our forest, I will not only kill him, but I will kill each and every one of you." She shifted her gaze back to Damek. "Be sure of what you ask, Astari. If you judge him wrong, all your lives are forfeit."

Before I could object, Damek nodded curtly. "I accept your terms."

I had a sinking feeling he had just signed all our death warrants.

Morning dawned in a cloudless sky. Birds sang gleefully as they darted from branch to branch. A small yellow one landed on the interlocking twigs that formed the edges of the window to my room, chirping at me as if telling me to leave now, while I still had the chance. The sun had barely broken the edge of the horizon, yet even now Valnorians were crossing the many bridges from the surrounding forest to this center tree.

Everywhere I looked, I saw vibrant life, except when I looked inward. I felt this cancer growing within me. But unlike a disease that drained strength from the victim, this infused me with a bitter potency, one I neither wanted nor understood.

Queen A'Lenora had spared my life, at least for now. But I wasn't sure she had done me or my companions a favor. She didn't kill me, but she placed me on house arrest, as it would be described on Earth. She permitted me to leave this small room only when in the presence of an Astari. For safe measure, she also had two Valnorian soldiers guard the entrance and follow me. She explained that she had instructed them to kill me if I did anything to harm others or their forest.

I stepped over to the sink to splash water on my face. Everything in this room was part of the living tree, even the hollow branches that carried water. During my sleepless night, I had plenty of time to wonder about this place and how the Valnorians had fashioned such an elaborate tower. This center tree was immense, and I had glimpsed only a small part of it. I could just imagine how many lived here or spent their days on this one tree, working at things I couldn't comprehend. Surrounding this tree was the rest of the vast forest with hundreds, maybe thousands of homes that were all part of the trees themselves. It made me wonder if any of these people lived on the ground.

A sharp knock on my door brought me back to the

present. Without waiting for me to respond, Bevon stuck his head around the tangle of leaves and branches that swung open to his touch. "A fine day is waiting for us, Earthfriend. Come, let us sample the Valnorian food for our morning meal."

I thought about telling him just to bring me something, or better yet, that I wasn't hungry. But his face was so cheerful that I didn't have the heart to dampen his feelings. He was only trying to help. "You realize that I may pillage or rape their women if I'm allowed to roam around this place."

He smiled even more broadly. "I am sure that's exactly what they fear. I will tell you what. How about you put on a stern expression at some of them so we can observe their reaction."

Bevon always cheered me up or made me feel safe, even during the worst of times. "I have the feeling they would reward me with a knife to my gut."

He considered this with mock seriousness. "You may be right. Let us talk about it over breakfast. I'm hungry."

We made our way through a series of walkways and up several levels as the Valnorian guards shadowed us from a respectful distance. I had to keep reminding myself that we were actually in a large tree. If I didn't know better, I would have believed we were in a building with a peculiar style of architecture. I often caught glimpses of the fields surrounding us far below as we passed along the outskirts of the tree.

Bevon led me to a room with rows of tables and chairs. Several dozen Valnorians were eating as they chatted together in small groups. Most noted our entry, but I didn't see anyone expressing surprise or alarm. "Remember, keep your face passive," Bevon chided.

We moved over to a counter where other Valnorians handed us a flat wooden tray upon which was a collection of unique foods. "The others should be along shortly," Bevon explained as he eyed an open table. When I went to sit, I felt as if I were back in kindergarten with its too-small bench and a table that I could barely fit my legs under. Bevon didn't seem to notice my discomfort that the Valnorian furniture was sized more for his stature than mine. "I've been told Valnorian cuisine is quite good," he said as he eagerly inspected his tray of food.

I looked down at mine. Like everything else in this place, the food was unrecognizable. All I could see were lumps of different colored pieces of something that ringed a bowl of warm mush. Bevon, however, was fascinated with his food as he sampled one and then another. I recalled the bland bar of food that the Valnorians had provided after they intercepted us, so I wasn't expecting much. But the savory taste pleasantly surprised me once I took a few bites. The flavors differed greatly from Astari food, but I soon scooped all of it off the plate, wondering if I could go back for more.

"Here they are," he nodded as the rest of the Astari entered with Cassie, Matt, and Diane.

"We should have known you would be here first," Riyaad said with a touch of humor as he eyed Bevon.

"It is not my fault you are so slow," Bevon countered.

After taking a tray of food, Cassie sat next to me while Diane and Matt positioned themselves on the other side of the table, each of them looking as silly in the small furniture as I felt. Damek waited until everyone had settled before saying, "We will meet again with Queen A'Lenora later today." He glanced at me before continuing. "I am hopeful this goes better than our first audience with her."

I thought again about yesterday's encounter, and my emotions spilled over. "Why do you think today be any different? In fact, why are we even here? It's obvious these people don't trust me, and because of that, they probably feel the same about you. It seems unlikely that you're going to accomplish anything." I was bitter about the queen's attitude. It wasn't my fault that this happened to me.

Surprisingly, Cassie spoke first. "Phil, you can't expect everyone to fall in love with you immediately. We have to win her trust somehow. I remember a time when you first met us, and you thought we didn't care for you. You almost didn't join our Utopia Project because of that first impression."

"That was different. Nobody's life was on the line then."

Matt fixed his eyes on Damek. "What's your plan now? Much has changed since the time you first left Loralee to find allies."

He nodded. "Yes, things are worse; the Bots are stronger. But that doesn't alter the need for our distinct races to work together. If anything, it should make our task easier."

Matt scrunched his face, an expression he used when not convinced about something. "Seems to me, you're unlikely to get any support from them. I kinda agree with Phil." When Damek didn't respond immediately, Matt added, "They're afraid. You can see it. The devil is at their doorstep, and the Valnorians are hunkering down. They would probably welcome you if you came here with an army of Astari ready to fight. But right now, they don't care about the Floating Isles. Maybe they never did, but certainly not now. They only care about protecting their home, and I don't think they're going to consider any grand scheme to bring together the races like in times past."

"But they should care," Damek shot back. "It's our only hope."

"Matt's right," said Diane. "You're only going to win their support if you can stop the Bots from destroying their forest. They may have been willing to cooperate in the past, but I don't see it now."

Damek's gaze shifted back and forth between them. It took some time, but he lowered his head as he stared at his uneaten food. "I knew from our reception that something had changed. But I was still convinced they would understand the good that could come from working together. It saved all of us in the past. I believed they would see the value."

Matt rubbed his beard, which like mine, was nearly full. Neither of us had shaved since leaving Haven. "Like it or not, we need help from someone to stop the Bots. But I don't think it's going to be the Valnorians. It seems like we're back to where we started so long ago."

2 2

THE ETHWOOD TREE

Damek looked around the room as if searching for an answer. I could see him struggle with the belief that the Valnorians would be no help. But I knew his nature was not to give up so quickly. "We are here now," he said, "and we have sacrificed so much to come to these woods. I want to use our time to learn more about them. Maybe there is still hope. After all, despite Queen A'Lenora's initial decision about Earthfriend Philip, she did eventually change her mind."

"Reluctantly and with concessions," Matt added.

Damek looked at him for a moment, as if recalling her demand that all our lives be forfeit if I did any harm. He nodded before continuing. "Nevertheless, we will meet with her again later. Maybe she will become more agreeable once thinking about it." He smiled as if even he didn't believe it. "Meanwhile, I suggest we explore this Ethwood Tree and learn what we can from the people here." He surveyed the room, which served as a cafeteria. "None of us ever had the chance to see this place before, and we may never again."

"I'm not in the mood to be a tourist," I said, realizing as soon as I spoke that I was dampening his mood. I softened my voice. "I understand your interest; the place is amazing. I just wouldn't enjoy it. At least not now."

Damek frowned but didn't object. As he stood up to leave, the others hesitantly followed, except for Bevon, who remained with me in spite of my objections. After the others went, I intended to return to my room, but Bevon eyed a group of Valnorians sitting across from us. "I see many here are drinking a warm beverage. I think I will try it. You?"

"I suppose." I didn't particularly need anything else, but I also didn't want to complain more than I already had.

A Valnorian entered the room just then and glanced my way before doing a double take. I recognized him as the leader of the scouting party that first intercepted us. He walked toward me and stood smiling before me. I wasn't sure if it was a friendly smile. "I was surprised that Queen A'Lenora decided not to have your head."

I didn't know why he cared. He didn't look menacing, so I answered. "No, I guess she figured I wasn't that much of a threat." But in my mind, I knew the only reason she changed her mind was because the Astari pledged that they would prevent me from harming anyone. For good measure, I added, "It's a good thing for me you didn't follow through on your orders."

He looked down at me thoughtfully. His interest in me was making me nervous, and I suddenly felt exposed. Yesterday, he had been moments away from executing me. He might now consider taking matters into his own hands.

I glanced over to find Bevon, thinking I had better catch his eye in case this escalated into trouble. But his back was toward me as he engaged in a conversation with a worker behind the counter. The soldier nodded to the seat on the other side of the table from me. "May I?" Without waiting for a reply, he sat in the chair that Bevon had vacated. "You think little of us, don't you?"

He didn't say it harshly, but I still didn't like his message. I looked him in the eye. "I don't care much for people who want to kill me."

He thought about this for a moment. "I was about to do it. Consider yourself fortunate that your friends are so persuasive. It seems they could even change the queen's mind. And that's not easy."

"They had good reasons," I shot back.

He looked at me as if sizing me up. "I'm sure they did. But the Astari have always been known for their compassion." A darker expression came over him. "We do not have that luxury in these times."

I thought about what we had seen in the lands just outside the Sacred Forest, the dead zone, the storm that smashed into Haven. I guess I could understand his point. "I have no intention of harming anyone." It seemed I had needed to repeat this far too often.

Again he looked at me with a thoughtful expression, as if trying to see more than what was on the surface. "That may be true. But you must understand, you are not like the others.

It is clear to us that you have a taint from the Bots within you. I'm sure you feel it. That's what the queen fears. As do I."

I was sick of everyone telling me I had an infection, but nobody seemed interested in doing away with it. I remembered why I came along on this mission in the first place. "Then do something about it. Get it out of me."

For a brief second, he seemed surprised by my outburst, but then turned contemplative once again. He shook his head weakly. "I'm just a soldier. That is beyond my understanding. Lady A'Lenora would know more about that than I would."

He spoke with a hint of sadness in his voice. I was struck by how he called her Lady rather than queen. On a hunch, I said, "You love her, don't you?"

He didn't react strongly to what I said, which confirmed it all the more. A bitter smile came to his lips. "It seems you and I have that much in common. We both desire someone we can't have."

I stared at him, trying to puzzle out how he could know that. Was I so transparent? In spite of his initial animosity toward me, I decided he was a decent enough person. Before I could ask anything else, Bevon returned with two steaming cups. He sat beside me and greeted my guest warmly, as if they were old friends. "Hello, Woodsman Fendor'il. It is good to see you once again." Why didn't I know his name? How much else had I missed? Bevon handed me one mug. "They call this drink Kivak." He looked at Fendor'il for confirmation.

"Most of us can't live without it," he responded and pushed back his chair as if to leave.

"Please stay for a moment," Bevon blurted before

Fendor'il stood. "I readily admit, I don't know a great deal about your people or the Greylock Forest. I would appreciate you telling me more."

The Valnorian relented and sat forward in his chair. "What would you like to know?"

Bevon thought for a second. "For one thing, how have you fared against the Bots recently? Have they been a problem?"

The thin line of his eyebrows bunched together. "We've not seen much of the Bots. Others have done their bidding; we frequently spot surrogates trained by them to do damage to us and the forest. Races of beings and animals we've never seen before began to attack our people some time ago. It forced us to step-up the patrols on our borders to protect the residents." He looked at us a moment to gauge our reaction. "I expect it's only a matter of time before the Bots themselves flex their muscle."

"Have you sought others to help?" Bevon asked.

"I don't know who's left in this realm that might make a difference. And besides, that's not something for me to decide."

Once again, I caught a hint of resentment in his tone. I suspected the queen must have spurned his advances. Either that, or she could not return his love, at least publicly. I knew so little of their customs. "Tell us more about your queen," I asked.

He eyed me suspiciously. "Why?" he responded in a flat tone.

I decided to keep the conversation light. "Well, for one thing, since my life appears to be in her hands, it might be a good idea to understand her better. For instance, how did she become queen and how long has she been in control? She appears rather young for the role. Is she respected by the Valnorian people? Is she married, or do you even have such a ritual here?"

He looked at me as if dumbfounded. "Do you always ramble so?" After a moment, he exhaled as if he didn't want to answer. "This is the only thing you need to know about our queen. Her responsibility is to protect our Sacred Forest. Everything else is secondary. She is the strongest of our people to wield the power of Elthea. That's why she's the queen. Age doesn't matter." He spoke as if lecturing me. But then his eyes lowered to his hands on the table as he continued. "She has not chosen a partner. When Valnorians mate, it is often for life, although it depends on the feelings of the pair."

He looked suddenly uncomfortable. "Let me give you a word of advice. If I were you, I would not worry so much about the customs of the Valnorians as much as convincing the queen you are truly an enemy of the Bots. Otherwise, she will not trust you. This is no time for us to be worried about an attack from within such as someone like you."

He looked at me as I remained speechless, wondering how else in the world I could convince them otherwise. The trouble was, I wasn't sure myself.

After Fendor'il excused himself, Bevon and I went back to my room. I preferred to think of it as a cell. Once inside, an old emotion came over me, one I hadn't felt since my first year in high school. It was a time when I didn't fit in, and it seemed like everyone was against me. Nothing I did or said made a difference. It was as if I had a black mark stamped on my head so that everyone would understand that I was different. I felt that way again.

Bevon sensed my mood. He sat on the single chair, which consisted of woven branches, while I threw myself onto the bed, an ornate structure with a frame and posts that were like the trunks of trees. It even had a canopy of branches and golden leaves hanging over it. A mattress of thick moss and soft blankets formed the bedding. The palatial appearance of the bed did little to suppress my ill mood. "This is not going to end well," I said before he could attempt to cheer me up.

"You do not know that, Earthfriend. We are among people that don't yet understand you or how you became infected. We will work with them to make them understand that you are good. Or we will leave here to find others who will help."

A coldness settled in my heart. How could I convince anyone else that I was a decent person if I wasn't sure myself? "I tried to kill Cassie. That's not the action of a good person."

He frowned. "I thought you were past that. At the time you didn't understand they had infected you. How could you fight against something that you didn't even know about? Now you understand better."

I touched the infection with my senses. Since we entered the dead zone during our trek here, I had realized I could identify that part of me that differed from the real Phil Matherson. It was always there inside me, like some predator stalking me in the shadows. And what concerned me most was that I could feel it getting stronger. It was waiting, ready to spring into action at some command or maybe a sign of weakness on my part. I didn't know what it intended to accomplish, but I understood that if I allowed it to run unchecked, the festering sickness would claim me for good. "How can I continue with this hanging over me?"

It took him a moment to understand what I was asking. "I know you better than you realize. You will resist. It is part of your nature. And not just you, but the human race. Your history is rife with people who threw down those who would harm others. I believe you will do that now."

I looked at him with leaden eyes. He was the one person I felt I could speak to without recrimination or judgment. "I'm not sure I have the strength. You have to persuade the queen to take this out of me, now while there's still time."

He looked worried, which was not an expression I often saw on his face. All the Astari were even-tempered, especially Bevon. He stood up and walked over to the window to gaze out at the land beyond. "These people have changed since the days when we joined forces to vanquish the Bots. Maybe it was the losses they suffered during that war, or maybe they just turned inward as a way to recover, much like we Astari have done. Whatever the reason, it is clear they are now more concerned with themselves and their forest than they are with anyone else."

He stood gazing out the window for some time before he faced me again. "It may take time for the queen to become convinced that we should attempt to purge you of this affliction. Until then, you must keep it under control. Otherwise, we will have to leave here empty-handed."

He never said the words *or worse.* But I knew he was thinking it.

BEVON KNEW I WAS IN NO MOOD TO TALK, SO HE LEFT ME alone, saying he would be nearby if I needed him. I was grateful for the time to brood on my own, but I couldn't help wonder if keeping busy would have been a better option. I was once again falling into despair, as I had done during the months following my attack on Cassie.

I had thought about ending my life more than once since then. But I knew I never had the courage to take that step, not then and not now. My failure will be a fitting epitaph to my life. *Here lies Philip Matherson. He was too weak to spare others the harm from his affliction.*

I lay on the moss bed looking up at the ceiling, which was part of the tree, just like everything else. Even in my despondency, I could see the beauty in this place rivaled that of the Raised Isles. I felt as if I was missing out on something amazing by not immersing myself in Valnorian society as I had done on Loralee when we first arrived. My friends were off doing just that, causing me to recall a memory of our first day on the island of Tensheann when Damek had been so proud to guide us around the island.

An annoying trill of a bird drew my attention. The jabber of animal life was a constant backdrop since we set foot into this forest, but this one screeched louder than the rest. I turned my head to observe it sitting in the tangle of branches that formed the frame of the window in my room. The bird looked like any other in this land, colorful and lively. This had a red stripe across its back. I thought about shooing it away but decided it wasn't worth the effort.

Only after the incessant chirping continued did I look at it again. I noticed something around its neck, almost as if it were wearing a necklace. I wondered about this as I tried to angle my head to see the object before the bird flew away. The bird went silent as I paid attention to it. While I continued to observe it, the animal tilted its head toward me as if understanding I was looking at it. "You're a strange one," I muttered, swinging my legs around to stand, fully expecting it to fly away.

But it now remained quiet where it was, observing me. As I slowly approached, I realized it did have something around its neck. "What do you have there?" I said soothingly. "Is that stuck on you?"

The bird looked at me as if fascinated. I wasn't sure how I would remove it. My parents had several parakeets when I was a young child, but I don't remember ever handling one.

I inched closer, fully expecting it to dash away any second. But it remained seated on its perch. "Is this your home? Is that it?"

I didn't see any sign of a nest as I puzzled over why it remained. Standing right before it, I raised my hands as if in slow motion. The creature appeared transfixed as if drugged. Ever so slowly, I wrapped my hands around it, careful not to squeeze.

I almost dropped it once I realized it was cold to the

touch and hard as a rock. It was some sort of mechanism. "What the hell?" I muttered, still fearful that I might scare it.

The thing did not attempt to struggle. Since I came this far, I slipped the gold chain off its neck. The chain held a medallion with a turquoise gem. I scrutinized it while absently setting the bird mechanism back on the branches with my other hand. I brushed my fingers over the jewel, looking for some sign or marking that would provide a clue to its origin or owner.

My eyes shifted back to the bird. It sat where I had placed it on the branch and it looked up at me expectantly. "What is this, little fellow?" I murmured, half expecting it to respond.

As if in answer, the pendant in my hand warmed. My mind raced, thinking it might be a weapon or a bomb. The Valnorian queen wanted me dead, and this might be a good way to rid me of her problem without my blood on her hands. I inspected it another moment before preparing to fling it out the window. The jewel pulsed with an inner light.

A motion to thrust it away never came as my senses dulled and my body became numb. My perspective shifted as the turquoise gemstone came closer to me until I felt as if I were falling into it. And then, in a blink of time, I stood looking at the figure of a Draas. I recognized her immediately as Enia, the same one who had appeared to us underground. Her expression remained placid, as if waiting for me. Unlike the detailed settings we had experienced with the artificial realities, the air surrounding her was an indistinct gray of shifting swirls.

I knew with certainty that I was back in another reality projection.

Now I was angry. "How dare you? What gives you the right to bring me back here?"

She tilted her head as if puzzled. "You are not back anywhere." She spoke calmly, as one might to someone who didn't understand. "This is a remote chamber which allows me to speak with you again."

My nerves calmed as I remembered that the Draas didn't mean any harm to us while we were underground, at least that's what she explained at the time. Now I wasn't so sure. "What do you want?"

"I wish to give you something."

My anger ebbed, replaced with suspicion. "You've given us enough already with the ordeals we suffered in your chambers. It nearly killed us the first time."

She shook her head. "But you survived it. I stopped the sequence once I realized your capacity to activate it. But that is not why I wish to speak with you now. It is vital that you prepare yourself for the challenge that will no doubt come. If you succeed, I achieve my charge of safeguarding our home."

I felt sorry for her. Her people might never return, but she remained steadfast to her task. Even though I knew she was not alive, who was I to say that she had no feelings or aspirations? My beliefs about what was real and what was artificial had become blurred. The Astari, as well as the Bots, had evolved from binary code. "Okay then, what do you want to tell me?"

She seemed pleased. Was that something planted into her programming, or something more?

"I wish to convey to you a prophecy, one that may help."

"Are you kidding me? A prophecy?" I snorted a laugh. "That's the last thing I need right now."

She remained unshaken. "You may believe that. But when the storm breaks, and there is nothing else to anchor both your life and everything good it represents, this may be a beacon for you to grab onto."

She was speaking in riddles, which was exactly what I expected from any prophecy. With little expectation, I assented. "Tell me then."

She paused a moment, as if reconsidering her decision. "Listen well, Philip Matherson. More than your life may soon be decided." I took that as an admonishment, but I remained silent until she spoke again. Her voice took on a deeper tone. "Before the end, you will weep for the death of a friend, release a deadly force upon the land, and spurn a love. You always blame yourself for your failures, wanting to die rather than face what is within you. It is easy to die, harder to fight. Above all, remember the bond that exists between you and those closest to you. It is the only emotion that will save you."

I stared at the face of the Draas, unable to understand her words. Despite mocking her at first, I caught the glint of something important in what she said. "Please, explain what you mean."

The slightest shake of her head told me she would not. "Prophecies are not meant to be explained. The words must speak to your heart, or they are meaningless." I wanted to shout that there was so much I didn't understand, and this didn't help at all. But she waved her hand before I could say anything. "Farewell, Philip Matherson. Mayhap we will meet again someday."

The image flickered out, and I found myself standing in the room surrounded by the branches and leaves of the Ethwood Tree, more confused than ever. *Before the end you will weep for the death of a friend, release a deadly force upon the land, and spurn a love.* What did it all mean?

I looked down to see the chain of the locket still wrapped around my fingers. The bird that wasn't a bird flew over and settled on my hand. I could see it wanted the jewel back. I thought for a moment about refusing, thinking it was a last link to the Draas. But what would that gain?

I opened my palm, and it deftly slipped its neck through the chain. With a final chirp, it flew out of the window. I watched it glide out to the open air until it became indistinguishable from the flocks of other birds.

A new fear began to take shape inside me. Whatever was going to happen, it was going to be my fault.

THEY ENTERED MY ROOM WEARING THE SMILES OF people who had spent the last few hours enjoying themselves. I tried my best to look as cheerful as they were. I didn't want my friends to think I had once again turned gloomy. Besides, when I saw Cassie's radiant face, I couldn't help feeling the same.

"You really should see this place," Diane gushed. "We went nearly to the top. The view is amazing."

I grinned, even though my mind was still wrestling with

the words of the Draas message. I decided not to mention it. No use troubling everyone else with something they couldn't do anything about. "Sounds like you enjoyed it. Sorry I wasn't up for it today."

Wrinkles creased her forehead. "We were concerned about you."

I wasn't sure if she was just saying that because she sensed my mood or if she meant it. Either way, it sounded genuine, and I smiled. "Don't be. I'm fine." When they didn't look convinced I added with more emphasis, "Really."

Damek stuck his head in and announced, "Wait here Earthfriends, while we try to find out when the queen might see us again. Bevon, you can stay here if you wish."

Bevon nodded in assent as Cassie sat on the bed next to me while Diane sat on the now empty bench with Matt on the floor next to her. "We learned something," Cassie said, her eyes sparkling. "Long ago the Valnorians had trees that could actually fly. They used them to travel just like the Astari ships. Can you imagine what a sight that would be?"

It was always a joy to see her excited like this. Anything that involved something magical ignited her emotions. If only I could have the same positive result on her.

"They don't have them now?" I asked, thinking one of them might be a way to escape from here if relations became any worse between me and the queen.

She pursed her lips. "No, they said they don't have that ability any longer." She turned toward Bevon. "Why is that? I don't understand how an entire race can lose that skill."

"It's not that they forgot," he responded. "The power of Elthea has been lessening for some time. We don't understand why, but some believe it is because the Bots are drawing more of it for themselves. It may be there is only so much energy for everyone to use."

Something in his tone told me he didn't believe it. "And that's what you think?" I asked.

He looked at me a moment as if debating whether to say anything. Finally, he shook his head once. "I believe Elthea's Realm has more than enough for all of us."

When he remained silent, Cassie asked, "Then what happened?"

He shrugged. "I do not know. I am not sure if anyone does. I have only heard theories."

I thought back to the artificial reality rooms the Draas had created. They must have needed tremendous amounts of some force to sustain them.

Matt stirred as he sat on the floor. "The Bots didn't seem to have a problem when they created the storm or the dead zone."

Bevon winced as he considered this. "No," he replied slowly. "And that concerns me greatly. I am afraid it will not be a fair fight when the time comes. And it seems that day draws near."

A SINGLE SNOWFLAKE

I waited while Bevon kept me company, or guarded me, depending on your point of view. It was probably both as I remained in my room. Diane had said she could use some rest after their long march up and down the stairs of the tree, so they returned to their room.

We were expecting the queen to summon us once again, and it came that afternoon with a knock on the door. Bevon went to open it, and I saw an unarmed Valnorian standing outside. Behind him stood the two armed sentries. The Valnorian entered the room and stared at both of us as if intrigued. "I am sorry to bother you," he said meekly, "but Queen A'Lenora requests that you meet with her."

I was about to retort that it was likely a command rather than a request, but didn't see the point in arguing with him. It took me a moment to realize he was the only Valnorian who had shown any compassion toward us. "You're the one who guided us on the walkways, aren't you?"

A broad smile spread across his face. "Yes, I am surprised you remembered."

I thought about his good nature and the deference he showed us while he had guided us, a marked contrast to most other Valnorians. "Most others want me dead. You're easy to pick out."

His smile turned into a frown. "We Valnorians are not all of one mind." He considered me for a moment. "I suspect that the same is true of the people from your home." He gestured with his arm to follow him as he led Bevon and me out of the room. The two guards fell into step behind us.

I thought about what he said as we walked. "So not everyone thinks I'm a menace and wants to end my life?"

He slowed his step and fell into pace next to me. "I do not know how everyone feels about you; many likely don't understand."

This was a new notion I hadn't considered. I just assumed everyone here mistrusted me, or worse. "So why don't you hate me, or want me dead like your queen?"

He looked at me strangely. "Because I have never met humans before." He turned to Bevon, walking a step behind us. "Neither have I seen an Astari. I'm willing to believe we can learn much from you." He marshaled his thoughts while he wrinkled his otherwise smooth forehead. "Our people have grown too isolated, removed from the rest of Elthea. Who's right in judging whether our opinion is the only one that matters. We haven't explored other societies or listened to the viewpoints of other races."

I blinked, thinking how close his beliefs were to that of

Damek, who might have said nearly those same words. I shot a glance at Bevon, who returned it with a wry smile. Maybe this was a way to change A'Lenora's opinion about me. "But you understand why your queen wants me dead? I have an infection from the Bots."

He wasn't surprised, so I had to believe he knew this already. "Yes, I can sense it." His eyes narrowed, and I had to wonder if he was looking at the venom inside me. "The Bots are dangerous, and they can spread evil. But you are not one of them. I see the difference between who you are and what the Bots have done to you. That is why I feel differently from our queen."

I was beginning to think better about the Valnorian people. Maybe more of them were like this young man. I realized I didn't recollect his name. "You told us your name on the walkways, but I'm sorry I don't remember."

He laughed, and it sounded more like musical chimes. "That's not surprising. At the time you were all so fascinated with our forest and the Ethwood. My name is Ja'Krill."

For a time we climbed the steps of the tree in silence, and I dreaded another meeting with the queen. Our first hadn't gone so well, and I had little reason to expect this to be any better. "Let me ask you something else." He looked at me expectantly. His eyes were full of life, just like this forest. "If this—whatever is inside me—caused me to do something bad, say I killed or harmed another person, or maybe damaged the forest, what would you do?"

He stopped walking and looked out to a view of the forest as he considered it. "If I had no choice, I would do what any sane person would do. I would protect myself, my people, and my home. I would expect any free people to do the same." He looked back at me. "But that time has not come, and I can only hope it will not."

I turned my senses inward and felt the roiling energy growing stronger. I wished I shared his optimism.

JA'KRILL LED US HIGHER ON THE TREE THAN I HAD BEEN before. The top of the tree still towered above us, but at this height, it had thinned considerably, with fewer rooms filling the space in the middle.

He led us to a place open to the sky, something I hadn't seen in any of the other rooms. My companions had already arrived. They smiled when I entered, but I thought they forced their smiles for my benefit.

Ja'Krill remained at the entrance. "I have enjoyed our discussion, Philip Matherson. I wish you the best."

I was suddenly sad to see my only supporter leave. "Can't you stay? I would be thankful if you could remain."

He shook his head. "It wouldn't be proper. I was not invited. But I expect we will talk again."

He spun around and left us while the two guards remained just outside the entrance. Diane moved over toward me. "It looks like you've found a friend."

I smiled ruefully "Yeah, there are so few of them in this place." I looked back and saw that Ja'Krill was already out of sight. "Unfortunately, he may be the only one."

I scanned the room, noticing that it was much less formal

than the one from our first meeting with the queen. There was no throne, and it was much smaller. The leaves lining the walls were a mixture of red and gold, the color of a maple tree in October back in New England. The branches along the walls curved around large openings, affording a spectacular view of the surrounding forest. The furnishings, comprising a group of chairs with moss-like cushions, were part of the tree itself.

The view to the forest beyond caught my eye. I walked over and looked out an opening to observe the sight below, wondering once again how anything so expansive and complex as this tree could be part of the natural vegetation. At this height, the rope bridges that connected it to the surrounding forest were far below. We were higher than most of the surrounding trees in the woods, which extended as far as I could see.

"It's a spectacular view, isn't it?" I spun around to see the queen. The two guards entered behind her and positioned themselves on either side of the door. But unlike our first meeting, she had no retinue by her side. Her voice hardened. "Remember it this way, should you decide to destroy it."

"I have no intention of harming it. Even though you may not believe me, that's the truth."

She looked at me without expression. Gone was the formal garment she wore yesterday, replaced with a simple lavender robe that reached the floor. I expected her to fire another retort, but she shifted her gaze to the others, lingering the longest on my friends from Earth. "Tell me about your home. Do you have a forest such as this?"

I wasn't sure who she was asking, but Matt answered.

"Our world is full of wonders, but I must admit, we've already seen many sights in this land that surpass anything on Earth, including this forest ... or this tree."

Her face lost its harshness. "We call this Ethwood." She moved along the walls of the room, brushing her fingers along the bark of some thicker branches and resting them there for a time. It occurred to me that her motion was eerily similar to Torermak's gesture when he came in contact with stone. "This wood grew from the oldest of trees in this forest. Many Valnorians have dedicated their lives to creating it." She directed her gaze at Damek. "It was the first wood we raised following the devastation we suffered from the war against the Bots. Those monsters destroyed our forest before anyone could stop them."

"And now they turn their attention to us once again," Damek replied.

She furrowed her eyebrows. Maybe I saw fear in her eyes, but I couldn't be sure.

Damek tilted his head and focused his gaze out toward the tops of the forest trees. "They are coming after us again, all of us. The Bots killed many of my friends and family on the Isles of Loralee." His voice caught for a moment as he probably recalled once again the death of the Lady Elderphino. "But it won't be their last attack. Most recently, they battered the human village of Haven with an unnatural storm. And along our way here we saw large swaths of land devoid of life. They have a strength we cannot imagine."

She considered this without comment. Damek hesitated before adding, "It is possible the Bots are drawing on the life force of their dead ancestors."

Her face was so unlike a human, more elongated with a sandy color to her skin. Their joints could bend at angles that would be impossible for ordinary humans. But like the Astari and the Stonewraiths, some expressions seemed to transcend race. She pursed her lips. "That matters little now. Our concern is that the Bots are using new weapons and are intent on harming us. Already our defenses have been greatly tested. Unfriendly forces frequently attack the borders of our woods." She shook her head sadly and stopped to consider something. "Tell me, why do you come here now? Why these woods?"

It was curious that she hadn't asked this question yesterday, choosing instead to focus on me. Damek hesitated, likely considering Matt's warning that she wouldn't be interested in an alliance.

"We're here to offer our assistance," Damek responded.

The queen stood still and stared at him as she considered this. I could see she wasn't expecting an offer of help. She looked at him as if trying to read his mind. "Do you mean to tell me you've traveled all this way from your islands to fight with us?"

He shrugged. "No, that's not how it began. We started out seeking others who would join with the Astari so that together we might end this threat, once and for all. But we found the Ikhael people barely alive after an attack by the Bots."

Her eyes clouded over. "I didn't know that. A small party of Ikhael visited us here in the forest when I was a young child. Their good-nature and laughter was something I'll always remember. That, and how adamant they were about not using our walkways." She smiled at the thought, the first I had seen from her.

"They were courageous in the war against the Bots," Damek continued. "Once we discovered their fate, we decided to travel here and raise the alarm. But Bots attacked us along the way. They would have killed us if not for one of the Earthfriends who gave his life by destroying them."

She looked at me again. "Is that how he became tainted?"

I hated how she talked about me as if I weren't in the room. I was about to point that out, but Damek spoke before I had the chance. "No. Earthfriend Philip was infected some other time; we don't know exactly when. It was their companion, Earthfriend Eric, who gave his life for us."

She raised her eyebrows a fraction of an inch as she considered this, looking at me with newfound interest rather than bitterness. "And why do you travel with these Earthfriends now?"

Damek took a bit longer to reply. "Because they are our friends and they helped us when we needed it. Because they asked to join us to help defeat the Bots. Because the Bots threaten their home as much as our land. And because the Bots believe these particular Earthfriends are a threat to them."

She looked at us critically, as if not believing him. "Why would the Bots care about them?" She emphasized the word them.

Damek shrugged. "All I know is that the Bots consider these Earthfriends consequential in their plan to overrun this Realm and that of the human home."

A'Lenora paused for a time to consider this. She obviously mistrusted me. But I had to wonder if her mistrust outweighed the Astari offer of help. A thin smile creased her pale face. "I came here to tell you I had decided to send you away, to banish all of you from our forest."

She waited for a reaction from Damek. But it was Diane who spoke. "We almost didn't survive coming here."

Damek quickly added, "It is clear the land is facing another threat. We are on the same side in this conflict. Meanwhile, our races have fragmented into discrete entities, each living within the little paradise we each have created, believing we are safe from that which nearly destroyed us not that long ago. How could we have been so foolish?" I recalled Ja'Krill's belief that they were too isolated from other races and wondered how many others here might share that view.

"No, not foolish," the queen responded. "We hoped to build a better land, each in our own vision."

Damek had no response. He was likely thinking how most of his fellow Astari probably shared her same conviction. Meanwhile, she hadn't said whether she still intended to banish us or had rethought her decision.

At just that moment, I caught the sight of a single puffy snowflake that drifted from above us. It floated its way lazily downward, swirling around as a slight breeze buffeted it across the room. I thought it was a beautiful image, even in a place where everything else was so breathtaking. The thought entered my mind that it was too warm for snow. Was this another magical creation of the Valnorians, much like the cascading waterfalls on the many islands of Loralee?

A'Lenora's sharp intake of breath spoke otherwise. She watched it as fear spread across her face. It seemed she was trying to comprehend what she saw. Finally, in a throaty voice, she said, "It's begun. We're under attack."

24

THIS IS YOUR TIME

The queen swept from the room with her guards in tow. Her last words still echoed in my head. *We're under attack.* For a long moment, we all looked at each other, trying to understand what just happened.

But the Astari understood. "We must move the Earth-friends to a safer place," said Quintia.

"And where would that be?" Damek answered without emotion. "There is no safe place left in our land." He looked at me, and then in turn at Diane, Cassie, and Matt as if sizing us up. "This is your time. The winged Astari, Arianell, brought you here for a reason. She wanted you in this land. What you do now may determine the fate of us all." He turned his attention to the other Astari. "We offered the queen our support. Our word would mean nothing if we fled."

The rest of the Valnorian citizens understood that an assault was about to take place. I observed a tense resolve in their faces as they hurried up or down the stairway, which we could spy through the open door. I didn't perceive panic, only a token of fear. More than anything, I felt a gritty resolve from these people who would sacrifice everything, even their lives, to protect their families, friends, and the land they loved most. At that moment, I recognized that this exotic race of people, so dissimilar to humans, were not so unlike us at all.

I recalled a day from a year ago, after we had sailed from the raised islands to the mainland. On that day, Quintia had described the Valnorians by saying they had an inner strength she much admired. She felt they were always composed, even when all hell was breaking loose around them.

I could understand now what she meant.

What I couldn't understand was what steps they were taking to prepare for an attack. I could see no soldiers preparing for an onslaught, nor signs of men or women arming themselves. People were moving from one place to another with heightened energy that wasn't there before. But to the untrained eye, it might seem to be an ordinary day in the woods that rivaled the beauty of the Raised Isles or the lost city of the Draas.

The single flake of snow was all that we had seen of the pending assault. The sky was overcast, and the temperature had turned raw. To my mind, it still seemed strange for her to conclude that an invasion was about to take place. But I told myself that battles didn't have to be waged with two armies facing each other on a field of battle as they aimed their guns at one another. I only had to think about the cyberwar attacks that were taking place on Earth.

I suppose this was the cyberwar equivalent. What made

it even more unreal was that we were likely facing the same opponent that the Earth faced.

As we waited, not able to do anything else but wait, my thoughts drifted back to Haven. Rae had convinced me I could be cured of whatever hid within me. She believed the Valnorians might have a solution. At least that's the way I had taken her meaning. Maybe I had it all wrong. I was beginning to wonder if there was any salvation for me.

As more time passed, I grew restless, wanting to do something to prepare. "We don't understand how to fight them," I said. "How can we fight a storm?"

Damek glanced up at the sky before answering. "You understand evil. That's what we face. Look within yourself. Control of the Elementals is only a weapon that the Bots use, and like any tool, it has its weakness."

He might as well have been speaking gibberish. I looked at Matt for support. But he seemed to grasp this more than I did. And as he always did during a time of crisis, Matt spoke firmly and with authority. "We're here for a reason. Eric understood his purpose. Maybe it's time we find ours."

"But Eric died for his efforts," Diane countered.

Matt shared a long look at her before he nodded. "We must believe it will not happen to us." He shifted his gaze to look at Cassie and me. "We already decided not to hide under a rock. Like it or not, the Utopia Project changed our lives. I think we've come a long way since then. What's about to take place out there now would paralyze us with fright a year ago."

We continued to wait. The Astari stood passively, but the rest of us alternated between pacing or sitting on the collection of chairs. We expected an attack would come, but we did not yet understand what form it would take. That made it worse in many ways, both the waiting and the not knowing. Despite Matt's bravado, I could see the tension and fear build in each of my friends.

Cassie eventually broke the silence. She spoke meekly, as if afraid of disturbing us. "In a way, it's funny this is happening to us." We looked at her, none of us understanding what she meant. She didn't seem to notice. "There have been times when I wished with all my heart that I could go back to my previous life. I was safe in my shell, reading my books, not needing any friends." She intentionally looked at me. "But now, I know I could never go back to that existence. I don't always understand everything that's happening here in this land, but I know we can't run from it."

At that moment, I loved her more than ever. I wanted to embrace her, keep her safe from harm. But I knew that was a dream. I had already hurt her more than the Bots. I didn't want to make it worse. I was sure that I could do so much more damage. I felt it just below the surface of my senses; something was waiting, biding its time for the right moment. And that scared me more than any attack by the Bots. Maybe the queen was right in wanting me dead.

The Astari continued to gaze stoically out the open windows or up at the sky. It was rare for them to be so withdrawn. They knew what was going to come and were preparing for it in their own way.

I had the feeling the Bots were marshaling all their energy for this one strike. This time they were going to make it impossible for us to escape. We were part of their design, whether it was because they wanted those of us of the utopia team to be the face of their campaign to end life as we knew it on Earth, or revenge consumed them because Eric foiled their plans with the invocation. Whatever the reason, it didn't matter much now.

I felt the tension building inside me. Without thinking, I blurted, "I'm worried."

It took a moment for anyone to respond. Diane knitted her eyebrows together. "We're all scared. We know what they tried to do to us before."

I shook my head. "No, I know that. I'm afraid of what I might do. This time I'm different. There's something inside me, and it's growing stronger, consuming more of me like a deadly cancer."

I could see the uncertainty in their eyes, and I wondered if they mistook my words to mean that I had the power of an invocation such as the one Eric used. They understood that if I called it forth, the result would be my death, just as it caused the death of Eric, as it did the Lady Elderphino. But I somehow knew this was different. This wasn't a gift from the Astari. "I want to tell you this now before things happen," I added. "I'm afraid of dying, like anyone else. But I'm more afraid of killing each of you, or others."

The prophecy from the Draas drifted through my thoughts. *Before the end, you will weep for the death of a friend.*

"Stop thinking like that," Diane snapped. "You're beginning to believe what the queen said. What does she know anyway?"

I remembered the words of Enia during the moments

when the rest of them were in a trance. *You don't yet realize your capacity to destroy. And because of that, you are even more dangerous.*

My hope was faltering; I felt it slipping away like a thread unraveling. I tried to stop it, prevent it with sheer willpower. But I knew that wasn't enough. I knew in my heart that soon, all would be lost.

TIME SLOWLY PASSED AS IF THE LAWS OF NATURE HAD been violated and stopped working properly. And with each second, my foreboding grew. It was one thing to see the deadly Bots arrayed before us in an open field. It was quite another wondering when, and how, they would strike.

At one point, a Valnorian guard approached and handed Damek the weapons Fendor'il had taken from us. "Orders from the queen," he responded crisply before hurrying away without another word.

I still had no intention of arming myself, and I again refused when Damek passed them out. In my mind, it didn't much matter if we had weapons or not. I knew that when the attack came, we would face a deadlier threat than hand-to-hand combat.

Matt and Diane alternated between looking out at the walkways below, the forest beyond, or up at the steel-gray sky above. Except for the sights and sounds of Valnorians rushing from one place to another, everything appeared normal. That is, if you could call anything about this tree or these woods normal.

"Maybe she was wrong," Diane finally said. She spoke timidly, unlike her typical assertiveness. Nobody responded. What could we say?

After a long pause, Damek stopped gazing up at the heavens to answer. "No, she is not. Your senses may not be tuned to the ebb and flow of energy in this land. The Bots are harnessing it all around us."

I could feel it as well. It had ignited whatever was inside me as if the two were calling to each other. I wasn't sure how long I would be able to control it. That continued to worry me more than any assault from the Bots.

Cassie sat next to me, both of us lost in our thoughts. She hadn't spoken for a long while. Finally, she said, "I don't think I ever said I'm sorry for the way I acted." She tried to form a smile, but it came out more of a grimace. "It was wrong of me not to understand what had happened to you."

I knew what she was really saying. She was telling me goodbye, putting her life in order before the end. As we looked at each other, it seemed we were back at Woodbery College, a time before life became so messed up. I shrugged. "You couldn't have known, nobody did. I only realized what was inside me after we returned to this land."

She pressed her point. "But I should have known you weren't like that. I didn't know what to do, so I pushed you away. It was easier."

Sadly, that was the way everyone often acted; fear controlled our lives. "Cass, it's difficult to make sense of what's going on. Believe me; I've tried during these last couple of years." My lips curled into a smile. "Can you imagine attempting to explain what we've been through here? They would lock us up."

She returned the smile, and I felt my heart warm. At least for a few seconds, I pushed my fears aside.

I looked into her eyes, and she held my gaze. "It's strange how life turned out for us," I said. "Remember when we were at Woodbery? We thought we were under so much pressure to achieve something, whether it was good grades or preparing for a career. It was always hanging over us." I grunted. "What I would give to be back there."

She pursed her lips. "I wished things had turned out differently between us. When we came back to Earth a year ago, I thought it was a chance for a new beginning. I had hoped we would stay together."

I felt a pang of regret over what might have been. "We almost had that," I said softly. I so much wanted to believe that someday we still would. But I knew it wasn't likely. Not now. Not ever. "Let's take one step at a time. Just talking together again makes me happy."

Her smile was sad. "Everyone flubs up, one time or another. It seems ours was bigger than most."

There we sat; I felt we were all waiting for death to come. The Bots were going to have their way this time. How could we prevent it? Eric bailed us out before, but how could we count on a savior this time?

25

AGAINST ALL HOPE

The snowfall settled over us, a light dusting that portended a transformation of the life I knew. It quickly intensified into big, swirling flakes that covered the floor of the room where we waited, turning the deep brown of the wood into white. The snow was falling heavy enough to obscure even the nearby trees of the forest.

Rather than stay in the room with no ceiling, we took shelter nearby. We were off the stairway that led up or down the tree, so we were out of everyone's way. And the thick covering of limbs overhead protected us. Nearby openings in the wall afforded us a view of the falling snow outside.

A puzzled frown creased Quintia's face as she looked out a window. "Do the Bots think this snow will harm anyone? I don't understand what they are trying to accomplish."

But I understood. I felt a smoldering fire in the sky above. It was the same energy I had felt during the storm at Haven and when we entered the dead zone. The Bots were only beginning to flex their strength.

I felt empty inside, knowing our enemy was about to unleash some fresh horror on us. This time, the Bots had me in their crosshairs.

We didn't have to wait long before the brunt of the attack began. The giant tree shook with a horrible splintering crack. I braced myself against the wood of the wall, wondering if we would be pitched on our side as the tree fell to the ground. In the confusion, I inadvertently grabbed onto Cassie's hand. She turned to me with a wild look, fearful of what was happening. If only I could make that fear go away.

Outside, chunks of something fell from above; many pieces crashed into the tree itself while others fell to the ground. I had trouble identifying what they were. Everything was as white as the snow lashing against the outside of the tree. Then I recognized a body part. In the brief moment it fell past, I glimpsed the head and upper torso of a Valnorian, its face frozen in a grimace of pain or horror.

Bevon now understood the nature of the assault. "The Bots are attacking with waves of frigid air. It is freezing everything it touches."

I suddenly felt the bone-chilling air filter down toward us. Gone was the warm, humid air that had greeted us when we had entered the forest.

More crashing noises came from above. The ice shield was dipping lower. The Bots intended to freeze us all to death.

My heart began racing. I couldn't fight something like this. Who could? An overwhelming emotion told me to run toward the stairs and follow them down, away from the death overhead. I crouched low, an irrational feeling that the ice attack was going to touch my head any second and I would wind up like that dead Valnorian falling past us. The thunderous, bursting sound grew louder every second, a concussion I felt as much in my bones as I did through my ears.

Strong hands seized my shoulders. Bevon positioned himself inches from my face. "This is your time, Earthfriend. I have given you all that I can. In this, you must find your way. Always remember what you fight for." His eyes darted to Cassie for a brief second before he stood with the rest of his companions.

I looked at the other Astari. They were transfixed as if under a trance, and I remembered Bevon's reaction when the storm had struck Haven. They were fighting it as best they could. I knew all the Valnorians would be doing the same. But if their combined strength was no match for this power, what help could I be?

Bevon glanced down at me and nodded crisply. I wasn't sure if he was urging me on or saying farewell.

Somehow amid the cacophony of splintering, crashing wood, mingled now with the screams of pain and anguish of the Valnorians, I found a shred of courage and stood on my feet. Matt, Diane, and Cassie huddled together with their arms wrapped around each other. Diane made a motion for me to join them, but I waved her off. This was something I needed to do on my own.

The snow had stopped falling outside, replaced with a frigid cold. As my breath came in white plumes, I looked out to see the surrounding forest. The sight sent an uncontrollable shiver through me. A blanket of mist or steam roiled above everything as it slowly descended. Already it had pierced the tallest of the nearby trees, turning everything it touched into frozen, lifeless chunks as the pieces broke off and rained down on homes and people below.

I watched, mesmerized by the weapon of ice. But then I spied a new menace striking from the ground. Hordes of Bots streamed across the open fields and rope walkways surrounding the Ethwood Tree. And like insects intent on seeking their prey, more were already scurrying along the limbs of tall trees.

A voice in my head spoke. I had heard their demands a year ago. And now they had a new petition.

—*This is your moment to achieve greatness. Join us and be rewarded.*

Never in my life had I felt so bereft of everything that had made me the person I was. I felt something inside pulling me inexorably to a place I had never wanted to touch, a blackness I couldn't understand.

Massive slabs of the frozen tree and Valnorian bodies rained down around us. The Ethwood was dying. The surrounding forest was being destroyed.

Only a short time remained before we would suffer the fate I always knew was to come. The Bots had sealed our future the moment we received their first bewildering message nearly two years ago. It was now obvious they would never stop pursuing us.

And here it would end.

～

I looked at her one last time. Her face was awash with emotions as she looked up fearfully at the approaching ceiling of ice that moved invariably closer. She didn't see me staring at her. It was just as well. It is better that she remembers me as who I once was.

A burning sensation like a fiery flame pierced my insides. I doubled over in pain. The infection in me was struggling to do what it had been designed to accomplish. And I had little choice. I knew it had already been working to destroy me a little at a time. I was no longer sure how much of me was the original Philip Matherson and how much was the virus from the Bots.

"Earthfriend, Philip, are you okay?" Damek shouted amid the crashing and rending of the Ethwood. I straightened up at his words. "You must help us," he pleaded. "We cannot hold out much longer."

I only half recognized him in my state of mind. Another voice, stronger and more persuasive, drowned out Damek's appeal.

—*You deserve more than what they offer. Has anyone ever recognized your potential? Every step of your life you have been beaten down and scorned. You can change all that, here and now.*

A fire erupted inside me. I knew those words to be true. I had always tried my hardest to become a better person. There were so many examples. After graduating from college, I wanted to manage a political campaign. But nobody gave me a chance. And then when I needed my government job back after The Shutdown, they let me go. Nobody cared about me.

No one gave me a chance in hell to succeed. Why should I care about them now?

I saw everything more sharply, as if I had lifted a veil from my eyes. Everything was distinct and more defined. What I couldn't see before came into a brilliant focus. Pulses of energy flowed all around us. I could identify them as if I had another sense, even more pronounced than hearing, sight, or sound. I felt as if I could touch the energy and redirect it somewhere else.

The thing inside me was emerging in a way I finally understood. I hadn't been able to control it or fathom its purpose before this. I realized that it wasn't an infection after all. It was a blessing. Just as the Star Lights had given me a gift on the island of Tensheann and allowed me to see and talk with my departed brother, this was a boon that gave me vigor and strength I never had. If only I had been able to restrain it before, I never would have attacked Cassie.

I had it all wrong. I shouldn't have feared the thing that infected me. I should have embraced it and discovered how to use it. But I still wasn't sure how to control or direct its power. I had no map or operating instructions to follow. I only had my raw emotion.

I did the only thing I could: I observed. I noted how the Astari and the Valnorians were pushing back against an overwhelming might that was quickly draining them. I saw how they focused their minds like a third eye to place impediments in the path of the energy which was pushing downward. It was much like redirecting the flow of water from a faucet by putting a palm or finger under it. This was all so simple.

I quickly realized their mistake. They were only trying to stem the onrush of potency, and it was quickly overrunning them. It was clear to me that the combined forces of the Astari and Valnorians had no capacity to launch their own counterattack. Otherwise, they would have already done so. I suddenly understood what the Astari and other races had done during times past when they joined together to combine their life forces into a single, piercing weapon to smash the Bots. Even if they had agreed to do the same now, the Astari and Valnorians alone were far too few to accomplish anything that could make a difference.

On the other side, the energy that emanated from the ice storm was a thing of beauty. It flowed precisely and uniformly, as would a single entity. Those who controlled it understood much about how to wield a tool to achieve the best advantage. I marveled at how it smashed through any obstacles in its way. I saw the strength and purpose of the assault. The forefathers of the Bots were alive once again as they sought to claim what was rightly theirs. For all their strength, the Bots were only a poor imitation of the potency and might of their ancestors.

I caught a glimpse into the minds of the Bots. As I looked more closely, I discerned two distinct classes within the same race. One faction comprised the dominant, logical leaders, while the other embodied the working, passionate sect. Together, their logic and unrestrained emotion went way beyond anything I had ever experienced, especially their passion. These beings burned with a fanatical rage. The working clan had been shackled for so long, and they wanted more than revenge. They wanted to prove they were the superior people. The leaders wanted supreme domination over the universe. Nothing was going to stop either of them, united now in the Bots, from becoming the master race. It was their right. And these puny Valnorians were mere stepping stones on the way to achieving their birthright.

Elthea's Realm was now within their grasp. No other people remained who could oppose them. Even an alliance of the once great races, as happened in the past, could not stop them now. Earth was nearly under their control as they disrupted its infrastructure. It was the Achilles' heel of my world, and it would bring the people to their knees.

And then the Bots would be free to sweep through the universe and become its master. Only then would their revenge be sated.

The destruction of the Sacred Forest was well underway. They had already partially destroyed the Ethwood, with nothing to prevent its complete demise. The dome of killing freeze had settled to the level just above where we now stood. But out in the rest of the woods, the frost continued its descent so that from the top it looked like a circus tent with us in the middle.

Queen A'Lenora and a small contingent of what remained of her guard now stood before us. Her companion Fendor'il was by her side. I understood now that he was more than a soldier in her army. The queen's face was grave and her eyes wild. But more than anything, I saw defeat and exhaustion. She had no more to give.

Bots surrounded us, having made their way up from the ground, killing Valnorians who tried to stop their advance. There was nowhere to run or hide. No hope to even escape.

Everyone was looking at me now as if they understood I had changed. One of the humans spoke; I couldn't remember his name. "Phil, what's happening? Your skin."

I raised the back of my hand to see the gray and gold fabric, the same as that which covered the bodies of the Bots. Was I becoming one of them? Whatever it was, I didn't care. It meant little to me now. The voice that held my attention spoke again.

—*Demonstrate that you are one of us. Begin by killing their leader.*

I knew he meant the queen of the Valnorians. I had no weapon, but that didn't matter. She was no match for me. I moved toward her, but Fendor'il stepped forward protectively and pointed his feeble blade at me. Somewhere in the dim reaches of my mind, I remembered thinking I liked this person. But without another thought, I brushed the knife aside with a sweep of my hand and grabbed his throat, lifting him off the ground. I held him there for a second as he sputtered for air. Others screamed, none louder than A'Lenora. With my free hand, I grabbed hold of his weapon and then flung him across the room. He smashed into a wall and slumped unmoving to the floor. That one wasn't worth my time.

I eyed the queen, who now seemed to understand her fate. I brought the knife up to strike her in the chest, just below her neck. My muscles moved with a strength I never expected. I burned for her death. Rage consumed me as my old self fell away, no longer even a memory.

But before I could lunge forward and thrust the point of the dagger into her, one of the Astari moved to block my way.

He had ice-blue hair. I was about to strike him with my free hand to send him flying when he shouted, "Earthfriend. Remember my pledge."

The word Earthfriend meant something. I hesitated, and he continued, "You made me promise to kill you should you ever intend to harm anyone again. And I promised the queen I would not allow you to harm them." His eyes watered, tears were already sliding down his cheek. He said in a softer, almost pleading tone, "You have been my dear friend, but I made a vow. I will not go back on it."

"Damek. You must not," another Astari shouted.

I watched, almost in fascination, as he extended a knife from the hilt he held in his hand. A sob escaped from him before he drew back the blade. One of the human females screamed, "No!"

I remained rooted in place as conflicting thoughts raced through my mind. His words meant something, but I couldn't place the significance. Doubt struggled within me even as rage pushed me to act. The clash of emotions was just enough to forestall me from reacting. He poised his blade to kill; all he had to do was jab it forward. I stood paralyzed with uncertainty.

Before he could move again, something smashed into his back. His head and shoulders jerked up as if he were a puppet. While everyone's attention was on the two of us, a Bot had thrown a knife faster than anyone could react. The surprise registered on his face as he realized what had happened. Blood oozed from his lips as he exhaled and drops splattered to the floor from the wound in his back. The knife slipped from his hand and dropped to the floor.

His body relaxed, falling toward me. Reflexively, I supported him in my arms. He tried to speak but had trouble forming the words. Blood was leaking freely from his mouth onto his chin. He looked at me with glassy eyes. "Promise me." He coughed weakly. I didn't think he could continue. But he did. "Keep alive your utopia."

His body relaxed, and his eyes dimmed. I could see his life force flicker out.

Something snapped inside my head. His words unleashed the shackles that had constrained my memories, everything the Bots had tried to subdue. I now realized who I was. More than that, I grasped what had taken place.

I looked down with horror to see Damek dead in my arms. He was always the one I asked for advice. He would someday be the leader of all the Astari, this I was sure. He tried his best to keep me safe. And now he was dead because of me.

A guttural scream escaped from my lips, something I had no control over. I reached for the infection still inside me and realized for the first time that what I had felt before was a guise the Bots had devised to hide the actual gift. But I gave it little thought as I grasped what was flowing in my veins and was now a part of me. With all the strength I had, without thinking, I hurled it back toward those who had caused this, first at the Bot who had thrown the blade.

My mind went blank with rage. I pulsed with energy so vast that it had no limits. All of them would pay for this. I would see them suffer in hell even if it ripped me apart. I had a reservoir of strength to draw upon, and I would use it to smash every one of them and the weapon they had fashioned.

I felt the power course through me as if I had touched a live wire, one that didn't hurt me. It felt good, as if I were an addict who finally had a fix. The sensation emboldened me to draw more from the unlimited treasure. Concussions and flashes of light erupted all around me. I hurled it out of me without end, without thinking, thrilled by what I felt. All other sensations had fallen away.

I had a strength I never felt before. I never wanted it to end. I kept going without care. Every fiber in my body ached to continue, just as a finely tuned athlete pushes himself beyond all limits. Time had lost its meaning.

I thought I could continue without end. But rational thinking seeped its way back into my brain. My body weakened, and my strength ebbed. I could no longer draw on the source of power as I had. And as if awakening from a dream, one I didn't want to end, I realized I needed to stop.

I glanced at my companions, and that's when I saw her face. Cassie looked at me with the same expression she had after I had tried to strangle her. Her face was a mask of fear, as if I had turned into something alien. She didn't understand, couldn't fathom what had happened to me. But she knew I was different.

The thought made me pause, suddenly unsure of myself. And in that moment of doubt, I lost my grasp on the energy coursing through me. It dropped away and flickered out.

Even though my body and mind returned to the present, it still took me several long moments to recover. I blinked away the burning shock waves of light in my eyes and relaxed my muscles. The others stared at me with a mix of wonder and fear. Except for the Astari. They understood.

I was surprised to find that I was still standing and my skin tone had returned to what it had always been. And I still cradled the dead body of my friend Damek in my arms. If I didn't know better, I could believe he was asleep, so peaceful was his face. But I knew he would never take another breath, or chide me again for not doing something right, or inspire me to become a better person.

I firmly pulled the blade from his back and laid him gently on the floor as I kneeled next to him. Tears finally came, and then uncontrollable sobs. I had only grieved for one other person like this, and that was my brother Gary when I learned of his death.

After a time, I felt a hand lightly on my shoulder. I looked up through watery eyes to see Bevon next to me. "This was not your fault," he said gently. I knew it wasn't true, but there was no point in disagreeing. I would hold my feelings close to my heart. "He would have been proud of you. Remember that. You saved many lives."

Only now did I see that the Bots surrounding us were gone. So was the layer of misty ice. But I wasn't surprised. I somehow knew this would be the result of my rage.

Quintia and Riyaad strode forward to stand by Bevon's side. I slowly rose to my feet, uncertain what their reaction would be. Quintia's expression was grim, and her face awash with so many emotions. But most of all, I could see her concern. Was she afraid of what I had become, or what I had done? They both stood before me as if marshaling their thoughts. Quintia finally spoke. "If Damek were alive, I believe he would say, 'You did well, Earthfriend.'" Riyaad nodded his approval.

The only thing I could think about was that Damek was dead. "Is that what you think?" I said bitterly. "All this was my fault. I didn't understand what I carried in me, and I waited too long to use it. I could have prevented all this if I understood sooner. If only I had known the strength inside me."

Bevon shook his head sadly. "You could not have known. The Bots made sure of that by masking it. They probably intended for you to destroy Elthea's Realm once you helped them lay waste to this forest. But you did not. I don't believe many other people could have broken the control they held over you. That includes humans, Astari, or even Valnorians. Do not think you somehow failed. It was they who killed him. In their haste and their certainty, they once again miscalculated their actions. They became too concerned with winning."

I heard his words, but I realized it would take time before I could process anything. For now, I only wanted to feel the loss of a companion. I looked down at the body of Damek and let the tears flow freely.

26

WEEP FOR THE DEATH OF A FRIEND

The Bots weren't all destroyed that day. My fury had subsided a little too soon. Although many remained alive on the forest floor, they had lost their will to fight. Most scurried away like unwanted rodents as they fled the Greylock Forest. The Valnorians dispatched those who remained.

As for the lethal ice, it had subsided and melted away, leaving the top portions of most trees destroyed, along with the homes of those living there. The Ethwood Tree had lost much of its upper floors. I wasn't sure if it would survive.

Many Valnorian people did not. The Bots and the ice had killed untold numbers of them. Others had suffered terrible wounds and disfigurement from either the ice or by the blades of the Bots. This noble race might never be the same.

But there was always hope as long as there remained people in this land who understood the brutality of the Bots.

They would remember what the Bots had done to them and how a stranger gave them life. At least I hoped they would.

As for myself, I knew there was one life I could not save. And that left a hole in my soul that might never be filled.

These thoughts filtered through my mind as I stood at the base of the Ethwood, having carried Damek's body down the length of the tree. I insisted on doing it myself. I owed him so much more than I could ever repay. The guilt I felt over his death remained with me despite the sympathetic words from the other Astari. I had been too distraught to have any conversation with the rest of my friends. But now, as the shock was wearing off, each of them approached.

Matt surprised me by embracing me in a bear hug. He loosened his grip and looked me in the eyes. "Once again, we cheated death. You saved us."

My eyes watered, emotions still raw. I glanced down at Damek's body at the foot of the tree. "I didn't save everyone."

He wasn't sure how to respond to this. Diane was at his side. "We're all mourning his death, Phil. Please don't put it on yourself. That wouldn't be fair."

I considered her words. She still didn't make me feel any better, but there was no use arguing it. I would probably always feel responsible.

"What happened up there?" Matt asked. "Bevon said the infection had something to do with what you did."

I nodded. "They wanted me to become one of them by making me believe I was as evil as them. It was all to make me destroy this land and then our home. And they nearly succeeded. I almost couldn't control it."

"But you did. That's what matters."

I thought about it. "I could only break its hold on me when I saw what happened to Damek. Otherwise—" I left the rest unsaid.

"Do you have that strength to destroy them for good?" he asked. "Or did they take it away from you?"

Matt was always the strategic thinker in the group; he was frequently two steps ahead of us. I winced at the thought of ever using it again. "I'm not sure. It's not something I can turn on or off like a light switch. I'm not even sure if any of it remains." I turned my senses deep within myself. But all I felt was grief.

Cassie saw us talking and stepped toward us. She had become a friend again as our journey progressed. But how would she feel after she saw what I had done up there on the Ethwood? I had seen the horror in her eyes when I was in a rage. I now knew I had lost her once again, even if I saved her life. She understood I was something other than human.

Seeing her approach, Matt and Diane drifted away, letting us have our privacy. More than anyone else, the two of them understood the bond, however fractured it had become, that existed between Cassie and me.

She fidgeted with her fingers as she stood before me, her eyes lowered, unable to put anything into words. I decided to say it for her. "You were right about not trusting me." She looked up as if I had slapped her as she registered the shock of what I said, or maybe it was confusion. But I continued. "I don't know what I've become, Cass. I'm not the person you fell in love with so long ago." I didn't say the words harshly, but the sting of it remained on her face.

"You didn't ask for this. It's not your fault."

I shook my head and tried to soften my voice. "I never wanted power, or fame and glory, or to become the one who had to save others. Throughout my entire life, I had more basic ambitions." My breath caught, and I reflected on the flush of her cheeks, the curve of her neck. I would always try to kiss her neck when teasing her. That was during our good times. Our time together as lovers was too short. I could feel my throat close up, but I forced myself to continue. "I only wanted for us to live happily together." I stifled a bitter laugh. "Fairy tales always end with, 'And they lived happily ever after.' It seems that's not in the cards for us."

She furrowed her brow as she realized what I was saying. "I know I was harsh with you at first, but I was scared. I didn't understand."

I didn't want her to continue. "I don't blame you for any of that. I never did. I understand how you felt. I probably would have handled it much the same. But that's in the past."

"That's right. Nothing's stopping us from going back to the way we were." Her voice held a pleading tone, but I detected the uncertainty.

I shook my head sadly. "Yes, there is." I put my hand on my chest. "I don't know what's still inside me. After what happened here, I don't know what I'm capable of any longer."

Her eyes held a wild, untamed look. She didn't know how to take this. "Exactly. You don't know. Maybe the infection is gone. Or maybe these forest people can still cure you. That's why you came here in the first place."

I smiled ruefully. "They can't do anything. They never could. Besides, look around. Their treasured forest has been nearly destroyed. They will need all their strength and attention to repair it, even partially. There's no room for a lost soul like me."

"You don't even want to try?" She was angry now.

I didn't want to spell it out for her, but I had no choice. "Think back to how you felt when it first happened to me—when it first took control."

"I didn't understand it then."

"No, neither did I. But what scared you most was that I would do it again, that I would lose control of myself for whatever reason and try to harm you. You can't be sure that won't happen again. Hell, I almost killed all of you just now. What if this thing tries to control me again?" I took a deep breath and softened my voice. "That's all you'll be thinking about, Cass, whenever we're together. If I ever look at you funny, you're going to think it's happening again. You'll always be on edge, praying something doesn't set me off. Is that the relationship you want?" I wished for nothing more than to hold her in my arms and tell her everything was going to be okay. But that would be a lie.

Her eyes watered, and her chin trembled. "It's not fair. We've suffered so much. Why us?"

I wanted to say that life isn't fair, but I knew it would be trite. I smiled and tried to sound confident. "Recall how we felt when we were together on The Utopia Project. We were so optimistic. And somehow, all the emotions and good intentions we put into it have come to life. We never realized it at the time, but for better or worse, it has defined our lives."

I wasn't sure if I had convinced her of anything. I still saw the doubt and grief etched on her face. But I had nothing else to give her. As much as I wished, there was no going back.

"Come here," I said as I spread my arms. She stepped forward into my embrace without hesitation. She held me firmly, and after a moment I felt her sobs begin.

We continued to embrace that way for a long time. Letting her go was the hardest thing I had ever done.

QUEEN A'LENORA GAZED UPON ME WITH AN EXPRESSION I hadn't seen from her before. I wasn't sure how to read it. This had been a long day for her and her people, with the Valnorian forces still engaged in small conflicts against the remaining Bots. Those skirmishes, as well as more far-reaching issues such as the survival of her forest and her people, demanded her attention. I could see she was weary and appalled by the death she had seen. But she came to the base of the Ethwood Tree to pay her respects to Damek, talk with the other Astari, and to speak with me.

She stood looking at me for a long while. I let her play it out rather than speak first. "You nearly killed us all," she finally said. Her tone was level, and I detected no anger, only a statement of fact.

"You're right. What I had inside me was ready to explode. It only waited for a command from the Bots. I came close to killing you and probably everyone else. But you must believe me, before that moment I had no idea what I was capable of doing." I wasn't trying to plead for her forgiveness. Again, it was a simple fact.

She nodded. "If I had put you to death as I had wanted, I wouldn't be here talking with you now. And they would have obliterated our forest. Whatever the intention of the infection, you set your own course. You overcame it. And for that, I owe you a debt of gratitude."

I suddenly felt ashamed. "I don't deserve anything," I said bitterly. "They might never have attacked you if I weren't here. It was me they wanted."

She considered this. "Maybe. They might not have invaded us today, but they would eventually. And without you to stop them—"

I didn't want to speculate about what might be. "They killed my friend. That's the only thing I care about right now. And it was what brought me to my senses."

She pulled her eyes from me to gaze sadly at the body of Damek for a moment. "He was right all along. You humans have a purpose in our land that goes beyond my understanding. I should have listened to him."

I shook my head. "That wasn't why we came here. He wanted to bring you together, to bring all the once great races together to oppose the Bots. He believed it was our only hope."

She thought about this, and after a moment nodded her head once. "I will honor his wish." She looked up at the half-destroyed Ethwood tree. "We face something that is too dangerous for us to oppose on our own. I should have understood it from the beginning." Looking back at me, she added, "Tomorrow, we will say our goodbyes to those who perished. Damek will receive a service customary for the Astari." She paused again and added, "I wish I could do more."

I recalled the heartache at the service for the Lady Elderphino and the other Astari slaughtered on the island of

Tensheann. My voice shook as I spoke again. "Thank you. The parting ceremony means a lot to them."

She nodded and was about to turn away and then thought better of it. "One other thing. All of you are free to remain here for as long as you want. Of course, you may leave if you wish. Although now that this is over, I hope you will stay with us for a time."

I wasn't sure how to react, so I nodded without comment. I hadn't thought that far ahead.

She swept away, somehow looking regal without trying. That's when I noticed Fendor'il standing a short distance away. Someone had bandaged his head and wrapped his left arm close to his chest. I dreaded the thought of facing him again, but I owed him an apology. He eyed me warily as I approached. "I didn't mean for that to happen," I said before he could react. His bandaged arm appeared swollen. "Is it broken?"

He nodded as if unsure of how to respond. I didn't think he was going to speak at all. Finally, he said, "I heard what you did after you knocked me out. That's the only reason I'm not going after you right now with my one good arm."

I smiled, even though he spoke as if he meant it. "You couldn't take me with two good arms and a blade. What makes you think you could do it now?" I could see he was trying to decide if he should erupt in anger or take it as a joke. So I added, "You have to believe me, I didn't realize what I was doing at the time you came at me. If I could undo it, I would."

He relaxed tense muscles. Glancing at the queen who was speaking with Bevon, he said, "Well, I guess it's not all bad. She's a different person after this." I cocked my head, trying to figure out what he meant. He continued, "She's going to announce we're together. I didn't think she would ever consider it."

"I'm happy for you. See, it only takes you almost getting killed for her to realize how much she cares about you. I'm glad I could help with that."

He looked at me crossly. "Whatever you do, never try to help again. The next time I might not be around to accept her pity."

It was still too soon to laugh about anything. "I'll try to remember."

"Seems to me you also solved the problem with your lady." He glanced over to the place where Cassie, Matt, and Diane stood. "What with you being the big hero and all, I imagine she won't be able to resist you any longer."

I gazed at Cassie, feeling an old stab of remorse. "No, things didn't work out." I blinked away tears on the verge of flowing again. "Maybe someday, but not now."

He shot me a puzzled frown, but he didn't press the point. I put my hand on his uninjured shoulder. "Take care of her. She's a good queen."

He left me to my sorrow. I tried to make myself believe it wasn't all bad and that I shouldn't feel this way. Cassie, Matt, and Diane were alive because of me. So were Bevon, Quintia, and Riyaad. Although many had died, the Valnorians survived, as did their forest. But in my mind, the equation still didn't balance. The death of Damek outweighed everything.

I NEEDED SOLITUDE AND TIME TO REFLECT ON ALL THAT happened. My friends offered to stay with me, just as they had done through all of this. I could see the concern in their eyes, but I insisted I needed time to myself. I knew I had a decision to make, and I needed a chance to clear my head.

I walked to the edge of the field that surrounded the once-great Ethwood. Down here on the open ground, flowers bloomed, and insects sang their songs, oblivious to how close they had come to death. I shortly reached the edge of the forest, and I turned my head up to the towering trees before me. Even with nearly half their tops ravaged by the killing ice, they were still massive. The Valnorian people were already at work replacing rope walkways and searching through the remains of partially destroyed homes.

I leveled my head and stared at the abundance of plants and flowers that grew here on the ground, thinking how normal everything appeared from this perspective. Birds darted in and around branches, and small squirrel-like critters scurried along tree trunks and on the ground looking for nuts or berries. A larger animal, reminding me of a deer, walked from a covering of bushes as if it were a phantom of something from Earth.

I was about to turn away when a glimmer of blue caught my eye. Sitting on a nearby branch was the Draas bird with the pendant around its neck. The prophecy echoed in my head. *Before the end you will weep for the death of a friend, release a deadly force upon the land, and spurn a love.*

I wasn't sure I wanted to hear more of what Enia had to

say, if that was its intention. The bird glided toward me and flapped its wings as it hovered a pace before my face. I reluctantly extended my arm, and it settled onto it. When I didn't make a move to take the jewel, the bird angled its head and looked at me expectantly.

After a long moment, I reached out with my other hand and slipped the necklace off its neck. The bird immediately flew away to perch on a branch. I grasped the gemstone, realizing it felt warm to the touch.

The surrounding woods faded away, replaced by Enia sitting behind a desk in her room. Before she could speak, I held my hand to forestall her. "I don't want to hear about any other prophecy if that's what you intend to say."

Her forehead wrinkled. To me, she looked sad. "No, but I do want to say I am sorry. Our realm is diminished because of Damek's loss. I feel your pain."

Once again, I had to wonder if this virtual reality had feelings or was programmed to say the correct words. Did she ever feel loss or abandonment at not knowing if her people ever found their utopia, or was it a feeling she held in her heart every second of every day? My attitude softened. "That is kind of you to say." After a moment of silence, I asked, "Why are you here again?"

Her forehead smoothed, and she tilted her head a bit higher. "You have earned my allegiance because of what you have done to save our land. I am here to tell you I offer you my services, should you ever need them."

I wasn't expecting this. But I wasn't sure what she was suggesting. "What do you mean? You're restricted to your underground virtual reality chambers or this remote reality. What services can you provide?"

She nodded as if understanding my puzzlement. "The Draas have many talents that may be helpful to you. And you may need my help someday. The Bots will lick their wounds for a time. But they will never relent."

I thought about asking what talents she meant. But it was of little consequence right this moment. "What about your primary charge to safeguard your home if the Draas ever return?"

"There will be no home for them if the realm comes under the dominion of the Bots. You are now my charge."

I still wasn't sure what she was offering, or how I should respond. Sensing my confusion, she added, "Now is not the time to belabor this. It is enough that you understand I will come to your aid should you need it. Go now and mourn what you have lost."

She was right. I had no desire to think about possible assistance, whatever it might involve. "Thank you," I responded, not sure what else to say. But before she left me again, I asked, "Wait. How do I find you? I don't think I can ever make my way back to your home."

A smile came to her lips. "You need not try. This necklace will activate a remote reality once you touch its gem. Use it if you desire to speak with me. Keep it safe and always with you."

Her image faded, replaced once again with the leaves of the woods. I took a deep breath, smelling the richness of loam on the forest floor. My eye spied the bird that was not a bird. If I didn't know any better, I wouldn't have been able to tell it wasn't real. It let loose a single piercing chirp and flew away. I followed it until losing sight of it among the branches and greenery.

I WALKED FOR A TIME AT THE EDGE OF THE FIELD AND forest, lost in my private turmoil. I was about to turn away and move back to the Ethwood when I spotted a young Valnorian man with his back against one of the mighty trunks. His head was bent, knees raised, and his body shook from what appeared to be sobs. Most Valnorians preferred to spend their time among the upper boughs of the magnificent trees, so to see one sitting on the forest floor was unusual. These people had lost much today, and it was clear that, like me, he wanted to be alone.

I turned and began walking away, leaving him in his solitude. But a dozen paces later, I was still thinking of the man mourning his loss in private. Much of what happened here was my fault, so I turned to find out if I could offer any comfort.

He heard me approach before I came close. As he lifted his head, I realized that it was a Valnorian I had met before. His name was Ja'Krill. He was the one who led us to the Ethwood along the rope walkways and then to my meeting with the queen. Back then his eyes were bright with wonder at meeting us, but now his face was awash in agony as the tears flowed freely. Realizing who I was, he stood and tried his best to wipe his face. But his eyes and nose remained red, and his face drawn.

"I'm sorry if I disturb you," I said hesitantly. "But it seemed you might need some company right now."

He tried his best to collect himself, but when he spoke his voice cracked. "They're gone, all of them."

At first, I wasn't sure what he meant. "Your family?" I asked.

He nodded, and the tears flowed again. "We had such a beautiful house. Pa was always so proud that he acquired one of the higher limbs for us. At night I could feel the bed sway with the wind. It was such a comfort, like my mom rocking me when I was a babe."

He turned away to collect himself. I gave him a moment, unsure if I could offer any recompense. Here was yet another outcome of all our scheming and fighting against the Bots. Damek was dead, but how many others like Ja'Krill were grieving the loss of loved ones they would never see again?

He looked at me, not caring if his anguish showed. I winced, wondering if I saw an accusation in his eyes that I was to blame. "I hate them for what they have done. They took everything from me."

I thought again about Damek, and just as quickly my thoughts drifted to Cassie. In a way, I had lost both of them. "I'm sorry," I mumbled. "I wished I could have done more." I didn't have the heart to tell him I came close to destroying all the Valnorians and their Sacred Forest.

He didn't seem to hear me. "I don't know how I'm going to go on." His face was forlorn, no sign of hope. I felt a stab of sorrow for the young man. "Everyone I've ever loved, Ma, Dad, my sis and two brothers, all are gone."

My conviction wavered. Why did I ever approach him?

What could I possibly offer to make something like this better? There was nothing. But the image of my brother Gary came to mind. "I once felt as you do now. I thought I couldn't go on after my brother was killed in an accident. But somehow each day gets a little better." Images of all those I had lost drifted across my memory: Gary, Elderphino, Damek, and in a different way, even Cassie. "I wish I could offer you wise advice. But I have none, except try to be strong."

It was all I could give him right now. My words seemed to reach him. Tears still rolled off his cheek, but I sensed a calm taking hold of him. Thinking of Damek again, I added, "But now is not the time for moving forward. Now is the time to grieve for all the kind souls who have left us."

I held my arms open to embrace him. I wasn't sure if he would, but after a moment he stepped into them. I felt his sobs begin again, causing my eyes to well up as I thought about the death of my good friend.

We remained that way for a long while, two strangers of different races, mourning the loss of those ripped from our lives before their time.

27

PHIL'S DECISION

We stood on the banks of a river that flowed through the Greylock Forest near to the giant Ethwood Tree. The water rippled lazily, as if in no hurry to pass through the stately woods surrounding it. Even though most of the trees in the forest were severely damaged, they were still a magnificent sight.

In a clearing near the water's edge, lay a single body, that of Damek.

Many Valnorians came to pay their respects. They had suffered loss and hardship themselves, but they stood quietly around the clearing, heads bowed in prayer or contemplation. Many others ringed both sides of the river. I couldn't help draw similarities between what was taking place here and what I had witnessed over a year ago on the Raised Isle of Catalinar. It had been there that we paid our respects to Elderphino and the other dead Astari after the gruesome carnage by the Bots during the Midsummer Celebration.

How many ceremonies for the dead would we continue

to preside over because the Bots were intent on ruling the universe? In moments like this, it seemed it would never end. Like some bizarre dance, we were forced to repeat the pain of loss over and over again.

I discovered that the Valnorians preferred to bury their dead. They believed that the essence of the deceased fused with the roots of the trees to increase the potency of the forest. It was one reason they considered the forest so sacred. For them, the trees weren't only bark and leaves; they were the embodiment of their ancestors. Those assembled here would likely never have considered a funeral pyre, as was the Astari custom. The Valnorians never allowed open fires in their forest; preferring instead to use fireroot. But the queen made an exception in this special case.

Unlike the last Parting Ceremony I had witnessed on the Raised Isles, I moved through this one as if in a daze. I half expected to wake at any moment, realizing it was all a bad dream. I would see Damek smile at me, and he would ask why I was so glum. He would likely tell me a story about what he does whenever feeling down.

But that never happened. We kneeled next to him and touched our forehead to his. We listened in silence as the three remaining Astari sang a mournful dirge that built to a crescendo. We ceremoniously carried Damek's body in turns beginning with Matt, Diane, Cassie and myself, handing the body to Bevon, Quintia, and Riyaad as they placed him on a small raft at the waters' edge. Bevon took the torch and set the dry timber ablaze before nudging it toward the middle of the river.

We watched in silence as the current took him away from us.

I stood rooted to that place long after the pyre had extinguished itself as it rounded a bend in the river. In my heart, I felt adrift in this land, just like that small floating pyre. Damek had always been the one to guide us. He was our bedrock from the moment we first set foot in this land. What would I do with him gone?

After a time, Matt approached and stood next to me. He spoke gently. "Do you remember when he decided to set sail with us from the Raised Isles?"

I looked at him for a moment, wondering if he was trying to tell me once again that this wasn't my fault. I nodded, thinking back to that day.

"He told us how important it was that he do something for the good of the Astari. He didn't care that it might be dangerous, or that someone else in a position of leadership should be the one doing it. He felt responsible."

I recalled that conversation. Matt had questioned whether he was acting out of a sense of grief over the death of Elderphino. I smiled sadly, remembering those days. "We couldn't talk him out of it. But then he explained that he was training to lead his people someday. He said that we each had to take responsibility for the life we wanted to live."

Matt nodded. "He would have made an excellent leader of the Astari. He was much like his grandmother."

I smiled more broadly, thinking how he and Elderphino would always verbally spar with each other. "She was a wonderful role model for Damek, maybe for all Astari," I said. "I'm sure she would be proud of him now." Thinking about them brought fresh tears to my eyes. "I can't imagine him not being here. More than anyone else, he was a part of this land. He always knew what to do."

Matt glanced at the Astari, who were still speaking with the queen. "Just as Elderphino was a model for Damek, I suspect his companions have gained the same from him."

Diane and Cassie came over to us. I could see the hesitancy and pain in Cassie's eyes. Like all of us, she was mourning the loss of Damek. But there was something else. She didn't yet know how to feel about me: love me, hate me, fear me, or just forget about me. I could see the jumble of thoughts going through her head. She didn't deserve this pain. She did nothing wrong. Loving me was her only mistake. I put my arm around her shoulder, wanting to comfort her. But she turned it into an embrace. I felt my resolve slip away. Was I right in deciding we shouldn't be together?

Deep inside, I knew there was no other option. As much as I wanted her, as long as this was still inside me, there was no hope. I masked my feelings by gently breaking her hug and moved to Diane to do the same. "We're going to be all right," she whispered in my ear. "You're going to be all right."

I didn't want to debate it with her, at least not now.

QUEEN A'LENORA lingered even after most of the Valnorians who came to honor Damek had departed. She talked at some length with the Astari and then returned to the Ethwood Tree. Her forest and her people still needed healing. But I had no doubt that her bond with the Astari would be closer now that this threat had ended.

Once she had left, Bevon, Quintia, and Riyaad walked toward us. It might be my imagination, but they seemed to walk a bit taller and straighter. Maybe they understood that with Damek gone, it now fell to them to make the right decisions.

As Bevon stood before me, I could see in his eyes he had already moved past the grief he felt. He had once explained to me that the Astari Parting Ceremony allowed them to turn the page and recover from the bitter sorrow over a death.

Bevon noted our dour expressions. He hesitated a moment, unsure about what to say as he glanced at his companions before speaking. "For as long as we can remember, Damek has given us so much of himself. He was a rare individual. It will be difficult to continue without his guidance and leadership, but we will keep his dream alive. We'll not squander our time or fail to live up to our potential. He is still here inside each of us, and always will be."

I thought about how much of Damek's character had already rubbed off on me. "That's the best way to remember him," I said. "He was more human than most people."

Bevon took this as a rare compliment and nodded as if accepting a priceless gift. "Thank you. Being told this by another human means a lot." He hesitated before continuing, looking to each of us. "I told the queen that we would depart soon."

"To where?" Diane asked before he had a chance to say more.

"There are other races of people that we must find. Now

that the Bots have retreated, this may be our best chance to strike new alliances. It is the reason we left the Raised Isles. That hasn't changed."

I realized how much he sounded like Damek.

"But I thought you would have wanted to return home," Cassie said. "I would enjoy seeing Loralee again."

"I want to return, we all do. But not without completing the task Damek had begun. The Bots haven't finished. They'll strike again someday." He gazed up at the Ethwood, visible through the trees even though we stood some distance away. "Queen A'Lenora has agreed that the Valnorians will support us in times of need. But they need to recover and rebuild before they can do anything."

A few Valnorians, who still lingered along the river bank, began talking excitedly. They were looking at the sky. My stomach twisted, thinking it might be the Bots returning. I followed their gaze, expecting the worst.

But what I saw amazed me. The apparition of an angel floated gently toward us. Her wings were spread wide and barely moved in the calm air. I couldn't help but feel my spirits buoyed by the majesty of her sight. Arianell had returned.

Ever so slowly, she reached the treetops and continued to float toward us. She was smiling as she gazed down at us, completing the picture of an angel. Just before she reached the ground, she gently fluttered her wings a few beats. She kept her wings extended for a long moment once she stood on solid ground. Finally, she withdrew them so you would never know they existed.

"We meet again," she said pleasantly, sounding every bit

like a young adult. But a second later her smile faded as she cast her gaze on the other Astari. "We have lost a brave soul. No victory comes without a price. But this was bitter to accept. I share your sorrow."

Bevon and the others bowed respectfully. "We are going to miss him," Bevon responded.

She nodded in agreement before shifting her eyes toward us. It seemed to me that she lingered the longest on me. "I am sorry you had to go through this. But the Bots reacted as Elthea had hoped. You forced their hand, and they moved before consolidating their power. They weren't ready, and they failed while you, Philip, exercised the power given to you."

"But I still don't get it," said Matt. He glanced over at me. "Phil was the one who stopped them. The rest of us were only bystanders."

"Oh no, you could not be more wrong." She thought about it for a moment, as if debating whether to say more. "The spirit of Elthea has bestowed a gift upon each of you. Your ability, Philip, manifested itself now. But the Bots had no way of knowing when, or if, the rest of you would come into your own. They could not risk waiting."

I suspected as much, but she confirmed it. "This inside me was from Elthea?"

Her smile mingled with an expression of sadness. Once again, she thought about it for a long moment before replying, "You may have thought of it as an infection from the Bots, but it was not. The Bots believed they had corrupted Elthea's gift. It was because of their taint that you attacked your companion." She glanced at Cassie. "They assumed they could win you over and control you. But they were wrong."

My anger flared. "But they almost succeeded. Why didn't you tell me this before? Damek might not have died. I almost destroyed everyone."

"I am sorry, Philip." Her reaction was so disarming that I found it difficult to stay angry with her. "But you needed to act without foreknowledge of your hidden strength. The nature of your gift is such that you had to discover whether you stood on the side of good or if you harbored corruption in your heart. To explain it to you would have negated its value. You had to reach deep within and grasp your innermost feelings and not take a simple way out."

"And what if I didn't? What if I had believed the Bots were the answer to my salvation?"

Her expression didn't change. "That was a risk. But it was a gambit Elthea took." A thin smile came to her. "It seems to me that she is a good judge of character." Her eyes moved to Cassie, Matt, and Diane. "And that includes each of you."

"What gift do the rest of us have?" Cassie asked with a frown. After seeing me grapple with what I thought was an infection, I could understand her not wanting any part of it.

Arianell looked at her as if scolding a small child. "In due time, my friend. Do not be too impatient. A boon can be a double-edged sword, as Philip has discovered."

I still felt bitter about this happening to me, but then the images of Elderphino, Damek, and Eric came to me: three good people who had died trying to make this Realm a better place. I knew I should be grateful for the chance to help this land, and thinking that, my rancor cooled.

"For now, your role here has ended," said Arianell.

I then understood why she was here. My heart beat faster knowing that I was going to face a choice. And then she said it. "I am here to bring you home."

Cassie, Matt, and Diane apparently didn't expect Arianell's purpose. They looked stunned, and I could see uncertainty in their eyes. The last time we were in this land, we had no voice about leaving. It was part of the invocation that Eric let loose.

Diane spun around to look at the other Astari. "I thought we would travel with you to other places."

I bit off a remark, thinking how she desperately wanted to return home during our previous time in the land. Matt smiled at her, probably recalling the same.

Bevon also grinned, but it was Quintia who answered. "You have become as close as any friends." She broadened her gaze to look at all of us. "I marvel at how you have all changed since the first timid, scared people we found on the island of Palbender. We love you all. But you should do as she says. Your life, for now, belongs on Earth. Arianell has a close affinity with the spirit of Elthea. I trust their judgment."

"But will we see you again?" said Cassie. I could hear the disappointment in her tone.

Bevon answered. "Who can say? You have each given more than we could expect from anyone. Go now. Be content that you swayed the outcome of this horror in our favor."

Matt put his arm around Diane. I could see that none of them were expecting things to end this way. Quintia opened her arms and moved to Cassie to give her a warm hug. She then stepped to Matt and then Diane to do the same. Riyaad and Bevon followed her lead.

But when Quintia made her way to me, I stopped her, waiting for the others to finish their hugs. She frowned, maybe mistaking my intentions.

When all the others had said their goodbyes, I knew this was the time. "I'm not going," I said, trying my best to keep my voice even.

Bevon exhaled and said, "Earthfriend, I understand your desire to stay, but this is not your life. You belong back home."

"No, you're wrong. I have nothing left there. Whatever this is inside me, here in this land is where I feel it the most. I had believed it was an infection, something that was destroying me. But now I find out it's something else, maybe something good. But that doesn't change things. Here is where I need to be so I can learn what this gift from Elthea will do to me or what kind of person it has turned me into."

Bevon looked at me as if wanting to argue, but I stopped him with a gesture of my hand. "This has nothing to do with sentimental feelings. It has everything to do with understanding who I am. The spirit of Elthea gambled that I would make the right decision. Now I need to find out more about myself. I've never given much thought to who I am. I know in my heart this is something I can only do here."

He looked at me without blinking. I wasn't sure if he was trying to figure out a way to persuade me to return to Earth, or if he was considering what I said. It was Arianell who settled it. "Earthfriend Philip may have a better understanding of this than do we. This is his choice."

Cassie looked at me, Arianell, and then Bevon, a bewildered, lost expression on her face. I felt so sorry for her. This decision was probably harder on her than on me. I went to her and touched a lock of her hair, easing it back into place. "This has nothing to do with you or the two of us. I need to find my way. It's as simple as that."

"And you can't do it with me or back on Earth?" she pleaded. "Especially now that you know it's not an infection? That changes everything. Doesn't it?"

I felt hollow inside, but I shook my head. "You wouldn't be happy, neither would I. This is the only option. I need to find out what I have. And most importantly, if I can control it." I could see a haunted look in her eyes as she searched for a solution or an argument to change my mind. My heart poured out to her. "Cass, our timing was wrong. It's nobody's fault. Before, when we returned to Earth, we thought we had a new start in life. It didn't happen that way." I put my palm on my chest. "This got in the way."

She stepped forward and hugged me. I let my arms wrap around her, feeling the comfort and warmth of her body. She looked up to my face. "How did all this happen to us? Not long ago we were only college kids. We didn't have a care in the world. And now this. Why did it happen to you?"

I searched her eyes as if I would find an answer there. But what I saw was more comforting. She looked at me with an emotion that I had thought I would never see again. I knew I had to make her leave now or I would change my mind. I kissed her on the cheek. "Some questions can't be answered. Take comfort in what we had. And please, stay safe."

She looked at me with the resignation of a person who

knew there is no other recourse. She gave me one last hug and stepped toward Arianell. Mercifully, I wasn't able to see her tears I knew were there.

My eyes blurred as Matt and Diane came to stand before me. "Are you sure you want to do this?" he said.

I blinked away the tears and nodded. "It's the only answer."

Diane hugged me before I could say more. "You deserve better. I hope you find what you're looking for," she whispered in my ear. Matt took her place and also hugged me.

They moved to the winged Astari. She gave me one last look. It seemed that she understood my decision more than anyone. She nodded once to say farewell.

"Come closer," she said to them as she opened her arms wide to embrace them. A moment later she extended her wings. I was curious how she would bring them home since I had blacked out shortly after she had grasped me on Earth.

She slowly brought her wings forward and wrapped them around my friends until blocking them from my view. In the next second, they all winked out of existence.

The only humans I truly loved were gone, maybe forever.

In all my life, I had never felt so alone as I had at this moment.

HOME

As we broke through the brush, the view opened to a wide field beyond. Sitting on a low rise at its center was the fortress. Seeing it again, I knew I had made the right decision. The stone wall and homes within it were as I had remembered.

The sun was high in the sky, and villagers were working the fields; many tending the gardens while others watched over the herd. The gates stood open, allowing people to come and go as they pleased.

"You still expect to find what you seek here?" Bevon asked.

I squinted in the bright sunshine, not sure if it was because of the sudden brightness after walking out from the covering of shade or because I wanted to see who was standing guard on the wall. "I don't know," I answered. Looking at my friend, our bond closer than ever after the months we spent crisscrossing the land, I smiled. "At the very least, they will offer us home-cooked food and a soft bed in an actual room."

"Then this is a superb choice," added the Valnorian, Ja'Krill, who had decided to accompany us from the Greylock Forest. "But it appears to be a dreary place."

We looked at him, not sure what he meant. Realizing our puzzlement, he added, "All that rock and stone. I don't even see a sign of wood. Do you think it safe?"

I smiled as I scratched my shaggy beard, wishing now that I had the opportunity to shave, or at least trim it before arriving.

"Oh, it's safe," Quintia added. "But you will need to become accustomed to having stone all around you."

He made a sour face, and the rest of us laughed.

We stepped forward only a few paces from the surrounding cover of trees when two rings of a bell split the tranquil air. "Is that a warning?" Ja'Krill asked, putting his hand on the hilt of his sword.

"Easy there," Bevon chided. "It is only to announce our arrival. Two rings for strangers." My Astari friend looked at me. "Do you think the watchman will announce us as friends before we reach the wall?"

I inspected those by my side. We had the appearance of travelers who had been on the road for some time. Our weathered clothes, unkempt hair, and on closer inspection, the lack of a proper bath for far too long, marked us as strangers. "Probably not. We're not the same people who left here months ago." Although I was thinking mainly about myself, it still applied to my Astari companions. "Plus, I don't think they've ever seen a Valnorian before. They'll likely not recognize us."

I continued to scan the top of the wall where more of The Guard had appeared as all eyes observed our approach. A lanky young man began moving along it as he pointed excitedly in our direction. I smiled, realizing it was Bryson.

Another person settled in beside him. With a mix of emotion, I observed that she stood at about the same spot when I had seen her last.

It was Rae.

She watched us as we approached. When we were closer, I touched my hand to my head in an informal salute. She returned the gesture.

Before we were halfway to the wall, a single peal of the bell rang.

I glanced at Bevon, and we both smiled. "We're back with friends," I said. It was a good feeling; one I hadn't felt in a long time.

I entered the gates of Haven with an optimism born from the ashes of another life. I still wasn't sure what this place would hold. But I was willing to give it a try.

AUTHOR'S NOTE

Thank you for reading my work.

If you enjoyed this book, please take a moment now to write a brief review. Leaving a review on the site where you purchased the book is a great way to thank an author and help others decide the book is right for them. Your rating and comments make a tremendous difference. Please spread the word.

You can subscribe to my newsletter at https://johnmurzycki. com/newsletter-sign-up-2/. I will never share your email address, and you can unsubscribe at any time.

I also appreciate hearing from you. Use the contact form on my website at https://johnmurzycki.com, or email me at john@johnmurzycki.com.

NEXT IN THE SERIES: ELTHEA'S PARADOX

Enjoyed Elthea's Gambit?

Read Elthea's Paradox, Book Three in The Story of Elthea's Realm series. Now available in paperback, hardcover, and ebook wherever you purchase books.

A reluctant hero stands against an evil spreading across the land.

Newfound powers awaken within Philip Matherson. But when he needs them most, the spectral energies of Elthea elude him. His worst fears come true as the Bots capture his friends on the utopia team.

The human village of Haven safeguards Philip, but their

sturdy walls offer scant protection against the might of the Bots. Without his powers, he is helpless against an onslaught by evil forces. At the darkest hour, help arrives from an unexpected source.

Even then, mysterious entities continue to conspire against Philip. His only hope is to rekindle the magical elixir within him until he discovers a hidden paradox surrounding Elthea's energies. It throws into question all his hopes and dreams. Can he save his closest friends while still protecting the supernatural wonders in the land of Elthea?

Not long ago, I spent my days as a marketing and sales manager, crafting messages for corporations, primarily tech companies. What I really wanted to do was write fiction—the magical kind that would take readers to imaginary worlds.

So I left corporate life behind and never looked back. Now I mull over enchanted realms and unlikely heroes who defend others against malevolent beings. I wrestle with words and fret about phrases, rewriting them until they evoke just the right emotion. "What if..." is always on my mind as I develop twists and turns in a storyline.

This is the stuff of dreams, a life I always desired.

I make my home in the charming state of Massachusetts. To

learn more about me, visit my website at johnmurzycki.com and subscribe to my newsletter, where I will periodically ramble about bookish topics.

Connect with John:

Website: https://johnmurzycki.com
Email: john@johnmurzycki.com

Follow me on Social:

facebook.com/author.johnmurzycki

linkedin.com/in/johnmurzycki

bookbub.com/profile/john-murzycki

amazon.com/gp/product/B08PZ7LG95

goodreads.com/johnmurz

ACKNOWLEDGMENTS

I am truly fortunate to have such a terrific group of people who contributed to this book by providing me with valuable advice on my early drafts. Their edits and suggestions contributed to a much richer story.

Robert Sigsby is a good friend and a fellow writer. His two latest novels are *With Which The Waters Swarm*, an emotional story about a herd of sea animals fighting for their survival, and *The Ages of Oosig*, about a boy coming of age in the South Pacific during a bygone era. Both are remarkable stories, and they display the range of his writing skills. More than anyone, Bob has helped me become a better writer with his astute suggestions.

Audra Cohen Murzycki surpassed all my expectations with her perceptive ideas and comprehensive edits. It shouldn't have come as a surprise to me, having learned she was once a professional editor for a publication. It's obvious she hasn't lost her skill. I look forward to the day when she finishes her book.

Sara Jastrem, my former co-worker, also has her sights set on one day completing a novel. She always provides me with great suggestions on my plot, and detailed edits and grammatical corrections.

Chad Eastwood highlighted errors in his meticulous

reading of my draft. Doreen Murzycki, Chad's wife and my sister, gave me terrific advice on the book.

Daniel D'Attilio, a voracious reader, has very sound advice and comments, which I appreciate.

Thanks to Paul Silva Design for the perfect cover.

Most of all, thank you to my wife, Carol. Your early reads helped me stay on course, and your final proofread caught those pesky errors. More importantly, your encouragement gave me the motivation to keep writing.

Finally, I appreciate all you readers who love a good story. None of this would be possible without you.

PREVIEW OF ELTHEA'S PARADOX

BOOK THREE IN THE STORY OF ELTHEA'S
REALM SERIES

A twig snapped behind me, and Bevon turned his head. In a blur, he grabbed the collapsible lance at his waist, extended it with a snap of his wrist, and pointed it in that direction. The other Astari and Ja'Krill reacted at the same speed. I spun around to see a Bot standing a dozen paces away.

My muscles froze, unable to move. At nearly eight feet tall, the thing was enormous. It must weigh three hundred pounds, and all of it muscle. Its size alone would be enough to frighten anyone. But the hint of a face made it worse. It was more of a mask with no eyes or mouth, only the trace of where they should be, as if the creature was a reincarnation from an unfinished painting.

My stomach did a flip, realizing too late that I hadn't bothered to bring a weapon with me today. And now, I faced the cause of all the pain and suffering during the past two years. The Bots were responsible for killing Damek, for causing the deaths of Elderphino and Eric, and for brutally murdering so many Astari during the Midsummer Celebration. My friends fanned out protectively around me, each of them armed.

Even on a face without discernible eyes, I had the impression the Bot focused its attention on me alone. I wasn't prepared for the pounding in my head as the creature began forcing its words into my brain, whether or not I wanted to listen. I winced at the violation.

—*You are incapable of harming us, Philip Matherson. The time for the end of humanity is near. The final extinction of the human race has begun.*

I forced myself to remain standing against the hammering blow of words. Whatever happened, I would never give it the satisfaction of seeing me grovel at its feet. What it was saying? This reference to the final extinction sounded ominous. Before I could frame a response, the pounding continued.

—*We have your friends. You will join our cause and do as we say. Or else...*

The bottom fell out of my world. They had Cassie, Matt, and Diane? One reason I wanted them back on Earth was for them to be safe while I tried to puzzle out my capabilities. It seemed every decision I made was wrong.

"You're lying," I said, hoping my words carried a shred of truth.

—*We have important plans for you, Philip Matherson. It would be better if you came to our side willingly, but detaining your college companions ensures that you will comply. We have a new strategy to supplant your race. At one time, we needed you to convince humans they should yield to our superior intelligence. But humanity is already ours.*

It was bluffing; it had to be. My pulse quickened as I felt

the bile rise in my throat. I would rather be dead than help these creatures. But I needed to remain alive long enough to free my friends.

Bevon's voice rang out. "You will never succeed! The Astari have stopped you before, and we will do so again. You think yourself invincible, but you are not."

If Bevon's intention was to anger the Bot, he succeeded. The creature moved toward him without hesitation and pulled out a blade holstered on its back.

Riyaad shielded me by positioning himself in front of me. "Stay behind, Earthfriend."

Bevon decided not to wait for the Bot. He rushed toward it with his lance held straight ahead. Bevon had the advantage of a longer blade, but the Bots had the speed and strength of a dozen Astari. At the last moment, before they crashed into each other, Bevon angled his lance to the left, intending to swing it rather than stab.

The Bot easily countered the feint, meeting Bevon's blade with its own and forcing the tip into the ground. The Bot twisted around and lifted its leg to stomp on the lance. The blow ripped the weapon from Bevon's hands.

I knew what would happen next. With Bevon momentarily defenseless, the Bot would stab him. I had only one chance to stop it. Using my anger and hatred, I reached for the weave of energy as I had at the home of the Valnorians. Maybe I needed to use my emotions as fuel to call upon the life force. Was that the secret? I needed to destroy this monster before it killed another of my friends.

I saw the scene unfold in slow motion. Bevon's face registered surprise that the Bot had jarred his lance free. The Bot swept its blade forward toward the defenseless Astari. I focused all my thoughts on killing the creature. The deadly energy would spill from my outstretched hands as it had once before. Bevon's life depended on me.

Nothing happened—no blast of energy, no superhuman force to stop the beast from murdering him. I watched in horror as the scene developed.

A buzz like the sound of bees split the air. An arrow appeared in the Bot's neck. The creature jerked its head up in shock. In quick succession, another shaft thumped into its chest. Both Quintia and Ja'Krill were reloading their bows. Riyaad took advantage of the opening and bounded toward the beast, plunging his lance into its mid-section. Green liquid flowed from the wounds as the Bot slumped to its knees. In another moment, it fell face forward on the ground.

I felt myself shaking. All that remained of the nightmare was the dead Bot's body with its dire warning. *We have your friends.*

www.ingramcontent.com/pod-product-compliance
Lightning Source LLC
Chambersburg PA
CBHW051212190726
48288CB00006B/1922